A Coastal Christmas

Lynna Clark

Text copyright© 2016

ISBN 9781521018989

Lynna Pittman Clark

All Rights Reserved

Unless otherwise indicated, all Scripture quotations are taken from the *Holy Bible*, New Living Translation, copyright © 1996, 2004, 2007 by Tyndale House Foundation. Used by permission of Tyndale House Publishers, Inc., Carol Stream, Illinois 60188.

The Blue Meadow Series:

Dedication:

"Now all glory to God, Who is able
through His mighty power at work within
us to accomplish infinitely more than we
might ask or think."

-Ephesians 3:20

Thank You Lord Jesus for getting me through
these long months of chemo; for clearing my
brain enough to edit this book; and for the
words You so sweetly poured forth as I wrote.
Bless each reader with a clear picture of Your
precious love.

**"When doubts filled my mind, Your
comfort gave me renewed hope and
cheer."** –Ps.94:19

Chapter 1: Early December

For the first time since Blue died Lydia found herself looking forward to Christmas. Watching how happy it made Jesse made her happy too. Together they made a list and delivered baked goods to nearly everyone they could think of. While Jesse seemed to slip off to work on something for her, she had no idea what to get for him. In her thinking nothing was good enough for her wonderful man.

Finally it hit her. She waited until he was finishing up a repair job for an elderly widow then she headed to his farm. Her trusty old tractor made quick work of plowing up a hillside into the shape of a heart. He'd always loved her Claudia Garden. Now he'd have one of his own minus the ashes of dead loved ones.

As quickly as she could she planted clumps of liriope and Lenten roses to outline the edge. Just inside that she buried daffodil bulbs followed by tulip bulbs of all colors except pink. In the middle area she sowed a wide variety of wildflower seeds so that he would have blooms for every season. Even in winter the Lenten roses would provide some color. Hurriedly she finished and headed from the pasture toward his house on her tractor. She stopped and climbed the steps to his back deck and was happy to see that her gift held the shape of a heart even without blooms. Though it was a bit whoppy jawed she was very satisfied with the results. And best of all he would be able to see it from his house.

She pulled the note from her back pocket and left it under the tile coaster by his chair on the deck. Slowly she drove the tractor home happy that she was able to get the work done in an afternoon. Though it was only about five it was already getting dark when he passed her on the road.

She threw up a gloved hand and wondered if he'd recognize her.

~~~~~~~

Jesse hurried home after finishing the work for one of his favorite customers. It seemed she'd sat down on the toilet one day to find that it rocked rather easily side to side. Upon further inspection Jesse discovered that at some point the person who repaired her bathroom had stacked concrete blocks in the crawl space to support the toilet rather than replacing the floor. He sighed at the shoddy work and wondered what would've happened had she fallen through. Immediately he tried to shake the visual from his brain.

When he finished he ran by the hardware store for paint hoping to get Lydia's Christmas present done before they left for Texas. As he topped the hill between her drive and his, he passed a tractor headed in the opposite direction. The driver threw up a hand and smiled. He looked in the rearview mirror to see a braid falling from the ball cap onto her army jacket. He backed the truck up beside her.

"Girl you lookin' fine in that flannel shirt. Why you wanta be waving at me nearly makin' me run off the road?"

She laughed at his crazy talk. "Did you get Mrs. Powles' toilet steadied up?"

He laughed too. "Yep. Bless her heart. That could've been bad. See you in a bit."

"Give me time to take a shower. My boyfriend's coming over later and I want to look nice for him." She winked and started the tractor.

Jesse offered, "It's too cold to let your hair air dry. I'll dry it for you."

She shook her head and laughed. "Uh... no thanks." The tractor lurched and blew out black smoke as she left."

Crazy man! You do not want to see what happens when you use a blow dryer on my fuzzy head.

By the time she rolled into her drive and neared her house it was dark. Suddenly the place lit up with all manner and color of Christmas lights in the trees lining the last half of the drive. Drop cords were strung from tree to tree to tree until it was a virtual Redneck Utopia. She burst out laughing as she approached the house. Packing peanuts were strewn all over the front yard. When the guys heard her old tractor coming they dropped down on the ground and made snow angels in the wannabee snow. She laughed so hard she nearly wet her panties.

"Merry Christmas Mommy!" Shawn and Kurtis called behind her as she took the tractor to the barn. She laughed and thanked the Lord for her very wonderful life.

Chapter 2

The bakery business exploded the weeks before Christmas. Jesse stepped up to help her often in the evenings. He wondered if they needed to take a few days to rest before leaving to visit his parents. She seemed very tired and her eyes were underlined with dark circles. When he finished the last job he'd promised to complete before Christmas he cleaned up and headed to her house. He found her in front of the stove stirring something in a large pot.

She smiled at him as he entered the back door. "Hey Cowboy. How was your day?"

He couldn't wait to circle her waist and hug her from behind. "It was good. I'm through til the first of the year." He kissed her cheek and whispered, "You feeling okay? I know you're working awfully hard to finish up all your orders."

She placed the big spoon on a saucer. "I'm not feeling well but it's kinda good news." He noticed that she blushed as she continued. "I'm actually having a regular period and it's only been a month since my last one, so maybe…" She looked up at him and smiled. "It kinda gives me hope."

"Anyway, it's still weird for me to talk about but I'd rather you know in case I bite somebody's head off. Poor Shawn is usually the one to catch it."

Jesse turned her around and smiled. "I'm sure he deserves it." He waited til she looked at him. "Honey I'm so glad. But I'm sorry you're hurting." He kissed her lightly and drew her to him. "Maybe rather than leave on Monday we could give you a few days here to rest. We could wait and leave early Wednesday and still be there by Christmas Eve. Let's sit down and talk about it a minute."

She turned the burner down and walked with him to the couch. The room was pretty bare since the broken furniture had been removed. At least she had the purple sofa and her old wooden rocker.

He held her hand and asked, "Which sounds better, rest a couple days before leaving then drive two long days? Or leave sooner and drive less per day? Talk to me Darlin'."

She wondered about telling him her fears. He waited knowing there was more.

Finally he asked, "Are you worried about meeting my folks or staying at their house or what?"

She answered smiling. "Nah. I'm actually fine with that. I figure Texans are about as hospitable as they come and as good as you turned out they're bound to be nice."

She sighed and felt very foolish over the issue. "I'm worried about staying in a hotel room by myself on the trip. I still have nightmares about the break-in even after all this time. But I don't know what to do about it. I'm such a fraidy cat."

He held her close. "I'll take care of you. We'll just get a room with two beds. No biggie." He kissed the top of her head as though it were a done deal.

"Are you sure Jesse?" She really didn't want to put them in a compromising situation.

He looked at his girl. "Honey we'll put some boundaries in place. And if I feel like I'm about to mess up I'll take a cold shower. How's that?"

She laughed. "At least we'll both be good and clean before we hit Texas."

He laughed and hugged her again. "So when do you want to leave Darlin'? We'll do it any way you want."

"You may never hear this from me again so soak it in. Just surprise me. Figure out what you think will be best and tell me when to be ready. I'm with ya babe!" She smiled up at him so thankful and relieved about the overnight arrangements that the rest seemed unimportant.

"Good! Then we'll leave Monday. Honestly I can't wait to see my mama and daddy. I've missed them so much. They're gonna love you!

I'll make your bakery deliveries tomorrow so you can work on your laundry and stuff. Then we'll rest Sunday and be ready to go bright and early Monday morning."

His kissed her cheek with a big fake loud sloppy kiss. "I'm so excited! We're goin' home baby!" He walked outside to some unknown chore.

His excitement about going home made her wonder. The trailer where she'd grown up as a girl was less than pleasant so it wasn't a place she missed or longed for. The first happy home she'd known had been Blue Meadow. She and Blue had begun making a life together twelve years earlier with the intentions of staying forever. But after he died it didn't seem like home any more. The break-in changed things too. Many times she still feared staying there even with the guys around. She returned to the kitchen and stirred the big pot of soup.

Lord… sometimes I feel like I'm losing my mind. Maybe it's the hormones or Christmas or… I don't know. Maybe I'm just a bad person. I don't feel like celebrating or decorating. Christmas music makes me sad.

She sighed and tasted the soup.

But I have so much.

The thought of Jesse made her smile.

What a Godly man You've brought into my life. Lord, if I know him next year at this time we'll still be dating and speaking of marriage as something way down the road. Sometimes he drives me crazy with his patience.

She laughed.

That's okay. Jack rushed things and so did I. Oh LORD I'm so glad I didn't wind up married to him! So would You please take this heart of mine and give me comfort? I feel so out of place here… so useless. Like I don't belong anywhere. What's that about Lord? Maybe it's a lack of purpose or something. Please help Lord. Take these Christmas blues away. I think I might be in another spiritual battle. Last time I ended up hurting Jesse's feelings so bad. Please handle this for me. It's not about Jack. At least I'm finally sure about that.

She sighed and wondered if the Lord could hear her at all.

Please just help. And while You're at it, my back is killing me. Could You reach down and work on that before we take off on a road trip?

The door burst open and Shawn made her jump.

"Good grief Liddy! Who all you feedin' tonight? That's a big ol' honkin' pot of soup!" He took one look at her and knew to go back outside to remove his work boots. At least he had refrained from telling her that she looked like crap.

A wonderful aroma came from the oven and she realized she'd forgotten to set the timer. Snatching the oven door open she was happy to discover that the homemade yeast rolls had not burned.

Thank You Lord. I think if I had scorched the bread after all the work I put into it...

She pulled the pans from the oven and placed them on the work island.

...that might've pushed me right over the ledge.

Jesse walked through the door in his sock feet. "Wow. Something smells really good. Is that homemade bread?"

He stepped behind her as she turned the rolls out into a basket lined with a tea towel. As usual his hand rested on the small of her back. And as usual it was warm gentle comfort.

"This is my first attempt at yeast rolls. Here. See what you think." She placed the butter dish beside the basket.

They each took a bite of a hot roll. Butter oozed from the center and Jesse hurried to catch it by cramming the rest into his mouth.

"Oh Darlin'! This is like manna from heaven!"

He made her laugh again and part of the cloud lifted. Her phone buzzed in her pocket so she wiped the butter from her hands.

It was Jack.

She showed the screen to Jesse then gave him the phone. Walking into the den he answered and she could hear part of the conversation.

"Hey man. How you doin'? Good. Still stickin' close to your Pop? Good job. Yep. It turned out really nice didn't it? The girl's got lots of talent that's for sure. I'll tell her. Nope. She handed her phone to me so it was her doing."

Jesse looked at her through the doorway to see if she wanted to speak to Jack. She shook her head no.

"Nope, listen. I'm praying for you Jack. Part of that prayer is about moving on. God will show you the next step. Take one day at a time but focus on moving forward, not backward okay? Stay strong man."

When Jesse returned to the kitchen Lydia realized that once again Jack had called at a time when she was most vulnerable.

"Jack Senior really loved the painting you sent him. Apparently Jack volunteered to convey the message. I can't blame him for trying. Do you want me to call him back and tell him not to call again?"

Lydia took her phone and blocked Jack's number. "Nope. I got it. Thanks Jesse-man." She made herself busy stirring soup.

Jesse turned her around to face him. "Thank you honey. Are you okay? I know that was hard."

She smiled. "I AM okay. God helped me by sending you in here at just the right time Jesse." She surprised him with a very tender kiss.

"Wow!" he whispered. "All this love and yeast rolls too. Merry Christmas to me!"

He made her laugh again and the cloud lifted a bit more.

Shawn re-entered the kitchen nearly tip-toeing. He could tell Lydia was not to be pushed but he wondered why. Normally that particular look only hit about every three or four months.

"Something smells good Liddy. What's in the pot?" He lifted the lid without commenting on their embrace.

She smiled up at Jesse then handed a spoon to Shawn. "It's called German Soup. Norma makes it all the time so I got her recipe. Try it and see what you think, but no double dipping."

Kurtis came through the door carrying his shoes. "It smells like bread baking in here. Is that for the bakery or us?" He asked hoping.

"Bless your heart. You have to live with all the yummy smells but don't get to taste it. This time it's for you. Here, try a roll. Hit it with some butter first." She held out the basket and lifted the cloth.

Shawn reached for one too. "Man Liddy! Usually when you're in a grumpy mood we don't get the good stuff. What's wrong with you? You in love or something?"

She teared up and didn't know why. "Yep. Head over heels in love with the sweetest Godliest man on the face of this earth."

Shawn had to add. "Sorry Jesse. I hate she's found somebody new."

Jesse laughed but looked at her tenderly. "I've got something for you girl. I didn't want to wait for our party Sunday. Stay here and close your eyes when we come in. Guys come help me with it."

The three of them returned a short time later with the gift. Jesse watched her face. "Okay. Open 'em."

In the empty place where the kitchen table used to be was a handmade farmhouse table. Jesse had built it then painted it white. The matching bench fit perfectly under the windows. Now her little area could easily seat six.

She covered her mouth and again teared up. "Oh Jesse it's perfect. Now we can have supper at the table together again like a real family!" She hugged him tight. "Thank you honey so much. I really love it!"

He smiled at her happiness. "Aw shucks ma'am. I'm glad you like it. I started to paint it purple to match the couch but I settled on this crazy white instead."

She laughed at his funny words and said again, "I love it. You're so wonderful." The tears were coming full force so she instructed as she left. "Y'all find some bowls and dip the soup. There's cheese in the fridge too. I'll be right back."

The reflection staring back at her in the bathroom mirror confirmed what she already knew. Her hair was a mess and her eyes revealed the pain. For a moment she thought about hiding in the bedroom while the guys had supper. Instead she prayed again asking God for help. Thinking of her pretty new table she realized it represented a new beginning of sorts. The old one was gone along with all the memories it held. A smile crossed her lips as she allowed herself to hope for better days ahead.

The four of them held hands around the table as Shawn prayed.

Lord thank You for Liddy and for our home and for our family and for this giant pot of soup. I sure hope it's good because it looks like we're gonna be eatin' on it for a while. Amen."

She looked at him through the tears. "Shawn…"

She explained while Jesse laughed. "I made extra on purpose so we can freeze part and you guys can eat it while I'm gone."

Shawn winked at Jesse while Lydia wasn't looking. "Don't worry. I'm planning on having Tessa stay over while you're in Texas. She's a pretty good cook." He busied himself with eating and waited on Lydia to call fire down from heaven.

She pointed a spoon at him but said nothing. Her death stare said it all. Kurtis and Shawn had a good laugh and eventually she laughed too. It dawned on her again that she was leaving her boys during Christmas. But she consoled herself by looking forward to the party she'd planned for just the four of them on Sunday.

Later that night as she reflected on Shawn's mealtime prayer she smiled. He'd thanked the Lord for HER of all things. She realized that he considered their family to be real even though in her brain she sometimes did not. Thinking again on her purpose in life she wondered if maybe God had already given her the very thing she'd always longed for: A real family, a home, loved ones around a table serving the people

God placed in front of them. Why did she always assume it was something different? As she tried to get comfortable she prayed.

Thy will be done Lord. I have to say that while I love these guys I had a different image of what my family would look like. But how blessed I am to have them. I really am spoiled rotten.

She smiled at their funny conversations and their crazy protection of her.

And Jesse… oh be still my heart! Bless my kind and gentle man. Give him wisdom and patience in dealing with me. It's bound to be a challenge.

She teared up at the thought of his kindness with her continual physical problems, her crazy fears and frequent tears. It occurred to her that the very patience she appreciated in those issues was also the same patience that delayed talks about their future. She prayed for patience too and looked at the verses on wisdom that had helped her when she struggled with Jack.

An old King James verse came to her as she looked for the passage. *"Let patience have her perfect work."*

James 1:4 in her translation called it endurance. The word seemed fitting yet still reminded her that the Lord's plan involved waiting, patience, and endurance. It tied right into the very wisdom that she longed for.

She prayed again as she switched off the heating pad and the lamp.

I don't much like waiting Lord. But help me, as Jesse would say, to not run ahead of You with my own plans. You are wise. Me… not so much.

She smiled again and fell into a deep peaceful sleep right in the middle of the bed.

Chapter 3

Jesse met her on the swing Saturday morning and was surprised to find her dressed and ready to make deliveries with him.

"I thought I'd run by Barry's too and give him an estimate on his kitchen. You okay going by there with me?"

She had to think for a minute as Barry always reminded her of Tate. "Sure," she answered though she wondered about the fear. No matter what came up she could count on Jesse.

They made the bakery deliveries then found Barry's home. She realized she'd actually been there before with Blue. The place was much neater back then and she wondered how long Barry's wife had been gone. The kitchen was a wreck as it seemed Barry didn't have a clue that leftover food and takeout boxes belonged in the trash and trash belonged outside. It was all she could do not to tear loose and clean the whole place up.

The glance she shot Jesse made him smile. He felt the same way but had learned years ago not to be surprised at what he might find inside a home.

Lydia watched as Jesse measured the space and took notes. Barry seemed happy she was there and asked her opinion.

"Do you think Susan would like the colors you used? I don't really have any idea what she'd want. I just know I liked how yours looked when I walked in."

Lydia wondered, "What are some things she picked out in your house? Did she choose the stuff on the walls or the dishes? Is there anything she seemed to be partial towards?"

He motioned her to follow him. "She loved this quilt. I'm not sure why she didn't take it with her. I don't even know what color that is with the blue. Would that work in a kitchen?"

"That really is pretty. It's sort of a terracotta color, like a clay pot. What do you think Jesse, maybe something earthy with touches of dark blue?"

He shook his head. "Sounds good. I'm not a designer but I like the looks of that. How long has she been gone?"

Barry sighed. "She took the boys to her mother's about a week before Thanksgiving so it's been a month. I came home from work one night and she had packed up and left. I'm not even sure what's wrong."

Lydia surprised him when she asked, "Have you let her know she's worth fighting for?"

Barry stood there thinking. "I don't know what to say to her. She's so ticked off at me that I'm mostly trying not to get her all riled up."

Jesse laughed and Lydia shot him a look. He quickly explained. "A woman riled up? I've never personally experienced such a thing."

Lydia smiled. "Do you think you could send her a text and ask her out? Sometimes it's easier to respond when you've had a chance to think about it."

She looked at Barry sympathetically then added. "Actually I have no idea what I'm talking about. Jesse is great at this kind of stuff. But from a woman's perspective she needs to feel like she's worth the trouble. If you keep letting this go she's not going to just pick up and move back home because you redo her kitchen. Find out what she needs inside. No need paintin' a barn that's gonna fall down anyway."

They walked back to the kitchen where Jesse began measuring again. Barry stood with Lydia and watched.

"When you and Blue used to hang out with us we always talked when you left about how much fun you had together; always holding hands and laughing. Susan said one time that she wished we were like that. Copper, how did y'all get along so good?"

Jesse said a silent prayer for her as she tried to answer.

"We did have a good time together. I think because we were such good friends first. And just so you know we had our share of fights. But it was Blue who always took my hand. I never had to wonder if the man loved me. We were careful not to throw off on each other to our friends. He never made fun of me with his buddies. The man continually built me up so that I felt like the most beautiful woman he'd ever met. He laughed at my jokes, he asked my opinion and he forgave me."

She could feel the tears coming so she deflected the attention. "Jesse drop some wisdom on the man. I'm going to find the little girl's room." She left quickly and wished she could've thought of something to busy herself with outside. Fresh air would have been a very welcome relief.

She briefly thought about adding,

And the man had brains enough to take out the trash before it stunk to high heaven.

But she refrained.

Once she pulled herself together enough to return she heard Jesse speaking to Barry about building the marriage on Christ.

"Without that solid foundation it's like Lydia said about painting a barn that's falling down. There's just not a lot of wisdom in that."

He promised to pray for Barry and his wife then handed him the kitchen estimate. "My phone number's on there so feel free to give me a call if I can help you and Susan. I do counseling too but you need to know ahead of time that I'm divorced. You may want to call Lydia instead. She actually knows more about having a happy marriage than I do." He laughed to cover his own pain and shook Barry's hand.

Lydia gave Barry a hug and was glad to be leaving. The kitchen mess had her unnerved and the bathroom was even worse. When they were finally in Jesse's truck he looked at her.

"You okay?" he asked with a sympathetic smile.

She shivered. "I need a shower. And not like a 'sleeping in the same room be careful not to mess up shower.' Holy cow! Why has it never occurred to the man to wipe off the counter tops? No wonder Susan left."

Jesse laughed out loud at her craziness. "Oh girl you are gonna LOVE staying with my parents." He looked out the window so she wouldn't pick up on his mischief. The truck fell deathly silent until she finally spoke.

"Jesse honey, please don't tease me about that. I may need to stay in a tent or sleep in the truck or something. Oh my goodness!" She shivered again and opened the glove compartment.

Jesse was still smiling. "Whatcha lookin' for Darlin'? A Cootie shot?"

She dug through the console as well. "I need some antibacterial lotion. Or just swing by a car wash so I can jump out and hose off."

He laughed at her again and pointed to the door pocket. She found antibacterial lotion and slathered down.

"Gross," she made a face. "I'm so glad you're not gross."

He smiled and asked, "Do I need to take you to the vet's for a flea dip?"

She finally laughed. "Can you imagine if I got fleas in this mess of hair? They'd have to shave my head."

Jesse grew serious but still smiled. "That was very good advice you gave Barry about marriage. And it's the type counseling that is easily received because it doesn't come from lofty towers."

She was surprised. "Thanks Jesse. Just be glad I didn't say what I was thinking."

He laughed again. "Yep. I already praised God for that."

She smiled realizing he knew her all too well.

Chapter 4

After church Sunday the little make-shift family gathered around the new table and enjoyed leftover soup from Friday. Fresh diner rolls were a hit again as Lydia was definitely getting the hang of making them. Both a chocolate pie and an apple pie waited in the wings to help celebrate.

"Shawn's the baby so he opens his first." Lydia clapped as she handed him her gift.

"Can't imagine what in the world this is." He grinned at her and tore into the package wrapped in funny papers. "Oh man! This was Blue's!" He stood and hugged her. "Thanks Liddy! Now I can fry a bunch of fish at once." The extra-large cast iron skillet had been handed down from Norma to Blue so he could fry chicken or fish over a campfire.

Lydia smiled at him and added, "That's been in the family since Blue's grandfather, Norma's dad. You're finally a man Grasshopper."

Shawn hugged her again and actually teared up . "I'll hand it down to my kid someday. Thanks Liddy... and thanks Blue."

He swiped at a tear so Liddy added, "Don't put that in the dishwasher."

Shawn laughed. "I KNOW."

Kurtis was next. He opened a similarly wrapped package. It was the coffee pot Blue had used on their camping trips. Kurtis teared up too. "I remember thinking I was a man in the seventh grade because Blue let us drink coffee. It was pretty nasty but at least it was hot! Remember how cold it was that one night Shawn?"

He hugged Lydia as she explained, "You'll be happy to have that if the power goes out." She opened the lid and showed him the instructions she had included. He laughed when he noticed she had written in large letters:

IF THE POWER GOES OUT MAKE SURE LYDIA HAS COFFEE LEST THE DEFECATION HIT THE OSCILLATION!

Jesse added, "Wise instructions right there son. Don't ever lose that card!"

They laughed together then Kurtis handed a gift to Lydia. She opened a gift bag with a pretty candle in it. "Mmmm, this smells good... like... what is that?" She read the tag and laughed.

"Warm Sugar Cookies because everyone bakes cookies in the bathroom."

Shawn handed her a box. "This is from both of us because that candle ain't near big enough."

She opened the box to find an exhaust fan for the bathroom. "Yay! Just what I always wanted! Fresh air!"

She rose and hugged them both. "Thanks so much sweet boys!" They rolled their eyes but loved her happiness.

"Now it's Jesse's turn!" Lydia was so excited. The three of them rose to gather something from the sunroom while Jesse waited at the table.

She tried to make a speech. "This is from all three of us. We love you so much Jesse-man!"

They moved the four pieces of birch plywood together so he could make out the pattern. On a black background was painted a vivid sunset in oranges, yellows, purples and blues in a quilt pattern.

"It's for your barn. Shawn and Kurtis made the frame and they'll help you hang it. I hope you like it." She smiled at the look on his face then added. "It's the only thing I know how to paint!"

They laughed together then put the pieces on the floor of the sunroom so he could see how they fit together.

Jesse pulled them in for a group hug. "I love it guys! Thank you so much" He stood back to look at it again. "That's really gonna show up great on my old barn. I like it almost as good as my new Lydia Garden." He smiled again at the note she'd left him.

Merry Christmas Cowboy! I figure with me as a permanent fixture in your life you're gonna need a place to pray. ~Love, Lydia

His favorite part of all was the word 'permanent.'

Jesse broke huddle and announced. "Okay this gift is from me and Lydia and it's selfish. We love that purple couch so much that we want it all to ourselves. So come out to the truck to see what we got you guys." Shawn and Kurtis couldn't believe their eyes.

"MAN CHAIRS!" Shawn exclaimed.

Jesse added so they understood, "These are yours no matter where you go. But now you can watch the games in comfort like real men!" They laughed when he added animal grunts. "Now you get the privilege of hauling those rascals inside. They are some kinda heavy!"

Lydia smiled at her boys. In one fell swoop they'd become men. And thankfully it didn't involve any floosy women.

Once the den was rearranged Jesse unceremoniously unloaded a homemade coffee table and placed it in front of the couch. Of course it was painted white. Lydia smiled at him as he tipped it up for her to see a heart he'd carved on the underside. She looked closer to discover he'd etched with a moto-tool words that melted her heart.

To Lydia, a woman worth fighting for ~ All my love, Jesse

When the guys were nestled into their man chairs and fully engrossed in the football game Jesse motioned to Lydia. They walked together to the porch where Jesse could give her something in private. Lydia noticed the gift bag was from Victoria Secret and immediately covered her throat. Jesse barely whispered as he handed it to her. "I know it's a little soon for lingerie but I saw this and thought of you."

She bit her lip and wondered if she was about to stay home for Christmas. Surely he hadn't misunderstood. Peeking into the bag she pulled the fancy tissue paper out to reveal thick cotton flannel pajamas with long sleeves and long pants. She laughed so loud the boys wondered what was going on.

Jesse looked at her innocently. "What? Too soon?" Then he smiled mischievously and kissed her so passionately that she longed for the day.

Chapter 5

They packed his truck that night except for the food. Jesse laughed when he saw the bags on her bed. "Is this all you're bringing?"

She tipped her head wondering. "Don't they have washers in Texas?"

He laughed, "Yep. Mama's gonna love you girl. Don't forget to bring a blanket and a pillow for the ride down. Maybe you can rest some on the way. Did you pack your blow dryer? There's no wind in Texas. Your hair will never get dry without help."

She sighed. "Oh well. Wet hair it is darlin'. Even as big as Texas is, there's not enough room for my hair if I use a blow dryer."

He smiled as he picked up her duffle bag. "They love big hair in Texas. The bigger the hair the closer to God."

She laughed and handed him her few hang up clothes. "Leave room for my cosmetic bag. I'll add it in the morning. I know you'll probably pack everything you own. It takes a lot to keep you so pretty."

He loved her good mood and it made him so happy to be packing together. His heart could hardly contain the joy he felt when he looked at her.

"Whatcha thinkin' there Cowboy?" she asked when she noticed his look.

He shook his head and sighed. Reaching for her hand he pulled her close and stroked her back. "Girl you just don't even know how long I have waited for this day."

She loved his warm embrace. Looking up into his sparkling eyes she asked, "What's today? December the 20th?" She hoped it wasn't his birthday or something and realized she had no idea when it was.

He leaned down to kiss her cheek. "The day we could pack a bag and run away together. So I guess tomorrow is actually the day I've been waiting for." He stroked her cheek and smiled into her eyes. She smiled back at him with heart pounding.

"Okay! Gotta throw stuff in the truck and get home. Lots to pack to keep me pretty!" With that he was out the door. She laughed behind him and hoped he'd turn to look.

So when he came back for one last kiss she thanked the Lord that they seemed to be progressing nicely in the love language of her choice.

~~~~~~~

It was still dark when Jesse pulled up with the Tundra packed and ready to roll. The front door of the house was standing open as an invitation for him to enter. Her cosmetic bag waited by the door. He glanced at the time and smiled. Five a.m. never felt so good. She peeked around the kitchen doorway and motioned him in. The aroma of coffee greeted him and he realized he'd forgotten to tell her he didn't drink coffee when traveling lest he have to stop for frequent bathroom breaks. He stroked her back as she poured the steaming nectar of life into a travel mug for him. Finally she turned and smiled a sleepy smile.

"Good morning Cowboy." She hugged him happily and whispered. "Today's the day! Oh honey I'm so excited!"

He kissed her neck and she drew back to look at him with happiness. "Hang on. Let me run get a cold shower before we get this party started."

He laughed and whispered, "Sorry."

She shook her head no. "Don't you dare be sorry! You know I love it!" She hugged him tight. They loaded the food then she looked around wondering.

"Okay… what am I forgetting?"

He tried to help. "Got a pillow and a blanket?"

"Yep, by the door. I guess I'm ready."

She still looked around so he asked. "Where's your coffee?"

"Oh I don't drink coffee on a trip. It makes me have to stop for potty breaks too often. But I made you some."

He laughed and took the mug from her hand. "Then let's get this show on the road woman! We're burnin' daylight!"

She stopped and asked. "Do you think I could slip into the boys' room and tell them good-bye one more time?"

He shook his head. "I don't think that's wise honey. C'mon. They'll be fine." He took her hand and headed toward the door. She remembered her keys and tossed them on the kitchen island for them. To her it felt strange, almost final. But one glance at the happiness on Jesse's face gave her the push she needed to walk out the door and lock it behind her.

~~~~~~~

Though he encouraged her to curl up and sleep while it was still dark she couldn't. "No need in you having all the fun without me." She smiled at him happily.

He took her hand and kissed it. "I brought you something my daddy used to always get for us kids when we were on a road trip. Check the little sandwich cooler behind my seat."

She reached through the two front seats into the small cooler and found a carton of chocolate milk. "Oh wow! My favorite!" She opened it and took a big drink.

He laughed at her. "I brought cups if you don't mind sharing."

She nearly snorted milk through her nose. "Oh. I did not know that. Sorry to be such a Goober. You are going to rue the day you ever invited me on a 1287 mile road trip." She found the cups and poured one for each of them.

Jesse asked, "So your internet is working again?"

"I don't know. I haven't messed with it lately. Why?"

"Well, you told me how many miles AND you used the word 'rue.' Sounds like internet info to me."

She countered. "Hey. I know stuff. Rue is a word. I just hope it doesn't come true, bless your heart. So far as the distance…" She pulled an Atlas from her travel bag. "I've got a map! It's a pain in the butt to use but if we need to go off-roadin' to get around a wreck or something it might come in handy." She crammed it under the seat. "So how far do you want to get today?"

"It depends on how you feel. We can drive all day or stop after lunch if you'd like. How're you feeling?"

She sincerely wanted to be truthful but sometimes it was very difficult when asked that particular question. He always knew when she lied. "I'm hurting but not because of girl stuff. It's all done. But last night about three I woke up in a lot of pain and couldn't go back to sleep. I don't have any idea what causes it. Maybe I was all tense about leaving my boys or something." She laughed trying to change the subject.

He held her hand and looked at her. "I'm sorry honey. Please let me know if we need to stop to take a break or when you're ready to stop for the night."

She smiled at him and added, "I think you're good for what ails me. I feel better right this minute than I have in weeks." She was being honest when she said it.

They covered a lot of ground that day, personal as well as highway miles. At one point a song came on the radio and Jesse asked her to turn it.

"You don't like Bonnie Raitt?" she asked as she found another station. "That surprises me as much as you like that bluesy kind of sound."

He spoke softly as he checked traffic and changed lanes. "Oh I love Bonnie. But that song…" He looked in the rear view mirror and busied himself with driving. Lydia realized the song was *I Can't Make You Love Me*. Suddenly she felt his pain and moved to stroke his back. "Stupid Kenya."

Jesse grew quiet then finally spoke after a bit. "Stupid Jack." He looked at her sadly. It made her happy when he added, "I don't think any two women on the face of the earth are as opposite as you and Kenya."

She laughed. Though she agreed she wondered what he was thinking. "How do you mean?" She asked as she still stroked his back. "Of course the beautiful part is obvious."

He looked at her. "You're the beautiful one girl and don't you ever forget it! But I don't want to bring her on this trip. So push her out of the truck here in South Carolina and let's never look back."

Lydia laughed at his determination. She'd actually never heard him speak a harsh word to anyone, not even Jack. Then she remembered Jesse returning her quilt with Jack's blood on it. Maybe it was that meek thing that Norma had spoken of, strength under control. She realized she'd never even seen him mad and could learn a lot from the man.

Somewhere around Atlanta they stopped for their first fill-up. Restroom breaks were a wonderful relief. While she waited for him to pump gas she wandered through the snack aisles trying to find something he might like. She called and watched him check his phone. He smiled and looked toward the store. "Hello Darlin'. It's good to see you. It's been a long tiiiiiimmme…." He held out the notes just like Conway Twitty.

"Hey Goober. Can I get you anything from the snack bar? A drink or juice or something?"

"Nah. The stuff we have packed is fine. I'm gonna move the truck then hit the restroom and we'll be ready to roll."

She offered, "I'm comin'. I'll move it. Then I can drive for a while to give you a break. Maybe you can take a nap."

He hung up and she looked out the door as he moved the truck to a parking place. Walking past her on the way in he surprised her again. "Negatory on the help driving Darlin'. Ain't no way I could take a nap with you behind the wheel. The door is unlocked if you want to wait in the truck. I'll be right out."

She put her hands on her ample hips and gave him a look. He kept walking and only turned to smile when he entered the store. She couldn't believe it. In all the time they'd known each other he'd never put her in her place like that. She realized again how spoiled she was since typically he did everything he could to please her. She had to laugh as she thought.

I guess it's his turn for a change. I can get on board with that. It's about time the man had some happiness.

She brought chicken salad sandwiches from the cooler along with bottled water. A big bowl of Chex Mix waited to surprise Jesse. She used a Dixie cup to scoop a nice helping of it onto the paper plate which held his sandwich.

When he crawled into the truck he hesitated to look at her. She bent low to catch his eye and they finally laughed together. They spoke at the same time. She smiled, "You first."

He took her hand and sighed. "I've put off this conversation for as long as I can, but you scare the crap out of me with your driving."

She laughed at his words. "That's funny Jesse. I've never even heard you say the word crap before. I'm sorry. Did I tell you that Jason pulled me again on Thanksgiving Day? It was right after I dropped Tessa off so I was headed home, praying out loud about that phone call from Jack when I looked up and blue lights were all over me. I promised him I would watch my speed and I have. I guess you just haven't had the pleasure of riding with me since then."

He took her hand. "Let's pray. Lord thank You again for this trip… the things Lydia and I are learning about each other… and for this food. Help us both leave the painful things behind and move forward together. Keep us safe Lord… bless my girl Lydia. You know how long I've loved her. In the Name of Jesus I ask and pray, Amen."

He opened his water and took a long drink. "Thanks for the picnic. I'm glad I didn't hurt your feelings about driving."

She situated his food while he pulled out of the station. "Well you did hurt my feelings and I'm not even sure what it will take to make amends. But just so you know, I am an excellent driver."

She tried to look hurt but couldn't pull it off. He smiled at her and laughed. "Darlin' you're such a liar."

Lydia laughed too and realized she was seeing a different side of him. He was relaxed and confident but also a lot of fun. She liked him very much.

Chapter 6

"Wow! What is this stuff and why didn't you get it out sooner?" He asked as he munched away.

"Norma made, as she would say, 'a foot tub of Scrabble.' I could eat the whole batch. I've got her recipe so when we get back I'll practice and be ready to make it before the Super Bowl."

He made yummy noises and ate all that was on his plate before he took a bite of his sandwich. "That's good stuff right there! I'll have to be sure to go by and give Norma a kiss!"

"Hey… watch out Cowboy. Don't be givin' away my kisses all willy-nilly. Although if you kiss Norma you will forever find yourself up to your neck in Scrabble!"

"Mmm… might be a good trade." He changed lanes just as a car jetted up beside them nearly making them wreck. His arm went out instinctively to protect Lydia as he swerved to miss it.

"Wow! That was close. He never even slowed down." Lydia sighed with relief. "Good reflexes. I'm glad you were driving because clearly I couldn't have handled that."

He glanced at her a little shaken then noticed her smile. He shook his head also very thankful that she wasn't driving.

When they finished lunch she began to feel sleepy. The soft blanket and pillow called her name. "Hey Jesse if I fall asleep will you be okay? You're bound to be tired."

He patted her knee. "I usually make this trip alone. So you're just icing on the cake. I'll be fine honey." His tone was soft and she hated to miss the time with him. But her eyes would barely stay open.

"Turn the radio up as loud as you want; whatever it takes to keep you awake. If you start to get tired just find a place to stay and we'll call it a day."

Her words made him think of the future and the things he prayed for them. Glancing at her with the blanket pulled up and the seat back, he loved the way she looked as she snuggled down for a nap. Even with her hair up on top of her head the few escapee curls stole his heart. What a long way they'd come. Her phone lay on the console and lit up with a call. He reached for it before it woke her. The screen said "Mr. Stephens."

If he had not been worried about waking her he would've answered it. He let it go to voice mail instead.

He figured either one of two things had happened. Jack's dad had somehow found a way to mess up her account again or Jack was calling from his father's phone in order to bypass her block on his number. Both scenarios made him mad. But the gracious man within him considered the possibility that Jack Sr. was calling to thank her for her gift or Jack Jr. was calling with bad news about his dad. He prayed as he drove and wished they could not only leave Kenya in South Carolina but also Jack in New York. He glanced at her again thankful that she'd slept through the call.

Please don't let anything spoil our trip Lord. You know how long I've waited for this.

She woke an hour later feeling refreshed but needing to potty. Stretching as much as the truck cab would allow, she wondered where they were.

"You took a good nap! There's a rest area coming up soon. Want to stop?" Jesse smiled at her sleepy eyes and confusion.

"Yep," was all she said. She shoved her phone into her pocket and pulled the truck visor down to check a mirror. She took the clip from her hair and rewound it on her head. Pulling her boots on she silently hoped Jesse would hurry. When he eased into the welcome center slowly allowing all pedestrians to walk to their parked cars in front of him she could contain herself no longer.

"Park as quickly as you can. My eyeballs are floatin' baby."

He hurried. "Sorry honey."

She wondered if she'd sounded miffed and hoped not. She tended toward snarkiness when she first woke from a nap and she knew it.

He parked, locked the doors, took her hand and walked toward the restrooms. "I'll wait for you right here by the entrance when I finish."

She hurried inside without answering. But when she returned to the lobby and he wasn't there, she nearly panicked. Two minutes later he sauntered toward her with those long Texas strides. He smiled that smile that took her breath away and reached for her hand.

Her heart pounded at the sight of him. "Thanks for taking care of me Cowboy and thanks for the nap. I feel so much better. How're you feeling?"

He looked at her like a man in love and put his arm around her shoulders as they walked back to the truck.

"Happy."

He opened the door for her and waited until she was in. Before he closed her door he leaned in and kissed her. "Mmm Chex Mix. I need some more of that."

She laughed at him and asked, "Are you sure you don't want me to drive? I'm an excellent driver you know." He closed her door soundly.

After another helping of snack mix she cranked up the radio and sang with every song she knew and was glad that he did too. Occasionally one of them would reach up and change the station. When *My Girl* came on Lydia quickly turned it and looked out the window to hide her pain. Jesse reached over and took her hand. "Stupid Jack. And that's such a great song. Maybe you and I can dance to it and make it ours."

She looked at him wondering. "Let's just stick to the song about being a happy man. That's my favorite anyway." She smiled at him.

Jesse thought about her phone. "Did you see you missed a call?"

When she saw who the message was from she looked at Jesse. "That's either bad news or Jack using his dad's phone. I'm afraid to play the message." She sighed and hit play. Jack's voice and his dad's sounded so much alike that she didn't realize it was Jack Senior until he called her 'Lydia dear.'

She was glad Jesse could hear it too in case she fell apart he would understand. Jack's dad pleaded with her to consider coming to visit for Christmas. He assured her that Jack was doing well, that he missed her terribly and that a visit from her was exactly what he needed to encourage him to continue.

Lydia surprised Jesse when she sighed and said aloud to no one in particular. "No it is NOT what he needs. What he NEEDS is to man up and be the spiritual leader of his own life without blaming others for his bad choices." She looked at her phone and spoke to the man who couldn't hear. "HE'S NOT MY STINKIN' PROJECT." She deleted the message and tossed her phone onto the console and folded her arms in disgust.

After a mile or two she looked at Jesse and sighed. "Sorry. But Jack lectured me continually on what he needed then pushed me to break the rules so he'd have someone to blame. It makes me so mad when I think about it."

Jesse said nothing.

She shook her head and apologized again. "Sorry Jesse. You don't need to hear all that and I don't need to dredge it back up. Sorry. I'm gonna just send Senior a text to decline then I think I'll block his calls too. What do you think?"

He nodded in agreement. "Probably wise. When I saw who was calling I figured it was Jack using his dad's phone. Sooner or later he's gonna try that. So far as Jack wishing he could have you back I can tell him right now. That's not gonna happen. You're MY girl now."

He pulled her close and tried to kiss her while driving. It scared the life out of her but still made her heart pound.

"Thank you Jesse." She whispered still close to him. "I needed to hear that. A woman likes to know she's worth the trouble." She smiled and kissed his cheek.

Chapter 7

Surprisingly they were able to travel ten hours the first day. Jesse was very pleased. Somewhere around Mobile, Alabama they started looking for a place to stay. With the time change from Eastern to Central it was only a few minutes after two p.m. But Jesse was whooped.

She waited in the truck while he got the room key and realized she felt pretty weird about the whole look of things. Suddenly she worried about Jesse's reputation and testimony.

When he returned to move the truck he noticed how quiet she had become. Once Jesse parked the truck he took her hand and waited until she looked at him. "I wondered when it would hit you."

She nearly teared up. "Jesse, I don't know what to do. What if someone sees us going into the same room together? You are such an honorable man and I've put you in a bad situation. Honey I'm so sorry."

He smiled at her. "I was able to get us adjoining rooms. We'll leave the door open between us so you'll know you're safe. But it'll be wiser than sharing a room. Is that okay?"

She sighed with relief. "You're wonderful Jesse. Thank you." She hugged him tight. "Maybe someday I'll get back to being a brave girl. But at least I don't have to be brave just yet."

They grabbed their travel bags and headed inside. "Are you hungry?" he asked smiling as he unlocked her door for her.

"Starvin' Darlin'!" She tossed her stuff on the bed and turned to see him standing in the hall. "Oh. What?" She walked toward him.

He dropped his bags and kissed her tenderly. "This is why we need two rooms. All the cold showers in the world are not gonna cure what ails me."

She loved his embrace but was thankful too for the solution of two rooms. "Let me freshen up a bit. But I'm not kidding. I'm so hungry. Wanta meet me in about fifteen minutes?"

He still held her. "Yes ma'am." He kissed her again and headed to his room. "No longer though. If I get still I'm probably gonna be snorin'."

"Yet another good reason for two rooms!" she laughed behind him. "I'll hurry."

~~~~~~~

They'd determined before the trip to stay away from fast food as much as possible since that seemed to activate Lydia's mystery illness. Thankfully they found a mom & pop diner and enjoyed a really good home cooked meal within walking distance to the hotel. Strolling back together holding hands in the beautiful weather seemed almost dreamlike for both of them.

Jesse looked at her wondering. "They've got an indoor pool if you wanta take a dip."

"Let's walk by and see how it looks." She doubted that she'd want to swim in such a public place. Sure enough there were quite a few college guys playing there so she opted out. "Nah, too many people."

Jesse was not surprised. "Good. Cause I'd hate to have to rough up some of those young punks for thinking you're my daughter."

She looked at him and laughed. "You are a funny man. You know I'll be thirty in February right?" He nodded and hoped she wouldn't ask. But it was bound to come up at some point.

"I've been meaning to ask you, how old are you Jesse?" She'd tried to calculate it by the years he'd played in the NFL and had a feeling he was older than Blue.

He sighed. "I'll be thirty seven on my birthday. So I am definitely robbing the cradle." He looked at her hoping it wouldn't matter.

She smiled warmly at him and he relaxed a bit. "When's your birthday?"

"December 27th, at least that's when we celebrate it. My birth mother left me in a church so I never really knew exactly. But my parents set that date because it's also the day I was legally adopted seven years later. They call it 'Gotcha Day!' and always made a big deal of it. They've been so good to me."

She looked away trying not to tear up. "You're right Jesse. I'm gonna LOVE your parents. In fact I already do."

~~~~~~~

They were both glad for two separate rooms as Jesse wanted to catch a nap and she just wanted to veg in front of the television. With all the men in her house and no cable, HGTV was a vacation all by itself.

"What fresh Heaven is this?" she thought as she got comfortable and settled into bed for the *Fixer Upper* marathon.

Several hours later a knock came at the door between their rooms. "Come in!" she called. Jesse stood there sleepy eyed in shorts and a t-shirt.

"Can I come watch television with you?" he asked with no ulterior motive.

"Sure honey. Crash on that other bed. You can even have the remote. It's probably time for Monday Night Football. I've been sucked into the dark world of *Fixer Upper* and I cannot look away." She laughed and tossed him the remote.

He glanced at her as she sat on top of the covers in her P.E. shorts and tank top. "Don't you like your new pajamas?" He still stood in the doorway.

"They're too warm for right now. I'm kind of a hot box. I'll wear them more at home." She finally took her eyes off the beautiful Gaines family and realized he wasn't moving. She jumped out of bed and got under the covers. "Is this better?"

He shook his head. "Nope. I think it's worse. I'll just watch T.V. over here." He tossed the remote to her and left. She went to the bathroom and dressed in the thick pajamas. It was the first time she'd tried them on and realized they were huge. The sleeves dangled way past her hands and the pants wouldn't stay up. She held onto them and walked to the doorway.

"How about now?"

He looked at her and burst out laughing. "Oops. I must've guessed wrong."

She gave him the look. "Mmm hmm. I'm very insulted that apparently you thought I was size mucho mucho grande." She turned and left. Climbing back onto her own bed she made herself comfortable and figured she could change once he went to sleep.

A soft knock came at the doorway.

"Come in," she laughed.

He looked at her with his head down in shame. "I'm sorry. I don't really think you're large. They must've sized them wrong."

She laughed. "The size says 3X so… what should it say? That's fine. I get it. I'm not the little woman I used to be."

He tipped his head sideways and disappeared. When he returned he held up a smaller identical pair. "I must've got ours mixed up. Those are mine. I was gonna surprise you and come out matching but I can't get these on."

She laughed so hard at her silly man. "Throw those to me you Goober. What a funny thing to do! Jesse honey I just love you!" She bounded from the bed holding onto the pants, took the smaller version from his hand and returned to the bathroom. Thankfully they fit so she took the others to Jesse. Once he dressed in them he stood in the doorway like a little boy.

She laughed heartily. "We need a picture of this! But it can't go anywhere, okay?"

He nodded, "Don't worry. I won't be postin' this on my Facebook page." She took their picture then sent him a copy. They rested on separate beds, stealing glances at each other and watched football during commercials on HGTV.

Chapter 8

They traveled all the next day as well. Eleven and a half hours later Jesse's mama and daddy ran out the door to greet them. Lydia immediately felt at home and teared up at the sight of Jesse embracing his dad in a long tearful hug. They looked so much alike that she marveled at God's grace in putting them together. His dad was tall and muscular with short white hair and sparkling eyes. He looked so young for his sixty seven years. Jesse's mom was small in stature but strong and vibrant as well. With short white wavy hair under a ball cap Lydia hoped to look that good when she reached sixty. Both his parents were tanned as apparently walking on the beach across the road from their house was part of their daily routine. Their warm smiles welcomed her in.

She was surprised that the house was no bigger. For some reason she'd envisioned something huge and grand like Jesse's. Their home was similar to hers but stucco. The floors were tiled and cool to their bare feet. His mom also had everyone in the habit of removing shoes before entering. Lydia already felt like a kindred spirit. At some point Jesse and his dad had added a second level with two bedrooms and a bath where an unfinished attic used to be. Downstairs was a nice open space which included the den, dining and kitchen. Two more bedrooms, a small bath plus a master bathroom finished out the house. Lydia wondered if her house had enough attic space to add a room. Then she wondered why she'd want to do that. All that HGTV from the night before had her dreaming. She smiled at the possibility then reminded herself not to get her hopes up as God may delay or even prevent her hopes of marriage or having children.

"I love your home Mrs. Mills. I'm partial to white but yours has such a beachy vibe that I want to use your pretty ideas in my house." Lydia spoke to his mom as they carried bags inside.

"Call me Nora honey. Mrs. Mills makes me feel ancient. We'll put you and Jesse upstairs. You may have to share when the other kids start piling in."

Nora stopped when she realized how that sounded and laughed at herself. "I'm sorry. That didn't come out right. You may have to share with some of the girls when they come not with Jesse. Bless his heart he's always been such a shy thing. He'd die if he heard what I just said."

"I heard it mama. Don't be telling Lydia all my secrets." Jesse called from upstairs. "We may need to turn on some air. Lydia's a hotbox."

Lydia laughed at them both. "Jesse bought me flannel pajamas. I'm not used to wearing quite so much when I sleep. With all this hair I'll be wringing wet."

Nora laughed. "Wait til you hit menopause. Night sweats are not to be trifled with, nor the woman who is having them."

"I can still hear you mama." Jesse called down and both women laughed.

When they unloaded the things Lydia had baked Nora was genuinely pleased. Lydia explained. "I'm a terrible cook but I like to bake. But I kinda have to do it in my own kitchen where I can think. I hope I didn't steal your thunder by bringing all this stuff."

Nora laughed. "No Darlin'. I've got plenty of thunder. The grandkids will wipe this out in no time flat. In fact we'll probably hide some of it so their mamas don't get us for loadin' 'em up with sugar."

Jesse's dad came from outside with a plastic bin. He placed the box of gifts in a corner. Like Lydia's the house was too small for a tree. "Don't hide all of it. I want an oatmeal crème cookie. Jesse's talked about those so much that I have to have one before they disappear." He smiled at Lydia. "And call me Sam. Though I'm not the famous Sam Mills that played for the Panthers I'm definitely honored to share his fine name. Did you know that he was the oldest NFL player to ever return a fumble for a touchdown? He was thirty seven. That's old in football years."

Jesse came from upstairs. "That's old any way you look at it." His knee was killing him. "I don't remember these stairs being so steep." His dad laughed at him.

"That's why your mom and I kept our bedroom downstairs. Has your mother told you she's been running the stairs to get in shape? I have to say, she's lookin' fine."

She turned and smiled at him. "Just trying to get ready for Christmas football with the family. Lydia I hope you're ready Darlin'. This house is about to explode with children of all colors, shapes and sizes. Jesse's the oldest then we've got kids and grands all the way down to the newest which is what… three months old Sam?"

Lydia couldn't imagine. Sam asked her about her own family and Jesse realized he'd meant to tell them not to ask. He was happy that she answered with a smile.

"There's only daddy and me. I'm not sure where he is. I've been thinking about calling him but I'll probably talk myself out of it." She made herself busy unpacking the cooler. "Have you got a cup I can use? There's a drop of chocolate milk left and I want to drink it before Jesse does."

He came running toward her so she turned the carton up and tried to drink it fast only to realize it had soured. She spit it in the sink and grabbed a handful of water to rinse her mouth out. "Gross! That's what I get for being selfish."

They laughed at her and Jesse found a paper cup. "Here, drink from their water cooler. I can't handle the water down here so I know you can't." He handed her the cup and smiled at her knowing she'd been successful in changing the subject from her family. He didn't blame her but sighed when his dad brought it back up.

"If you've been thinking about calling your daddy then you probably should honey. I bet he misses those copper curls." He looked at her the same way Jesse did when he was urging her to do well.

Lydia smiled. "Maybe I will. In fact he used to call me Coppercurls. Then one day he shortened it to Copper and that's what I went by the whole time I was growing up. Jesse's the one that brought me back to using Lydia."

Pulling the phone from her back pocket she mouthed the words to Jesse. *"Pray for me."*

She walked outside.

"Hey Daddy, it's Copper." Her bravery disappeared and she had no idea what to say. She sat on a patio chair not realizing it was right under an open kitchen window. Jesse and his parents could hear every word.

"I know it has. Yep… got through that crapstorm. Nah… he disappeared chasing skirts. Nope… I don't. How'd you know about him anyway? Oh… good ol' Norma." Lydia tried to laugh.

"Daddy the main reason I called is to let you know that I've met someone. Yep. That's him. How'd you know?"

She sighed. "Well… I guess if I'd stayed in touch you could've dropped that wisdom on me sooner. Sorry daddy." She laughed nervously.

"Hey daddy… I'm serious about Jesse. I've never loved anyone like this before."

She listened then interrupted. "No… Blue was a good man and I loved him very much. Please don't talk bad about him." She sighed and wished she hadn't called. "I know… I'm sorry. Hey Daddy… you have a good Christmas. Where are you anyway?"

She laughed. "No you are not… Nope… it don't matter… I won't be home anyway so don't worry about it. Alright. Take care Daddy."

She hung up and buried her head in her hands.

Sam looked at Jesse and whispered, "He didn't say 'I love you.'"

Jesse shook his head. "He never has."

He walked out the door and pulled her to her feet. Taking her hand he led her across the street and down to the sandy shore. They took a nice long walk breathing in the fresh salty air from the bay. When finally they were out of sight from his parents' house he pulled her close hoping to soothe her aching heart.

"I'm sorry Darlin'. It seemed like a good idea but I know it hurts when you talk to him." He stroked her back as she cried and didn't know why.

Finally she pulled away and wiped the tears. "I will never ever measure up. I just wish I wasn't such a disappointment to him."

Jesse took her hand and they walked farther hoping she could let go of the hurt before returning to the house. She tried to make small talk. "I like your parents. No wonder you're so dang perfect." She laughed trying to deflect.

Jesse smiled. "I KNOW! They're kind of sickening being so nice and all." He stopped her again and pulled her into his arms. "Thanks for coming honey. Just leave your daddy wherever he is and Jack in New York and Kenya in South Carolina. We're gonna have a good time especially since we got here early. We've got two whole days before the rest of the crew starts piling in. It's gonna look like a bomb went off once they get here."

She relaxed a little. "Good. I'll feel right at home then. I probably need to call one of the boys to let them know we're here. I miss them already. You okay if I do that now?"

"Sure, although the sun is about to set. But I can watch it alone." Jesse knew that would stop her dead in her tracks.

She put her phone away as they walked toward the house and watched the sun sink slowly into the water. A couple deep breaths later and Lydia was ready to pretend that she didn't care about her father at all. She didn't even bother telling Jesse that her dad was currently somewhere in Texas.

Chapter 9

In anticipation of Jesse being home his dad planned a project. Apparently Nora had wished for an outdoor shower for a very long time. Sam aimed to give her one for Christmas with Jesse's help.

"That's a great idea dad. Have I told you that Lydia has one at her house? Blue made it large enough that one end of it stays dry. Do you have a plan yet?"

Sam looked at him hoping. "I figured I'd leave that to my carpenter son." Jesse laughed. They began stepping off the area on the patio and thinking about the drainage.

Lydia wondered whether to hang out with them or to go inside and try to chat with Nora. Before she could push herself to do the obvious Nora came outside. "What a nice evening. Sam has finally gotten the mosquitos under control so we sit out here at night a lot."

Lydia smiled at the thought. "I love being outside. In the mornings I usually hit the front porch swing if it's not too cold and so far this year we've had very mild weather. In the evenings I walk out back and try to catch the sunset. It's hard to do that just after five though. That's right when Jesse gets home so I get distracted."

She caught herself and wondered what Nora was thinking. Nora laughed and glanced at Sam. "Don't I know it Darlin'. These men of ours…" She looked at Lydia and smiled approvingly. "Let's walk upstairs and check your rooms. I want to make sure you have everything you need. We can turn on the A/C if it feels stuffy."

Lydia rose and walked with her wondering if she were about to get a lecture or something. The woman obviously wanted her to herself. Once they were upstairs Nora began closing windows and turning on fans. "It is rather hot up here. I'm glad Jesse said something. Honey please make yourself at home. The towels are in this cupboard. I don't think you'll need it but there's an extra blanket in the top of the closet."

Lydia wished she'd get on with whatever she had on her mind. It briefly occurred to her to say, "Just spill it." But she refrained.

Finally Nora spoke. "Sam and I have had lots of children come through our home. There's enough love for all of them and there's plenty of love for you too. So don't be surprised when I treat you like a daughter. It's just how we roll around here." She smiled with such kindness that Lydia knew she meant it. "I hear you've got two grown boys of your own at home."

Lydia was suddenly very homesick. "Yep. In fact I need to call them to make sure they haven't burned the house down yet. Thank you Nora. Now I know where Jesse gets his kindness."

Lydia walked back downstairs feeling weird about the whole new mother/daughter thing. But at least the woman didn't seem to resent her relationship with her son.

She called both Shawn and Kurtis and left voice mails. Checking the time she realized they were probably still at work. She sighed and prayed for a good visit. One thing for sure; she would sleep well that night. The two day trip had been exhausting.

Surprisingly the men were busy cutting boards when she and Nora checked on them. It seemed building the shower had become a top priority. Nora laughed and told Lydia, "It only took Sam three years to get started. Now it must be done the second Jesse gets here." She shook her head at her husband and headed into the kitchen to cook supper.

Lydia decided she'd rather hold boards or fetch tools than hang out with her new 'mother.' The lady was really nice but she wasn't used to all that. Suddenly she thought of Tessa and laughed. Lydia had given her the Nora treatment the minute she'd met her too. She decided to go into the kitchen instead. One could always use another mother.

~~~~~~~

"What can I do to help?" she asked.

Nora began unloading items from the refrigerator. "Would you put together the salad? Just make it however you like. I'm gonna do something with this chicken."

Lydia looked at the lettuce and thought. Jesse was teaching her to be honest but she wondered exactly how honest to be. If she actually did what she preferred to do with the lettuce she'd drop it in the trash. Instead she washed it and put it on paper towels to drain while she looked at the other stuff Nora had out. She wondered what to do with the avocado and if the mushrooms were for the salad. Nora noticed her hesitation and laughed.

"Are you having a hard time there Darlin'? I'll be honest with you. I bought lettuce because you were coming. I don't really care for it."

Lydia laughed too. "Good, because I don't care a thing about salad, unless it's full of bacon or something."

Nora was surprised. "Honey as skinny as you are I figured you lived off lettuce. We'll toss that back in the fridge and do something else. Got any idea what I can do with this chicken? Sam usually cooks for us but he's all excited about Jesse being here so I thought I'd give it a shot."

Suddenly Lydia knew she was going to be fine. Not only had Nora admitted to not being a great cook but she had also called her skinny. Perhaps if the whole 'mother' thing didn't work out surely they could be friends.

After a nice supper of baked chicken with mushroom sauce and corn on the cob, Nora and Lydia cleaned the kitchen and the men went back to work on the shower. Eventually the four of them sat on the patio together trying to envision the completed project. After a good bit of laughter over mishaps of Christmases past, Lydia finally felt confident enough to make a suggestion.

"Jesse have you thought about adding a sink on the outside of it? I love mine for cleaning paint brushes and especially for Shawn to wash up after working on cars."

He tipped his head at her and smiled. "Girl this project is already bigger than what me and dad can get done before the crud hits the fan."

She tried to look repentant, "Sorry. Didn't mean to start a ruckus."

Nora and Sam piped up and agreed together that an outdoor handwashing sink would be perfect. Jesse pointed a finger at Lydia and laughed. "You just got put on the naughty list."

She rose and stretched. "Well it seems my work here is done. I'm whooped. Will it hurt anybody's feelings if I go on to bed?"

It surprised her when both Sam and Nora rose and gave her a hug. "Good night honey. Sleep well." Sam kissed her on the head and Nora kissed her on the cheek.

Jesse walked her upstairs to her door. "How's it feel in here?" He stepped inside her room and pulled a blanket from the shelf in the closet. "It can get pretty cold with the air on. I'm gonna go ahead and cut it off so you don't start hurting." He showed her the thermostat at the landing and added, "I'm so tired I don't think anything is gonna keep me awake tonight."

He pulled her into his arms and held her tight for a nice long minute. "Sleep well girl. Did you know that I love you?"

"I knew it!" She whispered as she smiled. "I love you too Cowboy. Night night." She turned to go because for some reason she didn't expect him to kiss her in his parents' home.

He held her hand and pulled her back toward him. "Uh-oh. Did I mess up with the sink comment?" He asked wondering.

She laughed and answered, "No silly. That was funny. You just haven't kissed me since we got here and I thought maybe your parents had a no kissing rule or something."

He got a good laugh at that. "Honey they're probably making out even as we speak. This is the kissingest house you'll ever be in." He pulled her close again. "I just didn't want to make you uncomfortable."

He leaned in for a kiss. "Good night Darlin'. Thank you for coming with me. I hope you rest well. Now let me get back to the patio and see if daddy's figured out where he wants that sink."

Chapter 10

She forgot to check the closet. The door was cracked just a tiny bit and someone watched as she undressed. Quickly she shucked her clothes and threw them in a corner. Her old Panther jersey and a pair of undies would be really comfortable after two long days on the road. Cool sheets melted her body into such deep sleep that everything blended together. Neither Shawn nor Kurtis made it home after work. Lights from an ambulance beckoned in the distance but she couldn't get her legs to move. Jack laughed at her for being afraid then kissed her til it hurt. She realized he didn't love her at all. The closet door opened slowly and the man stepped from the shadows. She still couldn't run but was finally able to turn. He grabbed her hair and jerked her backward. She tried to scream but there was no sound. Her daddy called from the other room but she couldn't obey. The smell of spoiled milk filled her nostrils and she thought she might be sick. The man shook her hard. Maybe if she screamed louder Jesse would hear and come find her. She screamed with all her might trying to fight off the man. If only Jesse would come.

~~~~~~~

Sam and Nora sat snuggled together on the patio swing which hung from a frame Jesse made for them last Christmas. "Every southern home needs a swing!" his mama had exclaimed happily at his gift. He'd been glad to give them a place to sit together outside. He had thought of Lydia when he made it even though she had no idea that Kenya had terminated their marriage. As slowly as Lydia moved in matters of the heart he was very careful not to reveal he was single lest she cut ties. His neighbor and friend had finally warmed up to him enough that they'd begun sitting together on her swing during counseling sessions. Thinking of the things he'd prayed for only a year ago when he'd brought the swing to his parents, he was amazed at the unfolding of God's plan. Finally it seemed his beautiful friend was as much in love with him as he was with her.

His parents were so pleased and happy for him. Jesse had always been such a gentle soul but had broken their hearts by marrying a girl they did not approve of right out of college. The few times she'd visited their former home in Waco she had turned up her nose at everything. Nothing was good enough and she refused to even share a meal with them. She smirked at their simple country lifestyle which happened to include seven children. Jesse tried to make excuses for her arrogance but they could tell he was unhappy. It didn't surprise them when she left after only three years. It also didn't surprise them that Jesse remained faithful to her praying for her return. Now finally it looked like the man was allowing himself the joy of loving someone who obviously adored him. They prayed daily that God's plan would somehow still include children for Jesse. They knew it had always been his dream to have a big family just like theirs.

His mom turned the conversation to Lydia. "Jesse honey she is so dear. Did you hear her tell her daddy that she's serious about you?" Nora smiled at her son. She knew he'd heard because his face had lit up.

"I DID hear it. That's a really big step for her considering she doesn't share much of anything with him. So daddy, what are you thinkin'? I made the mistake of not asking last time and I've paid for it ever since." He smiled at his father knowing already that he liked Lydia.

His dad took a minute to answer. "I'm going to pay her the highest compliment possible. She reminds me of your mother in that what you see is what you get. I don't think she'll be putting on airs for anybody."

Jesse laughed, "Nope. She really does remind me of you mama. Just so pretty in your easy goin' no frills way with your ball cap and flip flops. You would love her little farm house, so neat and simple. I'm afraid for you to see it though or you'll be having me build a sunroom." He shook his head, "I still can't believe she agreed to come down here with me. She's such a homebody."

Sam looked at him warmly. "The main thing is that she knows the Lord and she's growing. Are you two still studying Scripture together?"

Jesse nodded. "Every day. And I know she reads and studies on her own too. She's not the same girl she was a few years ago. Bless her heart. She's been through a lot but it's made her who…"

A terrifying scream pierced the night air.

Jesse leapt from his seat knocking over an end table and a pitcher of iced tea. He bounded up the stairs to her room and burst through the door. The light from the hall revealed a woman in the midst of a terrible dream who couldn't wake up. Jesse sat on the bed and pulled her close.

"LYDIA! Wake up honey! It's Jesse!" He shook her gently then hugged her again to himself. "Wake up Darlin'!"

She finally opened her eyes and saw Jesse. Relaxing into his chest she began to sob. "Oh my goodness. That was a bad one. I'm so sorry."

His parents watched from the doorway then tiptoed back downstairs. Jesse whispered and rubbed her back. "It's okay honey. I gotcha." He held her until she finally quit snubbing.

She looked at him tearfully. "Your parents are going to think I'm a nutcase!" She tried to laugh.

Jesse pulled her back to his chest and teased. "Shhh… don't worry about it. They're outside sending the cops home."

She pulled back so she could look at him. Finally she smiled and relaxed again as he stroked her back.

His gentle embrace and deep voice brought such comfort to her soul that she found herself over the terrible dream faster than normal. She was almost sleepy again.

"I'm okay Jesse-man. Please apologize to your parents for me." She sighed deeply and lay back down.

Jesse still sat on the bed and stroked her hair from her face. "I'm the one you should be apologizing to."

"Why's that honey?" She took his hand and kissed it.

"I can't believe you're cheating on me." He tried to look sad. "Wearing a Jake Delhomme jersey like I have no feelings."

She laughed. "Sorry. I'm loyal to the old guys. At least it's not Kuechly."

He wiped a tear from her face and kissed her forehead. "You gonna be okay? I can sleep in the other bed in here if you want me too. We'll leave the door open."

"Nah, I'm fine. Thank you for taking care of me. I'm sorry I'm such a psycho." She tried to laugh but wondered if it were true.

He kissed her lightly. "Maybe leave the lamp on since you're in a strange place. I love you honey. I'll be praying you rest well."

She smiled at her beloved gentle man. "I love you too sweet Jesse."

Chapter 11

No one said a word about the nightmare the next morning. Sam invited Lydia on a walk with him and she gladly accepted. Nora ran the stairs while Jesse got a shower and hoped his knee would quit throbbing. Bounding up the steps in terror had taken its toll but he didn't dare speak of it lest Lydia feel even worse. He found himself thanking the Lord that his dad was in good enough shape to walk as he knew Lydia would relish being on the beach at sunrise. His mom bounded up and down the steps and he wondered how many trips she'd make before being done.

He sat at the kitchen table making a list of supplies needed. Apparently Lydia had made the coffee as it was much better than he was used to having there. The weather was already warming up nicely and the forecast promised a beautiful Christmas weekend. He hoped he'd be able to play football on the beach with the family. He hated feeling old especially in front of his younger girlfriend.

He smiled to himself at the thought of her. His brothers were going to be so happy. And his only sister Magdalene would be thrilled for him. Plus all those grandbabies would warm Lydia up to his dream for them. He prayed and watched for his dad to return with his girl.

Lord it's been so long since I first started praying for her! Thank You for working in both our lives. I still can't believe You convinced her to come down here with me! You're so good Father. Help us the next few days in particular. Thy will be done.

She and his dad came through the door laughing. His mom bounded down the steps for the last time and smacked her husband on the rear.

"Whew!" she sighed as she fanned herself. "It's rather toasty for December, even in Corpus! What's the weather like in North Carolina right now?"

Jesse responded while checking his phone. "It's unseasonably warm but not this warm. So mom, would you and Lydia run pick up supplies so dad and I can throw down on the shower? He's got most of the stuff for the plumbing but I need a couple more things if we're gonna add a sink." He shot Lydia a mischievous look. "Little things like a sink."

His mom laughed. "Yep. Can I take your truck? You know I love driving that big ol' thing through these little tight roads down here. Everybody scatters when they see me coming."

Jesse didn't think twice. "Sure." He tossed her the keys then noticed Lydia's surprised look. "And whatever you do, do NOT let Lydia drive." He smiled a teasing smile.

The women downed a quick bowl of cereal then headed out together like a couple school girls. Lydia was thankful that his mom wore a pair of faded jean shorts, a tank top and a ball cap since she had on the same except she wore a t-shirt. They searched the aisles for the items on Jesse's list stopping to call him for clarification several times. Lydia found herself laughing at Nora's craziness and easy going manner. Like Jesse she wasn't easily aggravated. But like Lydia she didn't mind saying what she thought. Unlike either one of them shyness was NOT an issue. At one point Lydia found herself holding a rolling step ladder while Nora scampered to the top to search for a particular faucet she wanted. A nice looking salesman playfully reprimanded her for being on a ladder which was clearly marked 'Employees Only.'

Lydia was embarrassed but impressed with her new friend when she delivered her own set of instructions to the man. He stumbled all over himself trying to please. When finally the faucet of Nora's choice was retrieved in an unopened box she rewarded him with a very nice smile. She glanced at his name tag. "Thank you so much Rick. Now could you please help us find…" She took the list from Lydia and Rick became her own personal shopper.

As they loaded the truck Nora commented, "When I start feeling old and unattractive, I take a trip to the home improvement warehouse. I almost always feel better about myself by the time I leave." They laughed so easily together that Lydia began wishing Nora lived closer to her. She could picture them doing all sorts of things though she'd never in her life had a girlfriend that she trusted.

Lydia thought of her one female friend.

Except for Ann at the diner. I can always count on her.

Nora interrupted her thoughts. "Did you bring your bathing suit?"

Lydia nodded. "I did… but I don't know that I'll put it on. Jesse's never seen me in a bathing suit so I'm not real sure about that."

Nora laughed. "You are so much like Jesse; so private. Honey you are gorgeous with your long legs and beautiful eyes. And that smile of yours has captured my son's tender heart. I'm so glad he's found you. He kept telling his daddy, 'Pray for this girl. She's just a friend but…' and then he'd go on to talk about you for an hour. Sam and I have prayed for you for years. I'm so glad we've finally met."

The woman nearly ran a guy off the road who dared to venture into her lane. Lydia laughed and recognized herself once again. She wondered if Nora had ever been as rough as her and ventured asking.

"Do you and Sam ever ride motorcycles?"

Nora sighed. "I took a class and nearly killed all the other students. My legs aren't long enough to reach everything properly and I couldn't get the hang of stopping. Weaving through the cones was easy. I loved the speed and learning to ride. But I was last in line and when it came time to use the breaks, I couldn't figure it out and went plowing into the whole row of bikes. They took my keys and kicked me out. But at least I didn't cry."

Lydia laughed louder than she wished she would've and knew exactly what she was talking about. "Yep. Using both breaks can get tricky with all that power especially on a heavy bike. But maybe y'all can come visit sometime and we'll take you to the Blueridge. I'll ride with Jesse and let you and Sam take mine. Maybe we could take a trip this spring when the mountain laurels and rhododendrons bloom."

Nora looked at her pleased. "That sounds like so much fun. It's a date! Maybe I can get some of that hot pepper jelly you found for Jesse. He went on and on about that stuff. You'd think I could find some down here as close as we are to Mexico."

Lydia wondered if Jesse's parents knew every single thing there was to know about her. But somehow it didn't matter. Instead it made her feel very loved that Jesse had talked about her so much. She decided to open up a bit more.

"I'm sorry about last night. I tend to have the most terrifying dreams when I'm really tired or in a new place. I know it's terrible to hear someone screaming like a banshee."

Nora answered easily. "Don't worry about it. Honey it's a wonder you haven't lost your mind with all the stuff you've endured. Be careful not to get too hot. I used to have bad dreams if I used a heating pad or an electric blanket, but not as bad as yours I'm sure."

Lydia realized that she was sweated wet when she woke. Perhaps that was part of it too. "Life is a mystery sometimes. I'll definitely keep that in mind." She nodded. "I've also figured out that part of the pain that comes on suddenly is due to MSG. The first time Jesse and I went out we ended up in a clinic thinking I was having a stroke. There must've been monosodium glutamate in something at the banquet. I'm learning by keeping the labels of the stuff that seems to bother me."

Nora agreed. "Watch out for cottonseed oil. That gives me chest pains and they've started adding it to crackers and peanut butter and all sorts of things like shortening. You're wise to read the labels."

The guys had made great headway when they returned and were happy with the purchases. But Jesse was happiest seeing the two women he loved best in the world laughing and talking together as friends. It seemed yet another prayer had been answered.

Chapter 12

The four of them worked most of the day on the shower until it was nearly finished. Nora proclaimed with authority, "Okay people. It's break time. I know you men would work without stopping but I think it's time for a dip in the pool!"

A look of dread came over Lydia's face. Jesse noticed but Sam and Nora picked up a few items and headed inside to change. Lydia made herself busy straightening the job sight. Jesse looked at her and smiled sympathetically. "I understand honey. But it's better to get this over with while it's just us four than after all my brothers get here. Believe me, you'll be going into the pool whether you're fully clothed or in your bathing suit."

She sighed. "But if the water's cold I'll start hurting. Maybe if you tell them that..." She tried to stall.

He laughed. "Sorry Darlin'. The pool is heated. It's like swimming in bathwater. C'mon. It's just me honey. Don't be shy." He took her hand and led her inside.

She changed in her room and wondered what to wear over her bathing suit. Why was it so hard? She'd spent the whole day with Jack at the beach. Then she'd gone back there and shucked her clothes down to her swimsuit again just to walk with him. What had changed?

She looked at herself in the full length mirror. It was a modest suit but it was a two piece. Blue had never let her wear anything like that. Jesse was important to her and Godly. His parents were so good and noble. She'd never been around people she respected so much.

Lord please help me to not mess up. I don't know what I'm afraid of... except I keep wondering what they'd think of me if they knew all the stuff in my past... how I grew up... I'm sure not good enough for their son.

She wondered if Jesse had told them where he'd found her after Blue's death. Pulling a Carolina Tarheel shirt over her bathing suit she gathered her hair into a ponytail and sighed.

Jesse wouldn't tell them anything embarrassing about me. He's so protective and private just like I am. But even if he has they've sure treated me kind so maybe it doesn't matter.

She stepped into a pair of cutoffs and grabbed a towel. Jesse waited for her on the landing outside the bedroom door.

"Don't look at me." She smiled at him teasing.

He was glad she relaxed. The pool was going to be a welcome relief to his very tired body and aching knee.

When they rounded the house Nora stood by the pool laughing at her husband who bounced on the diving board. "Flip baby flip!" She urged him to show off his diving skill. He complied and Lydia could tell the man would do anything to impress his love.

Nora cheered loudly and clapped as he came up smiling. "You still got it baby!" She removed her dark green Baylor Bears tee to reveal a green and yellow plaid two piece. Lydia laughed and pulled her baby blue t-shirt off. Their bathing suits were almost identical except that her plaid bottoms were blue and white.

Nora called to Sam. "Look at us honey. Twins joined at the heart!" She dove in and swam easily to him. Jesse walked gingerly down the wide steps at the shallow end and sat down. It was the first time Lydia noticed he seemed to be in pain. She dropped her cutoffs and shirt on a lounge chair and stepped in beside him.

"Sorry you're hurting. Is it from the trip?" She asked as she sat near him on the step. As promised the water was perfect and soothing.

Jesse showed her the scar from his surgery. His legs were tanned and covered with blonde hair. His bare shoulder brushed hers and her heart leaped at being so close to him. He answered trying not to reveal he'd hurt it going up the stairs when she screamed. "The trip is probably part of the problem. I may have to have my knee scoped again. It's a simple surgery and it sure helped last time." He stretched his leg carefully. "You've told me before how much you love the water. Go ahead and take advantage. Once the whole family gets here there will be no relaxing swims after that." He smiled at her and had a hard time looking away. His mom called from the diving board.

"C'mon sistuh! Show me whatcha got!" She leapt into the air making the board spring when she came back down then turned forward in a pretty dive.

Lydia shook her head and laughed. "Good gracious at your parents! They're so young and I feel so old!" She smiled at Jesse and noticed his look toward her.

"Do you know how to dive?" He stalled trying to keep her near.

She answered still looking into his sparkling eyes. "I do but it's been a really long time since I've gone off a board. I'm usually diving from a dock or a boat." She reached up and pushed his hair from his face. The sun was warm on their backs and the water lapped at their legs. "Hard to believe it's December." She smiled at him that smile that melted his soul as she continued to stroke his hair.

"It's not always this warm. But I'm glad the Lord blessed us especially since this is your first time here." He took her hand and kissed it. "I know I keep saying it but thank you so much for coming with me." He glanced at her lips and longed to kiss her.

"Let me go show your mother how this is done." She pushed into the water and swam effortlessly to the other end. Jesse watched surprised at how graceful she glided through the water without a splash. The day she'd run to him from the barn he got the impression she was terribly uncoordinated. Apparently she was just being funny. He laughed at the memory and watched as she climbed the ladder near the diving board. His heart pounded at the sight of her. Jesse spoke to his Friend.

You did good Lord when you put her together. Mercy! I'm glad I'm having this time with her now before my brothers come so they can't see the goofy look on my face. Of course I'll probably look the same then too.

He smiled as she walked to the end of the board and jumped trying to make it spring. But she slipped and did a belly flop onto the water smacking it hard. Sam and Nora covered their mouths trying not to laugh. They looked at Jesse and mouthed, "Owwwch!"

He shook his head and watched her swim toward him. She came up laughing. "See, THAT's how it's done!" Her front side was red and splotchy.

Jesse frowned and looked as she sat down. "That had to hurt. Look how red you are. Want me to…"

He looked up at her and laughed. "I'm not sure what to offer at this point."

She laughed at him. "Nope, me neither." She looked toward Sam and Nora and stood with her arms in the air like a victorious gymnast. "I'm OKAY!"

She called over to them. "Whatdaya think? A ten?"

Jesse spoke to her low so his parents couldn't hear. "You're definitely a ten Darlin'."

She laughed and swam away from him. Her body still burned. Up the ladder she went for another try. Again she landed hard on the water. This time she came up red faced and sputtering. "It's okay! I've got this!" Straight to the ladder she went and back to the board. Standing on the end she looked toward Nora and Sam who sat on the side of the pool cheering her on.

"There's something wrong with your diving board. I hope you know that." She tried again and nearly got it. Her legs smacked the top of the water hard but otherwise it was definitely better.

She swam toward Jesse and sat on the steps resting.

"That was a good one!" He tried to encourage her.

She looked at him and laughed. "NO it wasn't. Look at my legs!" She stretched them out in front of her.

He nodded and smiled. "I see them." She heard his mischief when he added. "Stand up and show me again Darlin'."

She glided away from him on top of the water. Climbing the ladder she headed to the board. Stopping at the end she took a deep breath and tried to relax.

Nora called to her. "Dive without springing first. That'll give you the hang of it."

Lydia gave it a try and entered the water head first without a splash. When she came up everyone was cheering. She swam to the ladder and went back to the board. "Okay this is it. Do or die…"

She sprang hard on the board and went off the end. Her body landed on top of the water with a loud smack splashing Nora and Sam. She swam to where Jesse waited and sat beside him.

"I think that was good don't you?" She looked at him nodding.

His reply made her laugh. "Yep. Perfect ten. I just hate my brothers weren't here to see it."

Chapter 13

"So much for a relaxing swim!" Lydia thought as she showered upstairs. At least she'd get to wash her hair before bathroom space became a premium. But with Jesse and Sam working hard to finish the shower it might actually be done in time to help with the crowd. She tried to remember all the brothers Jesse had told her about. Recalling his one and only sister was easy. She was the youngest and apparently had been a big surprise. Nora and Sam discovered they were expecting when Nora was forty and Sam was forty seven. The pregnancy was tricky and of course considered high risk but the family had been rewarded with their only daughter. Baby Magdalene was showered with love and protection by her six older brothers. Jesse adored her and dubbed her Maggie from day one. He'd been seventeen when they brought her home from the hospital. Now she was twenty and shared an apartment with friends near Baylor University.

Lydia dressed and wrapped her hair in a towel. She found Nora downstairs briskly drying her hair with a towel as well. "I don't have a clue what we're doin' for supper." Nora tossed the towel into the laundry room and looked into the fridge. "Got any ideas?" With her short hair sticking up all over, she looked at Lydia for suggestions. For a moment Lydia was envious. It would take forever for her hair to dry.

"I could treat us to something if you don't mind driving. Jesse doesn't trust me with his truck." She unwound the towel from her head and began combing out her hair.

Nora looked at her surprised. "That's funny. I'm a terrible driver so you must be really bad." She laughed. "Yeah let's go get something. It'll be a lot quicker. We'll stay away from fast food. In fact there's an authentic Mexican place that makes great burritos. We'll hit the S.P.I.D and be there and back in no time."

Lydia looked at her wondering. Nora added, "The South Padre Island Drive; Believe me, you don't want to go there this time of day unless you have to. People down here are crazy! But let's do it anyway!"

Lydia grabbed some money happy to be treating the family to supper. She twirled her hair into curls while Nora drove in the wild evening traffic.

"Good gracious! Folks just change lanes all willy-nilly don't they?"

Nora laughed glad to have Lydia along. "You don't blow dry your hair do you?" She glanced at her while Lydia finger curled each strand.

Lydia replied, "Well I can but it's not pretty. It sorta turns into cotton candy. Not a good look."

Nora nodded. "That's how Maggie's hair is. Jesse's always loved her hair. It's dark brown and curly like mine was before it turned gray. When she came home last year at Christmas and had cut it all off I thought Jesse was gonna cry." Nora laughed again. "Bless his heart. He loves his sister. I can't wait for you to meet her."

Lydia wondered if she'd find it as easy to warm up to Maggie as she had to Nora. She actually enjoyed hanging out with the woman and even felt comfortable enough to ask.

"I just found out it's Jesse's birthday this Sunday or Gotcha Day as he so happily informed me. That is so sweet!" She smiled at Nora's happiness. "Do you have any idea of something I could give him? I'm a terrible shopper. If I were at home I'd just make him something. He always loves that."

Nora smiled and measured her words. She looked at Lydia with kindness and nearly teared up.

"Honey I think you've already given Jesse the best gift by coming down here with him. He just wants to spend time with you. So maybe take him out to eat or something private like that." She looked away hoping not to get emotional. The prayer of her heart was for her beloved son's happiness. He'd waited so long. The girl he had brought for their approval had definitely been a Godsend.

Lydia protested. "But I need something for him to unwrap."

Nora smiled at her innocence and refrained from saying what she thought.

Maybe next year Darlin'.

~~~~~~~

Jesse could tell that Lydia was stalling, trying not to go to bed. She yawned and even nodded off as the four of them visited well past her normal bedtime.

"Honey, why don't you go on to bed? We promise not to have fun without you."

She looked at him bleary eyed. "Oh but you will. As soon as I'm upstairs Sam is going to tell something funny about you growing up and I'm gonna miss it."

Jesse looked at her knowing that wasn't the issue. "Here. Lie down on the sofa. I'll wake you when it's time to go upstairs."

Lydia relaxed into the soft couch and took the throw he spread over her legs. Jesse pulled her feet into his lap and began massaging them. She was immediately out.

Sam and Nora realized she delayed sleeping because of the nightmare. Sam whispered to Jesse, "Dwell with your wife with understanding."

Jesse smiled at his dad and nodded. "Probably saved your life a couple of times if I know mom."

The three of them laughed softly and watched as Lydia smiled in her sleep. His dad had used the word 'wife.'

Sam and Nora turned in long before Jesse. He loved relaxing on the large sofa recliner with Lydia. She rested so peacefully that he hated to wake her. If only he could carry her upstairs without waking her he would. But his knee still throbbed and he didn't dare risk it giving way with her in his arms.

He leaned over and whispered softly. "Sweetheart… time to move."

She pushed him away forcefully and murmured. "Don't you DARE call me Sweetheart! I'm Jesse's girl." She didn't move. Jesse laughed as he thought.

That's right Jack! You can't hurt her anymore. She's Jesse's girl!

Chapter 14

Lydia slept so hard and so well that when she woke Christmas Eve morning she wondered how she'd ended up in bed. She still wore the clothes from the evening before and her lamp was on. She headed to the bathroom glad to find it empty. There was activity downstairs and she couldn't believe Jesse had gotten up before her. She quickly freshened up and tiptoed down the steps trying to hear.

The man was singing.

Stopping halfway down she listened.

"And I know… that I can't … tell you enough… that all I need… in this life… is your crazy love…"

He sang more words she couldn't hear but she recognized the song as the one they'd danced to at his house the night of their date. He sounded so happy that she sat down on the steps and waited as he sang.

"And if all I've got… is your hand in my hand, baby I could die… a happy man."

She smiled at his sweetness and headed to him. "Good morning Jesse-man. That sure is a pretty song."

He turned and smiled at her. "I made the coffee but it won't be as good as yours." He pulled her close and whispered. "Did you sleep well?" He moved her to music that only he could hear. They danced slowly in the kitchen and he hummed softly. "Baby I could die a happy man…" He twirled her and smiled.

She smiled up at him and added, "Or you could LIVE and we could both be happy."

He gazed at her. "Whatever. Just as long as I'm with you Darlin'." He pulled her close and kissed her tenderly. "Relax girl. Mama and daddy are walking. I just need to get some kisses in before my brothers get here. They will be all up in our business the minute they walk through the door. I hope you're ready!"

He kissed her again and the side door opened. "Merry Christmas Unka Jesse!" A little girl about four years old ran toward him and hugged his leg. She stepped back and peered up at Lydia. "Mama! Unka Jesse gots a girlfrin…"

Jesse's brother Pete came through the door loaded down. His wife Abigail was right behind him with a crying baby in tow. She handed the screaming child to Jesse with a pacifier as she explained. "He's been fed, he's just gassy." Jesse placed the baby on his shoulder and smoothed his little back.

Pete and Abigail did a double take when they noticed Lydia. Jesse smiled and introduced her. "This is my girl Lydia. Lydia this is Pete and his pretty wife Abigail. This little fellow here is my namesake Jesse. His big sister is JoJo."

Lydia smiled and was still caught off guard when they hugged her warmly.

"Jesse! I can't believe you didn't tell me she was coming." Abby was shocked. She had decided long ago that Jesse would forever be a bachelor. That was one of the reasons they'd named the newest grandson after him. Pete busied himself with JoJo hoping not to give away the fact that he and Jesse had talked often about Lydia. In fact she had been on his prayer list for a very long time.

Jesse looked at Lydia. "I just brought her down here because the family needs a redhead."

Lydia laughed at his introduction. He smiled and added, "Well that and the fact that I'm crazy in love with her."

Baby Jesse burped loudly and spit up on his uncle's clean t-shirt. Lydia grabbed a dishtowel and tried to catch the undigested milk. "Glad to see you approve of me baby!" She laughed and reached for him. "Jesse honey it's all down your back. Let me hold Little Bit while you fetch a clean shirt."

Abby apologized and gave Lydia a warning when she cuddled the baby on her shoulder. "He'll probably anoint you too. But at least it's a Carolina shirt."

Lydia laughed again and slowly stroked baby Jesse's back. He settled into her shoulder and nuzzled her neck. "Oh sweet baby. I am in heaven." She swayed slowly with him to the song in her head and watched as Pete's family unpacked. He and Jesse were similar in coloring as Pete's hair was very light brown but short and spiked. If she remembered correctly Pete's adoption had finalized long before Jesse's though he was four years younger. His wife Abigail had olive skin and silky dark brown hair. JoJo was the spitting image of her mom while the baby was fair like his dad. For a moment Lydia allowed herself to wonder what their children would look like if she and Jesse were so blessed. Quickly she shook the image from her head. Past experience taught her not to get her hopes up especially with a man who had never actually spoken of marriage.

She kissed the top of the baby's head and soaked in his presence. Jesse returned to where she still swayed with the infant in the kitchen. He circled her from behind with his big arms and held them close. For a long tender moment they felt like a real family.

~~~~~~~

The downstairs guest room was set up with a crib by the queen sized bed. Pete's family unloaded their stuff in there and Lydia wondered where the rest of the family would stay. Silently she wished that she could sleep on the couch with Jesse nearby like at least part of the night before. She still wondered how she had landed upstairs and it dawned on her that she'd met Jesse's first brother in clothes she had slept in. Her hair was up in a ponytail and of course she had no makeup on.

"Oh well," she sighed. "What you see is what you get." She smiled again at Jesse's words. He was crazy in love with her and said so to his brother's family.

Jesse came through the house carrying bags of groceries. He glanced at Lydia and smiled broadly. "Don't let that boy steel all my kisses." He came back to where Lydia stood with the baby and held them again.

She whispered to him while he stood so close. "How did I get upstairs last night? The last thing I remember was sleeping really hard on the couch and you rubbing my feet."

Jesse whispered, "I carried you right up the stairs. It was easy. You're light as a feather!"

She tipped her head sideways and looked at him suspiciously. "You and who else?"

He laughed. "Actually I would have liked to have carried you but my sorry ol' knee wouldn't let me. So I just held your hand and walked you up. You don't remember?"

She shook her head wondering. "I didn't smack you or anything did I?" Something was amiss but she couldn't quite tell. She hoped with all hope that she hadn't called him Jack.

Jesse teased. "You promised to bake me an apple pie for my birthday. That part I'm sure of." He held her and baby Jesse again and kissed Lydia's neck. "And you told anyone who would listen that you are 'Jesse's girl.'"

She sighed with relief. "Yep. That part I'm sure of too." She turned and kissed him not worrying if anyone saw them. With her free hand she reached up and stroked his scruffy beard. "I like your face."

Jesse laughed and whispered, "I like your face too, especially when you don't shave." He left to help finish unloading Pete's minivan and wondered how many car seats would fit in the back of a Tundra.

Chapter 15

Son number four was the next to arrive. Benjamin was as blonde as Jesse but much smaller in stature. His wife Kelly had dark brown hair and a gorgeous smile. The two of them laughed easily and parked a camper in the back yard. Their three boys ran in and out of the house like gangbusters. Lydia guessed they were maybe five six and seven. Kelly definitely had her hands full but handled it all with ease.

"No need getting our tinsel in a tangle," she laughed as she shooed them outside. "Boys you can go across to the beach but stay where I can see you. And don't get in the water." Jesse watched as they crossed the road then returned to the house to introduce Lydia.

"Ben and Kelly this is my girl Lydia. Ben you'll be happy to know that she loves to dance. So tonight I want you to crank up the music for us earlier than usual." Lydia looked at him surprised but Benjamin was happy at the thought.

"I can do that! I just happened to bring my sound system. *'We'll have a house party… wake up all the neighbors…'*" He was singing a song Lydia didn't know but it made her laugh.

Kelly gave Lydia a hug. "Now Jesse finally has someone to dance with! Poor guy has had to settle for me all these years while Ben played deejay."

Jesse smiled at her. "I have NEVER 'settled' for you girl." He gave her a squeeze and kissed the top of her head.

Sam came through the door carrying a crying boy. His two older brothers couldn't wait to tell what happened. "Toby stepped on a jellyfish but Grammy scraped it with a seashell then told us to pee on it."

Kelly fluffed Toby's hair. "You okay buddy?" She looked at her other sons. "Way to take care of your brother. Get someone to watch you across the road before you go back. Is Grammy still down there?"

Sam nodded. "She'll be watching for them." He headed out the side door with Toby in his arms. "We're gonna check out the new shower Uncle Jesse built, right Toby?"

Lydia watched as the Ben and Kelly took it all in stride. Pete's family had closed their door and was trying to catch a quick nap. The whole house seemed to explode with chaos. Jesse followed his dad outside and Lydia figured she may as well get used to doing her own thing. She grabbed a couple water bottles and joined Nora on the beach with the boys.

Handing her the water she laughed as two little boys suddenly were very thirsty. Nora sighed.

Lydia held out her bottle. "Here guys. You two can share this one. I haven't worked up a thirst yet like Grammy has."

Nora laughed. "I hope I didn't wake you this morning. I started running the steps then realized I probably sound like a herd of elephants. So I walked with Sam instead. Did you sleep well?" She took a big swig of water glad that it did not contain little boy backwash.

Lydia watched as the two boys drank from her bottle like they were dying of thirst. "I DID sleep well. I've got a question for you and I hope this doesn't come across weird. But would it be okay if I slept on the couch tonight?"

Nora wondered, "Why would you want to do that? Is it to make room for the family or is it because you would rest better there?"

Lydia sighed but knew she could be truthful with her new friend. "I'm so afraid I'll have another nightmare and wake up the kids with a bloodcurdling scream. In fact I may just sleep in the truck."

Nora laughed. "You are not sleeping in the truck woman. The mosquitos will carry you off. But you're welcome to crash on the couch. I don't know that you'll get that much rest as some of the kids stay up late and some get up really early. But as long as you can function on about six hours sleep you should be fine. If Jesse's not too weird about it he could take the recliner end and then you wouldn't have to worry about nightmares. Honey you were passed out cold last night when we went to bed." She laughed again and Lydia was very relieved.

"Well just so you guys are okay with everything. I'm sorry to be such a bumpkin. I guess most women my age would just crawl into bed with their boyfriend and not worry about it."

Nora glanced at her with raised eyebrows. "Not at my house they wouldn't!" She softened her tone. "I'm glad you are the way you are. That's why Jesse has finally let himself love again. He trusts you and that is a very special thing."

Lydia smiled and added, "Yep. I trust him too. And me trusting anybody is a miracle. But he's earned it."

Nora surprised her and asked, "Do you ever hear from what's-his-name?"

Lydia laughed. "Not since I blocked his calls." Right on cue her phone buzzed. She didn't recognize the number and realized she'd still not heard from Shawn or Kurtis. Her heart dropped as she remembered her dream about the ambulance.

"Hello," she answered. Jack's voice greeted her.

"Merry Christmas Sweetheart!" His voice was bright and cheerful so Lydia immediately knew nothing tragic had happened to his parents. She didn't even answer him but instead stood to her feet and hurled her phone into the ocean as far as she could throw it. Without a word she sat back down beside Nora.

Two little boys looked at her amazed. Peyton the oldest piped up. "That was a GOOD throw Ain't Liddy."

She laughed and high fived him. The middle boy Marcus offered her a fist bump and added, "Now blow it up." He opened his fist and made an exploding sound.

"Like this?" she asked as she imitated him. He showed her again and they practiced until they were satisfied. They dropped the empty bottle at Lydia's feet and ran off to look for more jellyfish.

Sam, Jesse and the wounded boy Toby joined them. Sam was happy to inform Nora that the shower head she picked out was perfect. "With the extension I just unhooked it and rinsed him without the water hitting him in the face. Ben and Kelly are impressed. That's gonna keep a lot of mess down in their camper."

Jesse plunked down beside Lydia and asked, "Where's your phone? I tried calling you."

Nora looked away trying not to laugh. Lydia sighed and tried not to lie. "It's somewhere."

Jesse looked at her wondering. "Somewhere?"

Benjamin's middle boy Marcus came to stand beside Jesse and rubbed his shoulder with a sandy paw. "She chucked it in the ocean really far away. Want me to swim out there and see if I can find it?"

Jesse looked at Lydia and laughed. "Nah, I'm sure she had a good reason. Maybe check the edge of the water and see if it's washed up."

Marcus wasn't buying it. "Maybe tomorrow. It has a long way to go." Off he ran to see what his brother was looking at.

Jesse still looked at Lydia and she finally faced him. "What?"

He put his arm about her waist and hugged her to his side. "Nothing Darlin'. Just don't get too far from me without a phone. I nearly panic when I can't find you."

Lydia, Nora, Sam and little Toby leaned forward in the line where they all sat facing the ocean. Looking at Jesse they said in unison, "Awww…"

Lydia pulled Jesse to his feet. "C'mon Cowboy. Walk with me, talk with me." She took his hand and they headed down the beach. Marcus ran to catch up. Lydia leaned down and whispered but Jesse could hear. "I need to talk to Uncle Jesse about something. Can you stay with Grammy and Poppy this time?"

He crossed his arms and frowned to express his displeasure.

Jesse instructed his nephew. "Marcus do as Aunt Lydia asked. When we get back we'll throw the football." The boy walked back to the family unhappy that his favorite uncle had chosen the new girl over him.

Jesse took Lydia's hand and asked as they strolled away from the family. "What's wrong honey? Is it time for me to give Jack a call?"

"Nah, he's gurgling at the bottom of the Gulf somewhere. I just wanted to ask if you'd sleep with me tonight." She looked at him and smiled mischievously.

Jesse cleared his throat and answered with a smile. "Well Merry Christmas to me!"

She laughed. "I got permission from your mom and everything." She noticed his look and decided not to carry out the joke too long. "Actually I want to sleep on the couch and she suggested you sleep in the recliner. I'm worried about screaming during the night and waking the babies. What do you think?"

He started to speak but she interrupted. "It's okay if you don't want to. I understand. I'm so weird."

He began again. "Well... I was going to suggest that last night but you were so far gone you couldn't process the question. I think it's a great idea but you have to wear your new pajamas."

She whined. "Nooo... honey I get too hottttt..."

He laughed at her. "I'm kidding. Actually this will be good. It will free up the two bedrooms for when the rest of the crew gets here.

"Thank you Jesse." she smiled up at him.

"Yes ma'am! You are welcome!" He exaggerated his southern drawl.

She decided to ask. "By the way. I'm still wondering where you got that Victoria Secret bag."

He noticed the look she gave him resembled the one his mother had used on him often. Searching for words he stammered, "Ohhh... somewhere."

She laughed at his discomfort and knew the man probably found it on a jobsite or somewhere. She couldn't imagine him as shy as he was actually entering one of the stores.

Chapter 16

The rest of the crew arrived during the day exploding all over the house with food and children. Son number three Adam arrived and interestingly his wife was Eva. She apologized as she warned Lydia. "Don't be surprised if Ben's boys refer to me as Evil. I own it. Crowds tend to make me cranky." She and Adam each had two boys from previous marriages and Micah, a seven month old baby boy together. They set up a tent in the back yard for their family and were very happy to discover the new shower.

Lydia watched their sons Seth, Caleb, Sammy, and Asher across the road til they joined the cousins on the beach. Grammy and Poppy hugged them then started a game of freeze tag.

She realized that Jesse had very accurately described his family as 'all colors, shapes and sizes.' This branch seemed more Asian with creamy white skin and lovely eyes. Jesse informed her later that both Adam and Eva's birth parents were Korean. They'd met at Baylor University but married later after each lost spouses. Adam's first wife disappeared and left him with two young sons to raise alone. It seems he picked the boys up from preschool one day and came home to an empty house. He thanked God that at least there had not been a custody battle. Eva's husband died of an overdose and she still blamed herself. He'd struggled with depression but they'd put off treatment hoping they could work through it. Her only consolation was that they had two beautiful sons together. When she and Adam reconnected a few years later she knew it was meant to be. Happily she assumed the role of mother to his boys as well. The two found themselves turning thirty and wrangling five sons under the age of five. Camping just completed the inevitable chaos.

College seniors Jonathan and Barnabas came through the door together smiling and happy to be home for a few days. African American by birth, brothers by adoption and lifelong best friends they shared a house near Baylor. Immediately Lydia noticed their good natured banter and relaxed personalities. They reminded her of Shawn and Kurt as Jonathan was larger and very muscular while Barnabas was just coming into his own. They beamed at Jesse and hugged Lydia happily.

"Finally!" Jonathan smiled down at her. "A redhead! Now the family has it all!"

Barnabas hugged her too. "Except for some redheaded grandchildren." He smiled at Jesse. "When's the wedding?"

Lydia noticed that Jesse laughed nervously so she tried to help. "Knowing Jesse, in about five years IF I don't scare the man off with my crazy!" She laughed and took them to the kitchen. "I brought homemade oatmeal cookies but you can't let the little ones see you eating them." She opened a container and was delighted that they reacted the same way Shawn and Kurtis would. Suddenly she realized she couldn't call them and they couldn't call her either.

Stupid Jack.

Finding Jesse amongst the mayhem in the den she asked sheepishly, "Can I use your phone to call and check on the boys?"

He had already pulled it from his pocket. "Let's walk outside. I need to call Maggie first. It's odd that she's not here yet."

Lydia noticed how worried he looked. She understood and followed him out the side door.

"Hey honey. Where are you?" He listened and she saw his face cloud over. "Are you okay? Get back inside and lock the doors. I'll be right there. I love you too honey. It'll be okay."

Stepping inside he informed Kelly that he and Lydia needed to run an errand. Ben commented that that was code for needing to leave lest they lose their minds. Jesse hurried to his truck and asked Lydia to watch for kids as he navigated around the other vehicles. She wondered what had happened but was thankful that Jesse immediately included her rather than taking off by himself.

When finally they were headed down the road together he filled her in. "Maggie's been in a wreck. She said it's just a bump up but her truck has been spun around the wrong way on the S.P.I.D and she's shaking so bad she's afraid to drive. She's not that far up the road. Bless her heart."

His heart pounded as he tried to get to her as quickly as possible. He saw her on the other side of the median and sure enough she'd swapped ends in her little truck and sat precariously on the side of the highway facing oncoming traffic. Jesse exited at the next ramp and quickly navigated back toward her. With lights flashing he parked and ran to her pulling her from the truck into his arms.

She laughed and cried all at the same time. "Only me! Who else could this happen to?" She wiped a tear then noticed Lydia standing behind Jesse. "Oh! She came! Oh Jesse I'm so happy for you!" She turned loose of her big brother and reached for Lydia. "Hello. I'm the crazy sister everyone warned you about. Hey! We have the same hair, except we've been wishing for years we'd get a redhead." She laughed and gave Lydia a hug.

Jesse asked, "What happened girl? Are you hurt?"

Maggie sighed. "I'm gonna be sore tomorrow but maybe I won't have to play football. Some jerk hit the back left bumper when he was passing me and it set the truck to spinning. I don't even know how I got off the road without getting hit again. My stupid airbag didn't even pop out. I have no idea how to get turned around in this little space."

Traffic flew past them and the wind rocked them where they stood. It was all way too close for comfort. Jesse handed his keys to Lydia and assured Maggie. "I'll turn your truck around and take it home. You and Lydia follow me once I get it headed in the right direction."

Lydia walked with Maggie toward Jesse's Tundra. She called back to Jesse over her shoulder. "Don't worry! I am an excellent driver!"

Jesse shook his head and wondered which was worse: giving Lydia the keys to his truck or watching his little sister climb into it with her. He could barely fit his long frame behind the wheel of the Frontier even with the seat pushed back as far as it would go. It took a while but finally he got Maggie's truck headed in the right direction. Lydia followed close behind and he noticed that she was being especially careful.

Maggie asked as they drove, "So how did Jesse finally ask you out? He's been trying to get up the nerve for about a year I think."

Lydia laughed then thought about her words. "Really? Hmmm…"

Maggie hoped she hadn't messed up. "Well… not a REAL year. That's just a figure of speech. You know… like when someone says 'It's been FOREVER since I've seen you' and it's only been like a couple weeks." She laughed nervously.

Lydia laughed too and it put Maggie at ease. "We've been friends for a long time but the first time I felt like we were on an actual date it kinda freaked me out. I think Jesse knew that would happen so he kept finding things for us to do together without calling it dating." She smiled at the thought. "He is so sweet. I almost didn't realize how much I loved him til it was nearly too late." She sighed at the thought.

"Yeah, I was really praying for you about Jack." Maggie covered her mouth. "Jesse's gonna kill me. We're really close and he was about to lose his mind when Jack came swooping in. He said he's really handsome. Plus Kenya started stringing him along after all these years. She must've thought she could get something out of him. I know we're not supposed to hate people but I really kinda hate her guts."

Lydia laughed. "I kinda hate all of her. Why does she have to be so dang gorgeous?"

Maggie agreed. "I KNOW! But you're prettier. You're way more what Jesse likes than her little skinny butt."

Lydia laughed and thanked her. "Hey, do you mind dialing a number for me? I need to check on my boys and my phone is currently somewhere else."

Maggie pulled her phone from her purse and dialed Kurtis' number. Lydia was sad he didn't answer but left him a message.

"Kurtis honey I'm getting worried about y'all. Call Jesse and let us know you're okay. My phone is on the bottom of the ocean with Jack gurgling out Merry Christmas. So be proud of me. Call me son."

She sighed and handed the phone back to Maggie. It played her ringtone just as she dropped it into her purse.

"This is Maggie. Oh hi Kurtis. I'm Jesse's sister. Hold on. Lydia's turning into busy traffic and she's driving the Tundra. Just talk to me while she tries not to give my brother a heart attack. Oh really? Is that good news or bad?" She laughed. "Well you can always spend Christmas with us. We'll hardly know you're here." She looked at Lydia who made herself busy driving so the two of them would keep talking.

"Shame on her! Sounds like a very foolish chick if you ask me. You're welcome. So what are you doing for Christmas? I'm sorry. Well I'm not kidding. You can come down here. We'll find a place for you. You're welcome. I go back January 25th. They call this winter break. Yep… Sophomore…" She laughed again. Apparently Kurtis was making a nice impression. "Sounds good. Nice to meet you too. Here's Lydia. Merry Christmas!"

She handed the phone to Lydia with a smile. He asked if Maggie could hear then he questioned Lydia thoroughly about her as he also informed that Mykaela had gone out with someone else.

"Well honey it's not like you're engaged. She probably still wants to see you." She laughed at his reply. "I agree. Her loss. Hey are you okay? How are Shawn and Tessa? Good. If you need anything call Jesse's phone. I love you too."

She hung up just in time to figure out where to park Jesse's big ol' truck. It really wasn't that hard to drive and she wondered what all the fuss was about.

Chapter 17

White picnic tables were pushed end to end on the side patio for supper. Thirteen adults, eight children and two babies bowed together holding hands as Sam thanked the Lord for their food, their home, the family, the beautiful weather but most of all for His Son Jesus. Lydia wasn't the only one who teared up at the thankful hearts and the prayer offered by the faithful man.

She glanced at Jesse trying not to stare at her beloved man. He was so happy and relaxed sitting on a bench crammed between her and Barnabas who he affectionately called Squeeze. When she asked about the nickname later he told her that Barnabas hated the nickname Barney so they started calling him Squeeze because of the big hugs he gave. But his real name suited him best as he was definitely an encourager just like the man in the book of Acts he was named for. After adopting their forth son Nora and Sam had decided to adopt once more. Then two baby boys became available at the same time. Happily they welcomed them both and for years people thought they were twins. They weren't quite three when Nora found out she was expecting Maggie.

As Lydia tried to remember the names of everyone she wondered if God could still have a similar plan for her own life. She suddenly didn't feel old and past her expiration date at all. Hopefully Jesse didn't either.

The sun set gloriously as they cleared the paper plates and wrote names on the plastic cups so everyone could find theirs later. The big family made quick work of cleaning up the huge covered dish meal then gathered on the front lawn. Jesse put his arm about Lydia's shoulders and pointed to the corner of the yard. Sam plugged up the lights and the giant tree came alive with Christmas cheer.

Jesse laughed as he whispered to Lydia. "We're the rednecks they talk about that leave their lights up all year long. Mama and daddy planted that tree five years ago when they first moved here and it's already so huge it's hard to get the lights all the way to the top. So we just leave them there and plug 'em up on special occasions."

Ben pulled out his guitar and led them in Silent Night. Between the laughing and mixed up words Lydia could hear the voices of the kids as well as Jonathan and Barnabas' harmony. As they sang a few other carols she realized it had been a very long time since she'd enjoyed Christmas carols... maybe since never. It felt like what home should be. She prayed for Kurtis and wondered if he was lonely. If she hadn't launched her phone like a juvenile she could've at least texted him. The family sang *We Wish You a Merry Christmas* and adjourned to the house. Mamas bathed tubs full of children and Jesse fetched his surprise. Lydia helped him make the rounds as he handed out matching pajamas for everyone in the house. The laughter and excitement over the flannel outfits was unlike anything Lydia had ever experienced. Nora capped it off when she and Sam came out of their bedroom dressed alike. "Crank up the air sister!" She looked at Lydia and fanned herself with a magazine. "Go put yours on girl. You're a part of this madness now so just make the best of it!"

She and Jesse headed upstairs to find Jonathan coming out of one room dressed in his and Maggie from the other. "Where'd that Victoria Secret bag come from?" She winked at Lydia knowing it would embarrass her big brother.

Lydia laughed. "I don't know. That's your brother's store, not mine."

Jonathan murmured to Jesse as he passed him. "Way to go Jesse! I'm hoping for a Victoria Secret Christmas special myself."

Jesse shook his head and laughed at the very large college kid dressed in the blue flannel snowman pattern. Lydia emerged in hers but had her hair pinned up on top of her head. She adjusted the upstairs thermostat then turned to look at Jesse.

"Best idea ever!" She smiled so big that he knew she meant it and might even appreciate his crazy love affair with his family. He knew for sure she did when she slipped her arms around his neck and kissed him happily.

Barnabas came from the boys' room. "Umm hmm... Merry Christmas to Jesse!"

Jesse offered him a high five and leaned back in for another kiss. He whispered into Lydia's neck. "Yep. Merry Christmas to me."

~~~~~~~

When finally all the kids were bathed and dressed in their new pajamas the family lined up on the stairs for a photo.

Lydia watched from the den as little boys tried to see if they could push their heads between the bars on the banister. Jesse helped situate people so everyone could be seen. Lydia snapped pictures with different phones while the mayhem progressed. Eventually the children sat and pushed their legs through the rails so p.j. bottoms and feet dangled over the edge. Little hands gripped bars and happy faces peered through. She and Jesse laughed at how the boy cousins stretched their eyes and grins as they continued to push their heads forward as far as they'd go. The bottom step was reserved for Jesse once everyone was situated.

Lydia offered, "You join the family and I'll take the pictures."

Jesse shook his head. "Nope! Like mama said, you're part of this craziness whether you like it or not." He took her hand and led her to sit with him at the bottom. Someone pulled out a long selfie stick and began clicking. It was no small task but everyone was assured that they'd be sent copies. Babies started crying, Eva felt the claustrophobia building and Nora nearly passed out from the heat that rose from all the flannel laden bodies. When finally they were satisfied that surely one of the shots would turn out the children were led down to the den where Sam brought out his Bible. The kids sat in a semi-circle at his feet as he leaned forward in his chair.

With great excitement he read the Christmas story pausing often to answer questions.

"Did the barn have cows like our cows?" Marcus wanted to know. When his grandfather commended him on such a wise thought, it began a flurry of questions from the others.

They talked about camels and donkeys and what the barn smelled like and if it had flies. The children seemed to have no problem with the virgin birth or angels bursting through the night air. But they had to wonder who watched after the sheep when the shepherds went to see the baby. And why didn't the hotel people just let them camp in the lobby?

Sam loved it all.

"You guys are the smartest kids ever! Good questions always make us stronger so never be afraid to look carefully into God's Word." He smiled and closed his Bible. Gathering his little ones into a huddle he prayed for each one by name as they wiggled and nudged closer during the prayer. Asher sat on Sam's lap and patted his face trying to keep his eyes closed. But it was hard to take his eyes off his Poppy. When finally they broke huddle the kids were instructed to give kisses. They began making their rounds kissing each mama and daddy and uncle and aunt. Lydia did her best but still teared up at it all. She sat on an ottoman accepting more hugs and kisses in one night it seemed than in all the rest of her life combined.

Little hands worked on her hair from behind pulling a clip partway out. Lydia looked to find JoJo trying her best to help. "It's too messy back here. Maybe you can make it pretty for when you and Unkie Jesse gets married."

Lydia could feel half of her mane fall and the other half tangled onto the back of her head. Abby, JoJo's mom covered her mouth at her daughter's words. "Leave Aunt Lydia's hair alone honey. Hers is different from yours. Now give her a kiss and tell her night-night."

JoJo complied but hoped to enlighten Lydia more another day.

Eva brought baby Micah over for Lydia to kiss goodnight. She reached for him and asked, "Can I hold him a minute?"

Eva laughed and handed him over. "Gladly! That'll give me a chance to run the boys through the bathroom again before we head to the tent. Thank God it's not raining!"

Lydia bounced the chunky seven month old on her knee as he giggled with delight. More hands worked on her hair but it hardly mattered. Eventually she turned to find Maggie separating the strands and working them into a soft side braid. Lydia smiled as Maggie licked her fingers and made curls fall across her forehead.

Jesse stood against a wall observing and loving every second. JoJo's daddy Pete stopped next to him and said softly, "Sorry about before."

Jesse shook his head, "No problem. Apparently she's not scared off as easily as I thought she would be. I can't believe JoJo used the 'M' word." He laughed nervously.

Pete looked at his big brother and shook his head smiling. "Maybe it's time somebody did."

Chapter 18

Lydia made coffee in one of the pots she found in the kitchen in anticipation of the dance party Ben had promised. Jesse joined her there and surprised her by kissing her neck. "I like your hair like that. Very pretty." He whispered from behind.

She turned and smiled at him. "Your sister is a doll. She and Kurtis actually got to talk while I was driving your truck with great precision and skill."

Jesse smiled at her. The coffee began dripping and the aroma filled the air. "That's good. She was supposed to be bringing someone home with her tonight but he ditched her at the last minute. So maybe her visit with Kurtis was encouraging."

Lydia looked up at him and thought he might kiss her right there in the kitchen with people all over the place. For some reason it didn't embarrass her to be so close to him even though his family could see. Her heart pounded at his gentle embrace. "Do you think Maggie and Kurtis would go good together?"

He leaned closer and kissed her forehead. "I do. Maybe I'll invite her to visit me over spring break."

Lydia smiled and wondered if they should wait that long before getting them together. "I heard her invite him here since he's ended up alone for Christmas. If it wasn't so far I think he'd come." She kissed Jesse's cheek then turned to check the coffee since Ben was headed into the kitchen.

"Do I smell coffee?" Ben asked hopefully as he opened the cabinet for a mug. "Is that decaf or regular?"

Lydia answered that it was regular since the other is a 'why bother.' Ben laughed and put his mug back. "I can't have regular this late or I'll be up all night." He headed back to the den.

Lydia looked through the canisters and found decaf. "Hey Ben! I'll make a pot of unleaded for the delicate people." Laughter came from his brothers as his wife called, "THANK YOU!"

Nora joined them and asked, "Where'd you hide all the goodies?" Lydia began pulling cookies and muffins from the cabinets and stepped back so Jesse could retrieve the Buttermilk Brownies from the top shelf. They spread the desserts on the snack bar and Nora set out mugs, sugar and creamer. "Do you think anyone wants to fix a plate? We've got tons of leftovers. I can always count on my kids to bring a boatload of food." She smiled at Lydia as she set out a stack of plates. Lydia began removing food from the refrigerator.

Folks filed through filling plates. As many as could sat around the table, while others crashed on the couch holding food on their laps. The noise level was kept to a minimum since a baby and his sister slept in the guest room. Lydia realized Maggie was missing and went upstairs to check on her. Jesse laughed as his brothers looked at him with thumbs up and smiles. Adam commented, "We needed a redhead. You did good this time." Ben added, "I was just going to say that." Nora reached over and smoothed her eldest son's back. She smiled that smile of approval that Jesse loved so well.

His father however got up to refill his plate all of a sudden so Jesse followed him to the kitchen. "Dad? Tell me what you think. It's important to me."

His father embraced him and whispered, "I think our prayers have been answered. But you're the one who's gonna have to live with her. A redheaded temper is like a woman in menopause. It's not to be trifled with."

Jesse laughed at his father's words and the family nearly woke the baby laughing when Nora added, "I heard that."

Sam whispered rather loudly, "Apparently menopause does NOT affect the hearing."

Lydia could hear the laughter downstairs as she stepped into hers and Maggie's room. Maggie was stretched out on the bed laughing with someone on the phone. She looked up as Lydia entered. "Kurtis says hey." Lydia smiled. "Tell him Goober says hey back."

She gathered a few things including shorts and a tee for sleeping. She was dying in the flannel pajamas although she had to admit that Jesse looked extremely cute in his. She hoped the pictures turned out good and wished she had her phone so she could receive one.

She looked into the full length mirror and wondered if she could get by with wearing a tank top with the bottoms instead of the heavy pajama top. She changed and stood before Maggie asking.

"Look's good!" Maggie went back to Kurtis but Lydia still gazed into the mirror wondering. Maggie smacked her on the arm. "You're fine! My parents aren't weird like that. You've got on a bra so don't worry about it. And put your shorts on under those pants so you can shuck those suckers if you decide to later."

Lydia could feel her neck turn red as she knew Kurtis had heard. She shook her head at the reflection and realized again what a bumpkin she was.

As she headed down the steps she sighed with relief to find the guys had all exchanged their p.j. tops for t-shirts. Apparently the consuming of coffee had encouraged their decision. Nora had even switched her bottoms for shorts. She still fanned frantically. Lydia followed her lead and stepped into the bathroom to remove her outer layer. She realized she liked her hair the way Maggie had braided it loosely over one shoulder. But she still couldn't pull the trigger on the pajama pants. Someone knocked on the door so she left them on over her shorts. Maybe being in a tank top would help her cool off enough to enjoy coffee. She passed Eva who handed over baby Micah as she entered. "Mind holding him for a minute?" She seemed to be in a hurry. Lydia took the baby who screamed loudly at the sight of the door closing behind his mama.

Lydia hurried toward the kitchen to get his screams farther away from the other sleeping baby. Stepping outside to the patio she heard Jesse's voice.

"Am I clear? NO. I gave you more grace than you ever wanted. Now it's time to leave her alone. I can always come speak to you in person if you'd like."

Lydia stepped back into the house and noticed everyone had gone quiet. Even baby Micah had calmed down. She felt her face flush as all eyes seemed to be on her.

"I think Jesse's having a 'Come to Jesus' meeting with somebody." She made a scared face and the family laughed nervously. She wondered what was wrong.

Lydia leaned over to Nora. "Did Jack call Jesse?" She nodded yes then added. "Jesse will fill you in. I'm not sure what's going on."

Lydia could tell that something had changed the mood. She sat on the sofa with baby Micah and tickled his nose with her braid until he laughed a belly laugh and sucked it back in loudly. Everyone turned and started laughing at his giggles until Jesse returned from outside. He was definitely shaken. Lydia noticed the look on his face and handed off Micah in order to meet him in the kitchen. He took her hand and stepped outside.

"Let's walk down to the beach." Jesse sighed deeply. The sticky hot air hit her full force so she stopped and pulled off the pajama bottoms and tossed them on the swing. Jesse didn't seem to notice. He walked slowly toward the shore with shoulders stooped. He stopped at the road and waited for her to catch up. She grabbed his hand and they crossed the road together.

The stiff ocean breeze was a welcome relief. A gorgeous full moon reflected off the water and waves lapped gently on the shore. Jesse said nothing and she noticed that he swiped at a tear. She stopped their walk and pulled him close.

"Honey I don't care what's going on. Just know that I love you with all my heart." She stroked his back and tried to read his face. "You don't have to talk about it if you're not ready but I'm here for you no matter what." She hugged him again then took his hand as they walked. He still didn't speak.

Chapter 19

They walked for a long way then turned back toward the house. Jesse still had not spoken but had brushed tears away the entire time. Lydia tried to give him some space but was starting to worry. What could possibly cause him this much pain? She decided to say one thing before they returned to the others.

"Honey was that Jack on the phone?"

Jesse nodded yes.

She stopped walking and looked into his tear filled eyes. "No matter what he told you please remember that Jack is a liar."

Jesse nodded again. "I know." He took her into his arms and whispered, "I love you honey, with all my heart. It's not about that. I just need time to process something."

Her heart pounded and she wondered what in the world Jack might've told Jesse about her. Was it about the massage or the shower or the hair cut? But really none of that was so terrible that Jesse would be that upset. In fact he already knew the bulk of it. She had confessed to Jesse as her counselor how much in love she'd been with Jack.

She wondered if she was about to lose him. She'd known all along that she wasn't good enough for such an honorable man. What had Jack said to ruin Jesse's happiness? If only she had a phone she'd call Jack herself.

Finally the house was in sight and she actually shivered in the cool air. A cup of coffee would be perfect if she could find a way to swallow. The lump in her throat was sizable. It worried her even more when they reached the house and he softly informed her. "I need to talk to my dad. I'm gonna take him for a ride and try to sort some things out. Try not to worry. I'm sorry I can't talk with you about everything just yet." He bent and kissed her cheek.

She held his hand as he started inside. "Jesse…"

He stopped but couldn't look at her. She went in front of him. "Wait out here. I'll get your dad for you."

He was glad for that and sat on the swing noticing her pajama bottoms. When she entered the house it seemed she'd broken up a prayer meeting. The glances at her were different and she felt ashamed for some reason. She motioned for Sam and he followed her outside. Jesse rose and handed her the bottoms. She felt the need to put them on but didn't know why. Everything was suddenly weird. She helped him navigate the Tundra out of the yard between all the vehicles then watched as they drove away.

Back inside the house she poured the last cup of coffee into a mug by emptying both pots. Adding cream she realized it was so quiet that she could hear the spoon clink against the cup.

What the hell?

Sorry Lord. Please help.

She wondered where to go and started outside when Nora invited. "Want to join our prayer meetin'?"

Lydia sighed with relief and sat beside her in Sam's chair. "Y'all… what's going on? Have I messed up or something?" She could feel the tears coming. How had she imagined she'd be welcomed so quickly into such a wonderful family? Maybe if she'd left her pajamas on instead of stripping down to a tank top and shorts. But Nora had. She glanced around wondering if anyone would be brave enough to put her in her place. Whatever they had to say she could take it, especially if it meant helping Jesse.

Finally Nora took her hand. "Here's what happened while you were upstairs honey. Jack called Jesse and when he saw who it was he hit ignore but accidently put him on speaker. Jack spoke quickly so Jesse wouldn't hang up. All he said was, 'It's about an abortion.'"

Lydia caught her breath and put her hand over her mouth at the word. No wonder Jesse was so hurt. Had Jack convinced him of something terrible?

Her head was spinning and she thought she might be sick. Nora still held her hand. "Honey whatever is going on, just know that we love you."

Lydia looked up in tearful surprise. She couldn't speak. As tears slipped down her face she bowed her head in shame. Before she knew what was happening she was surrounded by Jesse's family. Each had a hand on her shoulder and one by one they prayed. It was definitely weird but also strangely comforting. Peace flooded her soul and she was able to stop crying.

She sighed deeply with relief. Most of them moved back to their seats. Some held hands, Maggie wiped away a tear and spoke softly. "We're worried for you and Jesse. But we love you Lydia already. We love you."

Lydia could only imagine what was going through their heads and wondered whether to try to clear things up or just wait for Jesse. Surely he knew her better than that. Of course he did! They'd shared everything.

Sam came through the back door and motioned for Lydia. He put his arm around her and walked her to the truck. "It's gonna be alright honey. Sometimes a spiritual battle gets to be so strong that we just have to wonder what the devil is trying to hinder. You and Jesse have a wonderful future ahead of you that only the Lord could dream up. So hang in there Darlin'. Satan is working hard to keep you two apart. But we're not going to let that happen." He kissed the top of her head and opened the door for her.

Jesse waited and started the truck when she was buckled. He finally smiled at her. "I just hope we don't have a wreck wearing our snowman outfits."

She tried to smile back. He found a place to park near the Bob Hall pier where they could watch the ocean in the light of the moon. He unbuckled and she did the same. Taking her hand he turned in the seat to face her.

"As you know Jack called. He had a message for you. It seems one of the women he slept with is pregnant." Jesse sighed deeply. "She's very young and plans to have an abortion. Jack got her to agree to carry the baby to full term and sign the child over to his custody. But he will only commit to that if you'll be the mother."

Jesse looked at her and waited.

Lydia tried to process the news. "So… he wants me to raise his child, like adopt it?" She looked at Jesse not getting the proposition fully.

Jesse answered. "No… he wants you and him to raise the baby together. He wants me out of the picture." Jesse looked away trying hard not to tear up.

Lydia spoke with determination. "Why would I do that?"

Then she thought. "But the baby…" She teared up. "Oh Jesse! The thought of the girl having an abortion… what can I do?"

Jesse held her hand. "I don't know honey. But you need to understand that he wants to marry you."

She laughed. "I'm trying hard not to swear Jesse. Listen to me. I DON'T CARE WHAT THE MAN WANTS. He's not going to be a part of my life. I love YOU."

She sighed and added. "I guess I'll just have to trust that God will take care of the girl and that innocent little baby too. I can't fix this. But I'm sure God loves them way more than I do anyway."

She leaned back heavily into her seat. "I wonder if Jack's even telling the truth." She looked at Jesse.

"I wondered the same thing. He gave me the girl's doctor info and her due date. She's only a few weeks along."

Lydia did the math. "So even when he was still trying to convince me to go back to him he was sleeping around." She shook her head sadly. "I'm so glad the Lord took him out of my life."

Looking at Jesse sadly she added. "I have to say I'm surprised at you." He finally looked at her as she spoke. "Did you really think I'd drop you and run off to marry Jack? Honey! I get that you're not ready for marriage yet. It's okay. God will show you if and when it's time."

Jesse reached for her hand and struggled to find the words. "Honey… I'm sorry…" He teared up again. "I was sure you'd have second thoughts. I keep feeling like something's going to happen to take you away from me." He still struggled.

She waited and he finally added. "I guess I keep expecting to get dumped. I know how in love you were with Jack."

She leaned across the console and held him tight. "Take note Darlin'. I'm gonna be like Jesus and never leave you nor forsake you!" She smiled and kissed his face. "Now can I use your phone please? I need to settle this tonight."

He handed her his phone and she made the call hitting speaker so Jesse could hear. As soon as Jack heard her voice he began his well-rehearsed speech. He began with what a good life they could have together, how they could live anywhere she wanted, even on her farm. He'd build her a new house on the ridge or they'd stay in her old house and fix up the front bedroom as a nursery. He was sure to include the fact that he'd been in rehab, was being mentored by his father, and that he knew he could honor God with her help.

She let him talk and was not surprised at the sincerity in his voice. Long ago she'd come to terms with the fact that the man had convinced himself he was on the right path. Apparently in his thinking a few indiscretions along the way were to be expected. She continued to listen.

"Lydia I love you and I know you love me too. We'll have a baby right away just like you always wanted. So let me ask you officially. I'm getting down on my knees. Will you marry me? Please say yes."

She closed her eyes and prayed for the words to reply. Her heart was not nearly as cold as she thought and the words she'd planned were no longer appropriate. Tears began to slide down her face as she prayed how to answer.

"What if I say no Jack? What happens then?" She waited.

Jack sighed heavily and replied sadly. "Then you'll have to answer to the Lord for that. I can't raise a baby by myself and I can tell she's serious about the abortion. You've got to help me Lydia."

His answer revealed his heart and Lydia told him so. "It feels like you're using an innocent little life to get your way. You know how I long for a baby and you're using my grief to your advantage. If you really cared for your child nothing would keep you from protecting it. How sad, how terribly sad that your baby has become a pawn."

His tone became defensive. "That's a horrible thing to say. You know how much I've wanted a child since Ellen lost our son. I'll do whatever it takes to make things work between us Lydia. I'm begging you."

Her heart beat hard at the possibility of losing a child. She tried again. "Jack I loved you so much. But it's over honey. I'm sorry. I'll be praying for your baby… that God will deliver it to a family that can love it like their own. Or that you will have strength to do it alone. I can't imagine better motivation to stay sober than a little one."

Jack softly replied to her. "Then tell me you don't love me. You have to say it. I know what we had was real and you can't deny it. I was right about Jesse being in love with you and he got to you the second I was out of the picture. He knew you were vulnerable and he took advantage. So tell me Lydia. Tell me that all that time we spent in each other's arms meant nothing. Tell me you don't love me. I know better."

Her face flushed and the tears poured. "I guess part of me will always love you Jack, for taking such good care of me. But I would have ended up hurting you even if you hadn't left. Jesse has been my best friend for a long time. I just didn't know I loved him til you were out of the picture. Nothing's going to stop that now. Take care of your baby Jack. And if you care for me at all, please don't ever call me again."

She hung up and handed the phone back to Jesse. Buckling her seatbelt she looked out the window choking back the tears.

He surprised her when he reached over and unbuckled her seatbelt. Pulling her into his arms across the console he whispered, "I'm so proud of you honey. Let's pray right now."

Jesse prayed for the baby's protection, for Jack's thinking, for the birthmom, for adoptive parents, and then he prayed for Lydia. His kindness was overwhelming and she realized again that even when the family thought she'd had an abortion, they too were very kind. Neither they nor Jesse had expressed any sort of condemnation or judgment. She took a deep breath and tried to relax. Jesse still held her across the console but finally said 'Amen.'

They smiled tearfully at each other. "So Merry stinkin' Christmas Jesse!" She laughed and shook her head. "Good grief."

Jesse laughed softly. "We should've brought your truck. It's easier to get cozy in."

Lydia smiled at him and teased, "JESSE! Are you moving to the naughty list right here at Christmas?" She hugged him tight and was glad when he kissed her.

He started the truck and headed home. When they stepped from the truck they could hear "My Girl" playing over the sound system. She laughed a very weak laugh and said, "Perfect."

Jesse pulled her close and swayed with her on the patio. The sultry sounds of Motown lured them into a hopeful romantic mood while the cool air made them glad for their flannel pajamas.

Jesse whispered, "Jack can't have this song, he can't have this moment, and he can't have you. You're MY girl! Don't you ever forget it!"

She smiled up at him. "And I'm sticking to you like Jesus. You're MY sweet Jesse-man. Don't YOU ever forget it!"

He stopped and kissed her so tenderly that they both teared up again. Clapping came from inside the house. Apparently they had an approving audience.

Chapter 20

The family held hands and prayed while they were gone then started the music hoping for a romantic ending. For years they'd prayed for Jesse to meet the right girl. The breakup of his marriage had been devastating to him and he'd never brought anyone home until Lydia. The previous Christmas he'd revealed to his family that Kenya had finally divorced him and he'd asked for prayer regarding Lydia. For an entire year they'd been updated as to Jesse's relationship with her, even to the point of being disappointed when she met Jack. It was as if everyone had been aware of Jesse's love for her except Lydia.

So they understood when Sam gathered them to pray as Lydia made her decision that night. Knowing how much she desired a baby and how in love she'd been with Jack at one time, the family worried that Jesse might be hurt again. But Sam had faith.

"We're going to ask God to give her wisdom to see that He is in charge of the baby's life. Jack is trying to use her tender heart to his advantage. Let's intervene on her behalf as well as Jesse's. God has a plan for their lives that doesn't include Jack."

So when Jesse and Lydia danced on the patio then kissed it was only fitting that the family cheer. Ben played a few more slow songs as the couples danced together on the moonlit patio. Jonathan took Maggie's hand and moved with her and she thought of her funny conversation with Kurtis. Squeeze worked up the nerve to cut in on Jesse and dance with Lydia and Jesse was glad to rest his knee. He sat on the swing and watched them laugh together as he prayed.

Dear Lord... please don't let her change her mind. I love her so much. I don't think she has any idea how committed I am to her. And Jack keeps getting in the way of me telling her so. But I don't want her to think he's pushed me into something.

He recalled the day he found her unconscious near the Claudia Garden shortly after Blue died. She didn't know she was in the world. Though he got her to the hospital her baby was still born and she'd nearly grieved herself to death. Then he'd hunted her down during the terrible despair and gradually coaxed her back to life. When finally she returned to the farm he'd find any excuse he could to go by her house. Any time he'd spot her old truck in town he'd go to where she was in case there was a chance of helping her. For years he'd hoped and prayed. Now she was dancing with his little brother at his family home and his dad was making her smile by cutting in. Jesse continued to watch and pray.

"God I pray for Your timing in all these things. Protect her tender heart. Tonight when she sleeps help it be restful and peaceful. Strengthen her against guilt and the pressure Jack put on her to rescue the baby. Lord as she said, we trust You to rescue this child of Jack's. Bring him to his senses and take him out of her life for good. Lord I need You to intervene on my behalf. She's so young... so beautiful... could You please tune our hearts to the same thoughts... the same desires? I don't think we're in the same frame of mind timewise. Help us Lord. I love her so much but I don't know if she's ready to love me just as much. I can't stand the thought of messing up again especially not with Lydia."

He rose and cut in on his dad just as Bonnie Raitt sang, *"I Can't Make You Love Me."* Lydia understood his pain and held him close as she whispered. "You've already made me love you Jesse-man. It took a bit for me to come to my senses. But I'm never letting go." She smiled up at him and was sad to see he still looked unsettled. She wished for her phone so she could call Jack and give him the uncensored version of her speech.

But for the moment, she'd be content to hold the man she adored and ask God to step in and work everything out. Surely He planned for them to be married someday. No matter what, she'd rather wait for an honorable man like Jesse than to settle for a selfish man like Jack, even if it did mean putting off her dream of having children.

~~~~~~~

Nora had been right about half the family staying up late. Lydia started to go ahead and sleep in the room with Maggie but one look at Jesse told her the man needed her near. He seemed awfully tired and she wondered about his knee. Busying herself in the kitchen she readied coffee, set the timers for the next morning and put away the snacks. She noticed a bag of frozen peas in the freezer and found Jesse sitting on a straight chair listening to Squeeze talk about his coming semester and a girl he hoped to have classes with. She stood beside Jesse with bag in hand until he looked her way.

"Want to move to the recliner? It's finally empty."

He smiled wearily at her and limped that way. She wrapped the plastic bag of peas in a dry dishcloth and placed it on his knee. "There?"

He moved it a bit. "Thanks." He reached for her hand and kissed it. "How's your back?"

"It's doing remarkably well under the circumstances. So if anyone ever suggests the pain is due to stress you'll know better, especially after today." She smiled. "Need an Advil?"

"Two please." He hoped she'd still be sleeping on the sofa with him. If she moved to Maggie's room he'd know she was trying to distance herself from him again. So when she handed him the pain killer and a glass of water, then went up the steps his heart took a nosedive. He longed to hold her.

Squeeze turned out the lights except for the one on the stairs and headed to bed. Jesse closed his eyes and prayed. Lydia had not returned to him and he fell asleep fearing the worst. Many times through the years he'd make plans with her and she'd blow him off for work or just because she feared being seen with him. Often she'd made it clear that they were not a couple. Now that they'd expressed their love for one another he wondered if she would ever allow herself to trust again especially after the latest episode with Jack.

He remembered her words about never leaving him and allowed himself to hope. Yet she'd also said she'd sleep on the sofa near him but she didn't. He wished for a blanket as apparently his mom had lowered the thermostat setting and he was suddenly chilly. But he was too tired to move and his knee had finally stopped throbbing. He smiled at Lydia's remedy of frozen peas.

He slept fitfully and recalled her words to Jack.

I guess part of me will always love you Jack for taking such good care of me. But I would have ended up hurting you even if you hadn't left. Jesse has been my best friend for a long time. I just didn't know I loved him til you were out of the picture. Nothing's going to stop that now.

His heart took comfort in her words. She'd never told him that and he wondered exactly what she meant. A soft blanket covered his cool arms and he smiled at the thought of her. She kissed his lips and stroked his beard.

The white cotton gown showed off her large belly. She threw her head back and laughed at the thought of the little one that would come soon. He bent to kiss her tummy then held her close as she whispered. "Merry Christmas Jesse-man! I love you!"

Chapter 21

The wonderful aroma of coffee filled the room. Jesse stretched and sat up. By the light from the stairs he could see Lydia on the sofa end of the large sectional. Though she still wore the snowman pajamas apparently she was freezing as her arms were folded and she was curled into a ball like a cat. He took the blanket that had somehow found him and placed it over her. He moved to sit near then stroked her back as she turned toward him and stretched.

"Girl, I didn't know you were here. Why didn't you wake me last night? I would've rubbed your feet and shared my blanket." He pushed the curls from her face.

"Merry Christmas Jesse-man. I love you." She reached up and pulled him into her arms. He remembered his dream and gazed at her tenderly. "Yes! Merry Christmas to me!"

She laughed at his funny words then shivered. "Dang! I'm about to freeze to death! You could kill hogs in here!"

Jesse had to chuckle at her country talk. He'd actually never had the pleasure of slaughtering pigs but knew it had to be done in very cold weather. "I thought you decided to sleep in Maggie's room. Sorry I went to sleep without kissing you good night."

She smiled at him through sleepy eyes. "I have to say I felt a bit like Ruth trying to get Boaz to wake up and take her home to love her forever." She teased, "That's why your feet were uncovered. Did it work?"

He smiled not knowing what to say. "You crazy chick. In fact I had a dream about you." He stopped abruptly.

She tipped her head and looked at him suspiciously. "Oh really?"

He replied. "Want some coffee?" He moved from her arms and fetched each of them a cup. When he returned she sat on the sofa waiting wrapped in the blanket. He tried not to look at her. He couldn't tell her the dream lest it hurt her heart. He wondered what had possessed him to bring it up.

She didn't ask but gazed at him instead. "Maggie talked to Kurtis again and wanted to tell me all about it. That's what took me so long to get back down here. Sorry honey. And you don't have to tell me about the dream. Sometimes things like that happen for a reason." She sipped her coffee and remembered the dream she'd had about Jesse when she was still in love with Jack. It was the first time she'd considered loving Jesse and later decided the Lord had given her the dream to help assure her heart that it was okay.

He relaxed on the sofa beside her drinking his coffee. "Can I ask you something? Last night you told Jack you would've ended up hurting him had he stayed. What were you talking about?"

She wondered how much to say. "Well… it was starting to dawn on me how much I cared for you even before he left. And occasionally I'd have a dream about you. But that's all I want to say about that. I just know that God had a better plan for my life than Jack. It took me a while to see it was about loving you. I'm so thankful."

The back door opened and little boys poured inside the house. Adam helped seat his sons on the barstools and began pouring cereal. Lydia headed to the kitchen. "How do you take your coffee?"

"Straight up. Thanks! Eva likes regular too with cream and sugar. She's in the tent nursing Micah. I'll take it to her if you don't mind making sure the boys don't tear the house down. I'll be right back."

Jesse joined them pouring milk into the bowls.

Christmas morning had officially arrived.

~~~~~~~

Jesse pulled two griddles from shelves above the washer and dryer. Lydia joined him there off the back of the kitchen.

"Hey… I didn't know there was another bathroom back here. That would've come in handy last night!"

Jesse laughed at her and began mixing batter.

"What can I do to help?" Lydia asked as Nora joined them.

Jesse turned off the hand mixer. "Not a thing. This is mine and mama's Christmas morning ritual. But if you'll check on the boys and try to keep them alive that would be nice."

Ben came through the back door with his three boys. Lydia asked, "Can I take the kids down to the beach until pancakes are ready?"

A chorus of affirmation came as Squeeze offered to help. JoJo came from the guest room so Lydia and Barnabas took Adam's four, Ben's three, and Pete's girl across the road to look for shells. Maggie came bounding down the steps.

"I need to run an errand. Save plenty of pancakes for me. Be back shortly."

Jesse smiled at his little sister. "Don't call me 'Shortly.'" His mom shook her head and mumbled, "That just never gets old does it?" Jesse laughed and walked to the patio to watch Maggie back out then to check on the brood across the road on the beach.

Lydia and Squeeze threw a Frisbee while the boys tried to intercept it. JoJo stepped gingerly around something in the sand. Jesse counted kids to make sure they hadn't lost anybody.

He returned to find his mom removing pancakes from the griddle. He poured more batter as she mixed another batch.

His mom nudged him with her hip. "So did you and Coppercurls behave yourselves last night?"

Jesse laughed at him mom. "You know I'm nearly thirty seven, right?"

Nora pointed a spatula at him. "You know I'll always be your mama, right?"

Jesse gave her a squeeze. "Yes ma'am. For that I am eternally grateful. Thank y'all for praying. She did really well with Jack. I wasn't sure what to expect. The old Lydia I used to know would not have been quite as gracious. That's why it was so scary. She's got such a tender heart now that I half expected her to haul Jack's pregnant lover home with her so she could take care of all of them."

Nora turned off the mixer. "What did she do?"

Jesse flipped pancakes onto a warming tray and slid them into the oven. "She did the perfect thing. She left it to the Lord. I'm so proud of her. Jack did everything he could to get her back. The cool thing that came from all this is that I got to hear her tell him that she had feelings for me before he left."

Jesse looked at his mom and smiled.

His mom high-fived him. "Bless her heart. I know she thought we were nuts last night. I have to tell you Jesse, I really like her. Don't drag your feet son. She obviously adores you."

Jesse looked at his mom. "Be honest mama. Am I too old for her? I mean, do we look weird together? Are people going to wonder if she's my daughter?"

His mom laughed. "No, but what if they do? You're so funny Jesse. She is too. She was worried about wearing her bathing suit in front of you." Nora laughed more at that. "Too bad she's so dang ugly. I know you can hardly bear to look at her."

Abby walked in with baby Jesse to say good morning. "Tell Grammy and Uncle Jesse Merry Christmas!" She took her baby's hand and waved at them. Jesse handed his mom the spatula and took his namesake.

"Mind if I take him with me to get the others for breakfast?" He kissed baby Jesse's little head and stroked his back. The baby hiccupped loudly as though he might spit up so Jesse held him over the sink. "Don't barf on my shirt son. I've only worn it two days. I haven't quite got the good out of it yet."

He walked out the door with the little one in the crook of his arm like a football. Across the street he found Lydia running from Squeeze with Sammy in tow. She squealed in mock terror as the big brother chased them through the sand. Lydia and the toddler took a tumble and Squeeze pulled her up by the hand brushing her face off as they laughed.

Jesse felt so old. A fall like that would've ruined his knee. But when she looked up and saw him she ran toward him with that crazy run like she had at the barn. Only this time she fell into his free arm. He caught her and hugged her as she laughed. "Take me home Boaz!"

Together they headed toward the house for breakfast.

~~~~~~~

Jesse and Squeeze rinsed feet and hands while Lydia patted them dry and sent them to the picnic tables. Parents gathered their children and waited as Sam asked the blessing. Everyone dug in and thanked Grammy and Jesse for the pancakes. Lydia was surprised that the children didn't offer to leave the table though they'd woofed their breakfast down quickly. It seemed everyone waited for something. Once Sam and Nora were finished Sam opened his Bible and read the Christmas story again from Luke 2. The children added in the things they'd thought about the night before then Sam turned to Isaiah. From chapter eight he read verses Lydia had never heard.

"The Lord has given me a strong warning not to think like everyone else does. Make the Lord of Heaven's Armies holy in your life. He is the One you should fear. He is the One Who should make you tremble. He will keep you safe."

He moved on down the passage to verse sixteen.

"Preserve the teaching of God. Entrust His instructions to those who follow me. I will wait for the Lord... I will put my hope in Him."

Then in chapter nine he read familiar words which predicted the coming of the Messiah. "For a child is born to us, a Son is given to us. The government will rest on His shoulders. And He will be called Wonderful Counselor, Mighty God, Everlasting Father, Prince of Peace!"

Sam smiled a huge smile as the family listened. "How wonderful that we get to celebrate the birth of our Savior today! He came to set us free! The law showed us we could never meet God's great standard of righteousness. Jesus came to bear our sins so that we wouldn't have to! How great is our God!"

The sons cheered at their father's familiar words and the little ones cheered with them though they weren't exactly sure why. They just knew that the baby Jesus had grown up and was now in Heaven making a special place for them.

Sam turned to one more passage. "I saw this this morning and thought of our new family member from North Carolina. Their state motto is 'To BE rather than to seem.' That's a very good thing. We don't pretend to be good. We rest in God's goodness for Heaven and ask Him to make us better as we live. But we don't pretend. Here's what I mean. Look at Isaiah 29:13.

'These people say they are mine. They honor me with their lips but their hearts are far from me. And their worship of me is nothing but man-made rules learned by rote.' Dear children, it's a heart matter. Love God and love people. All the rest will fall into place. Don't pretend to love. Really love!"

He closed his Bible and prayed a blessing on his babies and his grown ones as well. He asked that the Lord would help them to be authentic and real before people so that others would be drawn to the Savior. When he said 'amen' the children burst into a chorus of "Happy Birthday dear Jesus" as Kelly brought a cake from the house filled with candles. Ben did his best to shield it from the breeze until the kids could blow them out. She sliced it and passed the pieces around.

Nora leaned over to Lydia and whispered, "Feel free to decline the cake if you're sufficiently sugared up for the day. Between that and the pancakes and the coffee I'll be wondering why I'm shaking in a few minutes." They laughed together as friends.

Jesse rose and looked at Lydia. Suddenly she remembered the gift she'd brought which was still in the back of the truck. He helped her get it out and stood with her at the end of the line of tables. She tried to make a speech.

"Okay… I'm no good at this so keep eating your cake and don't look at me." The family laughed and looked at their plates. She hoped she'd be able to say it without crying.

"I know y'all don't do gifts but I made a small barn quilt for Sam and Nora. Since you don't have a barn it's a pool shed quilt. The center white circle stands for you two. Then each colored section that goes from the center is one of your kids' families. I designed it after the verse in Psalm 127 that speaks of children being like arrows in the hand of a mighty warrior." She paused as Jesse turned the two by two foot board around. Nora teared up at the sight.

"Thank you guys for accepting me into your family. I've actually never been a part of anything like this!"

They laughed and made a few funny comments. Lydia tried to say the rest. "You've shown me what a real family should be like, especially last night when I needed you so much. Thank you."

They clapped for her as Jesse brought the painted board to his mama and daddy. Lydia was glad for the interruption when Maggie drove up. She bounded from her little truck with a guest.

Lydia caught her breath and ran to him. He hugged her for dear life. She couldn't keep the tears back any longer so she sputtered out the introduction.

"Guys this is my son Kurtis! Merry Christmas to me!"

Maggie clapped and smiled happily. "We surprised you didn't we?"

Lydia laughed. "Yes you did. How in the world?"

Kurtis leaned in to whisper. "That scholarship came through after all. So I used some of my savings to buy a plane ticket. I lucked up and got a flight straight into Corpus. You'll have to save a hug for Shawn. He got me to the airport at four thirty this morning."

Jesse came to greet him with a hug. "We've got pancakes and birthday cake for breakfast. I know it's your favorite! I see you've met my sister. Maggie, Kurtis is one of the nicest men I've ever had the pleasure to meet. So don't spoil him rotten while he's here."

She smiled at Kurtis. "It will be hard but I'll do my best."

Sam and Nora greeted him warmly then took the shed quilt to the side of the house facing the patio. Nora stepped back as Sam held it as high as he could. She looked at Lydia happily.

"I think I like it here where we can see it better instead of way back behind the pool. What do you think?"

Lydia smiled. This had to be the best Christmas she remembered in a very very long time.

Chapter 22

The family tossed paper plates in the trash and coffee mugs in the dishwasher. Jesse oiled the griddles and put them away for another day. Towels were gathered and children were again ushered to the beach.

Christmas football was about to convene.

They appointed Jesse quarterback of one team so he could stand still and not tempt his knee to give way by running in the soft sand. Kurtis was selected quarterback of the other. Adam became his best receiver while Nora became Jesse's favorite target. Sam loved catching her before she could get to the goal line and swinging her around like a little girl.

"Stop it Sam! That's not how you play! You're supposed to snatch the rag from my pocket." She laughed in spite of herself.

Sam smiled mischievously. "What's that dear? Did you say you're ready for a swim? The ocean's mighty cold this time of year."

Jesse tried to pass one quickly to his mom before his dad could get set. Lydia came through the middle and intercepted it running right past Jesse to score for her team. She did a funny touchdown dance but Jonathan and Squeeze took exception to it. Together they grabbed her ankles and wrists and turned her into a human swing launching her with ease into the surf. Though everyone was laughing Jesse hoped it wouldn't make her hurt. As she walked toward them wiping her face and shivering he wrapped her in a beach towel.

"I apologize for my brothers. Are you okay?" Jesse kept his arms around her and was glad when she laughed.

"I'm fine. You know I live with a couple Goobers don't you? Stuff like this happens to me all the time." She wiped her face and pointed at them shivering. She tried to think of something smart to say but couldn't. Her teeth chattered so Jesse pulled her close and rubbed her back to warm her.

"Goodness girl. Let's get you to the house. I don't want you to start hurting."

The game picked back up and Jesse walked her across the road to the outdoor shower. The hot water soothed her painful body and she tossed her tee shirt and cutoffs over the side.

Jesse asked, "Ummm… do I need to go get you anything?"

She burst through the door to where he waited. "Nope! Had my bathing suit on underneath." She laughed too much at his look then added. "You're the only man on the face of the earth who'd be relieved that his girlfriend had on clothes."

He shook his head at her. "You're embarrassing me." He sat down in a patio chair so she circled his neck from behind and kissed his cheek. "I'm sorry honey. I'm a harlot."

She walked to the diving board and jumped from the end springing into the perfect dive. She came up smiling. "Did you see that? I did it! You have to tell everybody because I don't know if I can do it again." She walked around to the other end of the pool and tried again.

Jesse stepped into the pool and sat on the wide steps. He watched as she sprang higher this time and came down in a pretty dive. She swam underwater toward him and came up smiling. "Did you see that?"

He smiled at her. "I DID see that."

She sat beside him. "Sorry for embarrassing you. I'll behave."

He tipped her chin up and looked into her eyes. "No, I'm sorry."

She smiled and wished he'd tell her he loved her. The business with Jack had unnerved him for sure. She wondered if he was having a hard time trusting her. But all she could do was all she could do.

"Thank you Jesse-man. So what's the matter? You seem to be struggling with something." She gazed back into his steel gray eyes. They'd lost their sparkle and she didn't know why.

When he looked away she knew she was right. Something was amiss. She waited hoping it wasn't about Jack. There was nothing else she could do about the man.

She swam away, pushed from the other end of the pool and swam back. "This water is perfect." She floated backward hoping he'd be able to open up before the family joined them. A few easy laps later she rejoined him on the steps.

"Is it something I've done? I am kind of a harlot." She tried to joke with him but was beginning to worry.

He looked at her tearfully then kissed her tenderly. Her heart beat hard and his embrace became more passionate. "Mercy Jesse." She breathed into his neck. "I was kidding about the harlot part. What in the world is going on?"

He sighed and looked at her. "Honey you're so young and you look so good with guys like Kurtis and Squeeze. I'm practically old enough to be their daddy. I have to wonder if I'm doing you wrong."

She shook her head at him. "Jesse honey, you might be a good bit older than them but you're only a few years older than me. This is about having a birthday isn't it?"

He sighed. "I will be forty in three years. And you'll still only be thirty three. When you turn sixty I'll be closing in on seventy. I'll have one foot in the grave and you'll still look like a kid."

She tipped her head and smiled. "Kinda like your mom and dad?"

Jesse thought for a minute then finally smiled. "Yep, just like mama and daddy." He smiled bigger. "I never thought about that. Dad is seven years older than mama and look at them. Maybe I just need my knee fixed then I won't feel so old."

Lydia laughed at him. "You sure don't look old. Honey here you are shirtless with your muscles showing, good gracious! You have no idea what you do to me." She smiled that smile that took his breath away.

He sighed heavily. "Thank you honey. You're so kind."

She swam to the other end and tried her dive again. The family would join them soon. She'd have to be careful to pay better attention to Jesse. She'd never thought of him as insecure. Maybe it was just in the matter of love.

~~~~~~~

No matter how hard she tried the dive kept turning into a belly flop. Finally she gave up, showered and changed into the last of her clean clothes before the indoor bathrooms became occupied. Coming through the kitchen she found Eva making sandwiches. They threw down together on a peanut butter jelly assembly line then carried everything to the picnic tables. Sam whistled and everyone froze.

"Nora Jane will you ask the blessing?" She did then Sam instructed.

"Boys line up at the new shower. Uncle Jesse will help you there. JoJo and ladies have the inside. When you finish, lunch is on the tables. Drop your wet suits and towels in a pile beside the new sink out here."

Nora interrupted. "Don't let me find wet stuff under the beds. Do what Poppy says... Jonathan!" Everyone looked at him and laughed then took off to do what they were told. Jesse instructed the boys by the shower. "Smallest to tallest: there you go. Asher, Toby, Sammy, Marcus, Caleb, Peyton, Seth."

Lydia sat in a patio chair near the shower while Jesse rolled wet bathing suits off his nephews, rinsed and handed little boys to her to wrap in towels. One by one they headed to their daddies to get dry clothes on then came back to sit at the table. Sam and Squeeze situated them at the table. Kurtis watched for a bit then began handing out chips. Maggie came from inside dressed in a pretty sundress with wet hair falling into dark curls. Kurtis tried not to stare as she poured cups of water and passed them around to her nephews.

JoJo emerged dried and dressed and joined her cousins at the table. She peered at Kurtis and wondered. "Do you have a girlfrin?"

Kurtis smiled at her and answered. "Nope. Do you have a boyfriend?"

She shook her head no then asked. "Maybe you can be my boyfrin. Bobby in my school likes Milly better 'n me."

Kurtis looked at her sympathetically. "I understand. That happens to me all the time. Can I sit beside you?" He grabbed a peanut butter jelly sandwich and smiled at her. He'd played very hard and was about to starve. "Mmm... this is good stuff."

Maggie sat on the other side of him and whispered, "Daddy's grilling steaks for us as soon as we get these kids down for naps." Kurtis looked at her and smiled. "Don't worry. I'll still have plenty of room."

Kurtis leaned down to hear JoJo tell him more about school as Maggie watched. His gentleness reminded her of Jesse. She was happy to discover Kurtis to be as cute as he sounded over the phone. He pushed his blonde wavy hair from his face and still listened as the little girl beside him spoke. When JoJo finally took a breath Maggie cut in. "Thank you again for coming. I'm sure that last minute plane ticket was expensive."

Kurtis looked at her and smiled. "Thanks for inviting me. You look really pretty by the way. I like your hair."

For some reason it caught Maggie off guard and she couldn't find the words to reply. So she just smiled. It was all Kurtis needed anyway.

When the kids finished lunch Maggie and Kurtis cleared the tables. As she wiped jelly from one of the benches Kurtis asked, "Could we walk on the beach or is it getting too windy?"

He wanted to give her an easy way out if she wasn't comfortable with him. He was happy when she smiled and answered. "Sounds good."

They walked down the beach away from the house and Kurtis asked, "So what happened after we talked last night? Did you hear how Lydia handled the thing with Jack's baby?"

Maggie sighed. "Bless her heart. She just basically told him to leave her out of it. I know she's worried though. And poor Jesse. He's not himself today. But the Lord will take care of it all. Like Lydia said, God loves that baby more than Jack does anyway."

Kurtis shook his head. "I could kill Jack with my bare hands. She almost went to New York to see him after Thanksgiving. It was the first time I've ever really been mad at her. So if the girl he got pregnant is just now finding out, he was still cheating on Liddy when he called her. Honestly if I ever see him again..."

He caught himself. "But me and Shawn have wished for years she'd wake up and notice Jesse. We've actually prayed about it but didn't tell her. She can be pretty hardheaded." He laughed. "I'm just glad she finally let him in."

Maggie agreed. "Jesse's loved her for a very long time. Now I think he's kinda floundering as to what to do. He was hurt so badly in his first marriage that I think he's afraid of being rejected again. Bless his heart."

Kurtis looked at Maggie. Her hair was twirling into a mass of dark brown curls as they walked. There was such a kindness about her that he commented. "You remind me of Liddy. She says, 'Bless your heart' all the time now. I used to be kinda scared of her when I was growing up. But now she's mellowed out since Jesse got hold of her."

Maggie tried to look fierce. "I can be scary when I need to."

Kurt smiled at her. "I'm sure you can. I'll try to stay out of the way of that." He took her hand and continued to walk with her easily. The two of them felt as if they'd known each other forever.

Chapter 23

Brothers stood around a grill with their dad. Mamas put their children down for naps. Nora gathered towels and started the wash while Lydia rinsed bathing suits and hung them on the line. At some point earlier Ben and Kelly had washed potatoes and tossed them in the oven to bake. They were almost ready. Maggie and Kurtis walked through the kitchen as Nora pulled salad items from the fridge.

"Want me to make the salad?" Kurtis offered as he washed up.

Nora looked at him thankfully. "I'd appreciate that. Just chop anything you can find."

Lydia came inside. "Real plates or paper?"

Nora looked up glad for the help. "Let's use real since we're having steaks. The bottom half of the dishwasher is empty so clean up will be easy enough."

Lydia set the table and looked for Jesse. She prayed for him and wondered how many times she had wounded his tender heart.

God help me to be more loving and kind. He's such a gentle man. Draw him to me in Your time. Help his birthday be very special. Heal his knee so he doesn't feel so old. Give us wisdom please Lord. I love him so much and I'm not sure how he feels anymore. He's let the Ruth comments go by without responding to them. I hope he's not having second thoughts.

She jumped when he put his arms about her waist from behind. He laughed, "I'm sorry. You must've been in deep thought."

She turned to look at him but didn't reveal that she was praying for him. His hand rested in the small of her back and made her heart leap. Instead of speaking she smiled and hoped he still felt the same about her as he did before he saw her with his family. She knew she'd probably embarrassed him more than once. How quickly things had changed with Jack. One moment he spoke of doing life together and the next he was gone. She wondered if she'd ever get over it. Part of her wondered if Jesse would do the same.

Jesse asked softly, "What's the matter Darlin'? Are you thinking about Jack's call?"

She teared up and wondered how he always seemed to know when she thought of the man. "No, I'm thinking of you and hoping you're okay."

He took her hand and walked her across the road. The wind picked up and whipped her ponytail behind her. "Talk to me Darlin'. I know when you're being less than truthful." He looked into her eyes and waited. "I also know how long it takes you to process things. Are you rethinking your answer to Jack?"

She sighed. "No Jesse, I'm not! I was thinking about the morning he left. He asked me to marry him then the next minute he was gone." She paused and looked away. "I lobbed one up for you twice this morning calling you Boaz and you didn't even respond."

He hugged his wounded friend. "Honey Boaz was old and Ruth was young. It hurt to be thought of like that."

She pulled back and looked at him surprised. "No he wasn't. At least that's not how I was thinking of it. But I'm sorry. I don't mean to embarrass you. Just forget it."

The wind was chilly and she shivered. Jesse held her against himself and rubbed her back. "No honey. I'm sorry. I've let my fears get in the way. I keep finding myself thinking of Jack too and worrying that you'll go back to him. I'm sorry. C'mon. Let's go eat a good steak and maybe get some rest. I know you didn't sleep well last night."

She swiped at a tear and sighed. He still hadn't said he loved her. If he was going to break up with her maybe he'd wait til they were home. But whatever happened at least she'd not been sucked into Jack's crazy offer. Maybe that was the only reason God had sent her to Texas over Christmas. She glanced up at Jesse as he held her hand and walked her across the road. She hated the thought of losing him as her love, but hated even more the thought of losing her best friend.

~~~~~~~

One of the brothers threw a football toward Jesse and he caught it easily. Lydia busied herself picking up swimsuits that had blown off the line. Once they were secured better she headed back past the pool just as Pete gave Ben a push.

Into the water she went. A chorus of laughter went up except for Maggie who rose to find her a towel.

Lydia swam to the shallow end and climbed the steps as she raised her hands in victory. "Don't worry! I'm okay!" She tried to smile. Maggie handed her the towel and she wrapped it around her. Pete apologized profusely but Ben couldn't quit laughing.

Jesse smiled apologetically but was glad she took it all in stride. "You okay?" He asked as she walked past him toward the house.

"Yep. Just fine." She couldn't look at him. Once she was through the back door near the laundry area she dried off as best she could. Nora was working on laundry so Lydia asked, "Do you know where I can find a dry towel?"

Nora nodded and retrieved one for her. "Here's the last one from my own private stash. Run upstairs and change. Sam's taking the steaks off the grill."

Lydia could feel the tears coming so she hurried away. "Don't wait for me please. It's gonna take a bit since I have to rinse this crazy hair."

Once she was in the shower she realized she had no more clean clothes. And her dirty ones were in a basket downstairs. The shower turned cold as the hot water heater had not had time to recover. Quickly she rinsed her hair and got out. Wrapped in the dry towel she stepped into Maggie's room shivering. With a wet towel around her hair and a semi-dry one covering her body she looked around the room for something to put on. If only she could find a decent bath robe.

Chapter 24

Jesse stepped in the back door to inform his mom. "Daddy's ready when you are."

Nora closed the dryer and hit the start button. "Jesse. What is wrong with you son?" She leaned against the washer and folded her arms. The look she gave him let him know she expected answers right then whether the steaks were ready or not.

He was honest when he replied. "I don't know mama. I guess I'm scared. I mean, have you looked at her?"

Nora was exasperated but she tried to be sympathetic. "What exactly are you afraid of?" She waited.

Jesse sighed and thought. "I guess I'm worried about rejection. You don't know how many times she's pushed me away through the years. And she called me Boaz this morning. It makes me feel old. I'm afraid being around all my younger brothers has given her an idea of what she COULD have instead of me. Plus she can always go back to Jack."

He looked at his mother hoping for advice but worried that she might agree with him. He knew he could count on her to be brutally honest. He was surprised when she laughed. "You're pouting because she called you Boaz? Really Jesse?" She shook her head and asked. "What exactly did she say?"

Jesse told her but as he repeated it he finally heard Lydia's real words. "She said she was hoping I'd take her home with me." He looked at his mom with sudden hope. "...to love her forever."

Nora sighed, "And you heard, 'Jesse you're an old man and I'm too young for you?' Wow. I thought I trained you better than that. If I were Lydia I would catch a ride home with Kurtis. No wonder she looked so sad."

Jesse stood there wondering what to do. How had he let his own insecurities ruin their day? Ironically it was exactly what Lydia used to do before she fell in love with him.

Nora interrupted his thoughts. "You need to get your butt upstairs and apologize before she feels too rejected to recover. It's not like she's never been tossed aside before. You know how that feels."

Jesse hugged his mother and said, "Save us a couple steaks but don't wait. Say a prayer while I go grovel." He bounded up the stairs and didn't think once about his knee.

~~~~~~~

Lydia gave up on finding a bathrobe. Maggie had packed rather lightly too and she hated pilfering through her things. A small wooden rocker by the window seemed to call to her. She sat there shivering and looking toward the ocean asking God what to do. If she had a phone she'd call Jesse and... she wasn't sure what. He definitely wasn't himself. She pulled the towel from her hair and began combing the wet mess. At least the towel around her body was tucked securely. Maybe Maggie or Nora would notice she was missing and come to her rescue.

As she sat looking out the window wondering what to do she spoke to her Friend.

Lord, why is my heart so sad? I love Jesse so much but I can't seem to help him understand that. The thing with Jack makes me so mad. What a selfish man. I can't imagine raising a child with him. But I asked You for a baby by next Christmas. Surely You didn't mean like that. Please protect his little one. Provide parents who will love him and treasure him. Wake Jack up in the meantime. And Lord please help Jesse trust that I won't go back to Jack. My heart hurts so bad. Please help Jesse love me. I feel so unworthy of such a dear sweet Godly man, but I love him so much. Please speak to his heart for me.

A soft knock came at the door startling her from her thoughts. Jesse's voice made her heart leap.

"Honey I need to talk to you."

"Sorry darlin'. I'm not decent." She called back to him knowing those few words would keep him away. The man seemed bent on keeping the physical aspect of their relationship to a minimum. His reply surprised her.

"Then grab a robe or something. I'm comin' in." He waited a few moments then entered.

She sat frozen in her seat. "Jesse what are you doing in here? I told you I'm not decent so don't fuss at me." She looked at him hurt and expecting a lecture like Jack used to give her.

He looked away. "Sorry. I just thought you were trying to blow me off. Be right back." He retrieved his robe from the boys' room and tossed it in to her. "Tell me when." He closed the door.

She turned her back to the door and dressed in his robe loving how it surrounded her with his fragrance. From her chin and shoulders down to the tops of her feet she was covered in white cozy warmth and softness. The sleeves had to be rolled up a few cuffs so she could find her hands, but having it wrapped around her reminded her of Jesse's embrace. It felt a lot like love.

He came when she gave him the okay and sat on the bed looking at her sadly. "I'm so sorry honey. Mama said I've been awful and she's right. Can you please forgive me?"

"For which part?" she asked tearing up. She sat in the rocker facing him.

Jesse looked remorseful and asked. "Well… what all have I done that needs forgiving?"

She shook her head no. "I'm not being sucked into that trap. You tell me. What are you sorry for?"

He reached for her hand.

"I'm sorry for feeling old and making it your fault. I'm sorry for being afraid you're still in love with Jack. I'm sorry for not hearing your words the way you meant them. I'm sorry for not trusting you to love me when you told me you do." He tried to pull her into his arms but she sat tight.

Tears slipped down her face. "Thank you Jesse." His words wounded her. He'd confessed so much more than she realized was wrong and he still hadn't said he loved her. So she asked. "Hey… if we break up…

will you still be my friend? I can't be losing my man and my best friend all in one fell swoop."

His heart hurt and he sat back down on the bed. "Lydia honey do you WANT to break up?"

She looked into his eyes and asked, "Do YOU want to break up? Because I can get home by myself if you're just putting things off. I know I don't deserve to be in your family. Everyone's so dang nice."

Jesse couldn't stand it. He pulled her to her feet and into his arms. "Honey listen to me. I love you with all my heart. The thing is NOBODY deserves to be in this family. We're all here because of love."

He held her close until she finally relaxed.

"Look at me Darlin'. I love you more than I can ever say. I can't imagine my life without you. So let's stop doubting each other, okay?"

She looked into his eyes and saw nothing but love. "Yes. Christmas Day. The day I promise to trust you. No more doubting. Cause if I can't trust you honey, then who can I trust?" She smiled up at him and whispered, "I love you so much Jesse. Please don't ever doubt it again."

They both teared up at the words between them. It felt like a very important turning point as Jesse kissed her tenderly.

She moved back a little then added, "But you've got to get out of here. If your mama catches us like this she'll kick me to kingdom come."

Jesse smiled down at her and whispered. "Yes ma'am."

She added as he turned to leave. "I need Maggie or Nora to help me. All my clothes are in the wash and my last clean outfit is soaked."

"Bless your heart. I'll send one of them up." He turned to look at her. "Or you can come down like that. You're covered. But I have to say… Merry Christmas to me!" He smiled at her mischievously.

She finally laughed. "Jesse please send one of the girls up here with some clothes. And be careful who you tell my dilemma. This is embarrassing."

He laughed. "Yes ma'am. Anything else?" He smiled at her glad they were back to normal.

"Yes as a matter of fact there is. I've never asked a man out before but Sunday is your birthday and I was wondering if I could take you somewhere nice, just the two of us. I need some alone time with you."

Jesse looked at her tenderly. "It would be my pleasure. I'll look forward to it." He smiled and closed the door behind him.

Chapter 25

Jesse motioned Maggie over and whispered Lydia's situation. She headed upstairs to rescue her new sister. Before she left she teased Jesse, "Are you two okay? Because if not I'm keeping her and getting rid of you."

Jesse smiled and thanked her for the vote of confidence.

Maggie found Lydia a cute pair of white shorts and a black V-neck shirt. Thankfully they even wore the same size underwear. Lydia checked the mirror and made a note to shop for a similar bra as it was definitely more flattering than the worn out stuff she'd grown accustomed to. She twirled her hair as best she could then headed downstairs.

"Where's my steak? I'm starving!" She smiled as she entered the patio area where everyone was eating. The look Jesse gave her made her feel very special.

"Over here Chickadee. I just pulled it from the oven where daddy had it warming." He patted the place beside him at the table. She sat and thanked the Lord for the food she was about to devour. Jesse leaned over and whispered. "Mercy Ruth! I can hardly breathe!"

She looked back at him smiling. Her beloved man was back. And it hadn't taken a terrible falling out to help them know how much they needed each other.

~~~~~~~

Together they loaded the dishwasher as others checked on children, put away leftovers and watched football. Lydia kept an eye on the washer and as soon as the load was finished she emptied it into the dryer and started her wash. Jesse came with an armload of his own and asked if she had room for his.

"Always sweet man. Cram them in there and we'll officially be a couple." Lydia smiled at him as he dropped his assorted clothes in with her own. As they sank into the soapy water Jesse said, "If I'd known that's what made it official I would've brought my laundry to you sooner. I think I've waited all my life for this moment."

Maggie heard what he said as she wiped up the kitchen counters. "Awww, y'all are so cute together." Kurtis smiled at Jesse and added, "Yep. You should see them at home trippin' all over themselves to be nice. Jesse sits on the porch and waits til someone tells him it's okay to come in. Liddy makes apple pie and leaves the peelings shaped in an 'L' so Jesse knows she loves him. It's kind of sickening."

Nora smiled at the things she overheard and praised God it seemed her intervention had worked. In her thinking God had obviously brought them together and Satan was doing his best to end it before it got to the commitment stage. If she had anything to do with it, her eldest son would be a happily married man when he brought Lydia back with him next year.

Noticing Lydia yawning again Nora offered, "Honey there's an empty bed in Maggie's room if you need a nap. Now's the time! I'll move your wash to the dryer when it finishes."

Jesse asked, "You didn't sleep well last night did you?"

Lydia shook her head no. "But honestly I'm afraid to take a nap. I'd die if I screamed like I do sometimes. Maybe I'll just sit on the sofa and rest." She glanced toward the den where all the men cheered their teams on.

Jesse looked at his mom. "Will you check the laundry in a bit? I'm gonna take my girl for a ride."

Maggie offered. "I'll keep an eye on it. We can't both run out of clean clothes." She smiled at Jesse glad that he was paying Lydia some attention. The girl obviously needed to rest. Kurtis was glad to see them leave as he'd been witness to Lydia's night terrors. They seemed to come when she was really tired.

Jesse grabbed a soft throw and led her to his truck.

"Where are we going?" she asked as she climbed into the cab.

"You'll see." He drove them to the pier where he'd given her the bad news the night before. As he parked facing the ocean the warm sun came through the windshield but he tossed the covers over her anyway.

"Now lean the seat back and get comfy. Rest well and don't worry about anything. If you happen to have a bad dream, I'm right here."

He locked the doors then leaned over to kiss her. "And when we wake up, I'll take you home and love you forever."

She smiled at him through the tears. The man knew exactly what she needed. Settling into the seat with the sun coming through the windshield she pulled the soft blanket up to her chin. Though the windows were up she could hear the waves breaking on the shore and children laughing at the edge of the surf. She almost hated to close her eyes. Glancing toward Jesse she found him looking at her tenderly. She reached a hand out to him. He took it and kissed it.

"Lydia honey I love you so much. I can hardly take my eyes off you. I'm not kidding. You take my breath away Darlin'." He leaned over the console and kissed her.

"Rest well," he whispered. "We've got a fun night ahead of us."

She looked toward him wondering. But the warm sun made her even sleepier so she gave in to the moment and drifted off without asking.

She stood at the front door and knocked. The breeze kicked up and she shivered. Fear gripped her heart when Sam opened the door and didn't recognize her. Nora came from behind him and explained, 'She can come in. That's Jesse's robe. I'd recognize it anywhere.' Sam hugged her tight and handed her a huge plate of food. 'Welcome to the family Darlin'. Any friend of Jesse's is a friend of mine!' Nora took the plate from her hand and raked the salad back in the bowl. 'Who needs rabbit food when you can have steak?!' She laughed with Lydia and took her arm. Jesse waited for her inside and opened his arms wide to receive her. 'Come on in Chickadee! I TOLD you I'd love you forever! What took you so long?'

"I'm comin' Jesse, I'm comin'! Sorry it took me so long." She murmured it out loud while she napped and Jesse smiled beside her. Whatever dream she was having sure beat the heck out of a night terror.

Chapter 26

Maggie checked the dryer and began sorting the clothes. Kurtis left the football game to join her. She asked him mischievously, "Want to completely freak Jesse out?"

Kurtis looked at her skeptically. "I don't know. Your brother is pretty big."

Maggie laughed. "He doesn't scare me. Let's take her panties and tuck some inside each pair of his underwear." She began her evil act.

Kurtis held his hands up as if not being a part. "I am not touching her underwear. She doesn't even leave her laundry out at home because me or Shawn might see it. You talk about freaking Jesse out. Lydia will have a cow!"

Maggie didn't heed his warning and continued her dastardly deed. Kurtis wanted to be a part so instead he folded her cutoffs and tucked them inside Jesse's shorts. Maggie liked it so together they inserted her jeans into his pulling from both ends. They knew it was silly but it was making them laugh and would definitely get a rise out of Jesse and Lydia.

Maggie asked, "Have you ever seen two people more suited for one another than those two? I just wonder what took them so long!"

Kurtis agreed. "I was beginning to wonder if she'd ever get over losing Blue. It's been seven years. Do you know about him?"

Maggie shook out a pair of Jesse's underwear and put one of Lydia's bras inside. "Just a little. Were y'all friends?"

Kurtis shook his head. "He was like a father to me. A very young father, probably like you feel about Jesse. So kind… showed me how to throw a football… how to treat girls. He led me to the Lord too."

Maggie stopped her mischief for a moment and looked at him. "He sounds like Jesse. Jesse led me to the Lord. I bet they would've been good friends. I wonder why they never met. Aren't the two farms beside each other?"

Kurtis got an odd look on his face. "Oh they met. Blue was really protective of Liddy so she didn't become friends with your brother til after Blue died. I think Blue could tell even back then that Jesse had a crush on her."

Maggie looked at him doubtfully. "Huh-uh! Jesse would never pursue a married woman!"

Kurtis spoke softer. "I didn't say that. I said I think he had a crush on her and Blue could sense it. And I think that's why it's taken so long for Lydia and Jesse to warm up to each other. They're both very sensitive to what's right. That's why it was such a surprise when she let Jack move in with her."

Maggie looked at him as though it was the first she'd heard of it. Kurtis quickly explained. "Jack was smooth, a really good looking man. And Liddy didn't live with him like they were married. But he really snowed us all. I could kick myself for not seeing it. I was so happy she wasn't alone any more. I'd kinda given up on Jesse ever asking her out. And I sure didn't think she'd say yes. But God had a plan!"

Maggie smiled. "Yes He did. Without all that I might never have met you." She looked at him and wondered what he thought of her.

He smiled back. "Yep. And here you are teaching me how to get into all sorts of trouble. Liddy's warned me about women like you!"

She smacked him with a pair of shorts.

"Watch it girl. If I weren't afraid of all your brothers I might haul you outside and toss you into the pool."

She dared him. "Try it."

He shook his head. "Like I said, I'm afraid of your brothers. You know they're watching us."

She glanced toward the den and saw several pairs of eyes looking back. She laughed heartily. I can't get away from them. Jonathan and Squeeze want me to move in with them til I graduate.

"Why don't you? You sure wouldn't have to worry about guys bothering you. I know I'd feel better since I'll be so far away." He looked at her tenderly. "Or you could transfer to my college and move in with Jesse. We could carpool."

She laughed. "Maybe I will! If you're sure we can carpool." She stood close smiling up at him and he really wished her brothers weren't so observant.

Ben left the game and walked through the laundry area. "Better go check on Kelly and the boys. So Kurtis what kind of music do you like?"

Kurtis wondered what the question was about but answered him. "Oh Motown, R&B, Aaron Neville, Zac Brown, Bonnie Raitt, or anything I can shag to."

Ben smiled approvingly. "You look more like the country music type. But I can definitely play some Motown for you. In case you haven't heard, our annual Christmas dance party happens tonight right after ice cream sundaes. So get your shaggin' shoes ready!" He left through the back door happy that Kurtis seemed to enjoy the same music he did. Kurtis called behind him, "Be sure to play Thomas Rhett's *Crash 'n Burn*. Liddy will love you forever."

Maggie asked, "What's shaggin'?" She began stacking the folded laundry into a basket.

"It's a Carolina thing, a dance that started around the beach. Liddy taught me how and we have the best time together." He laughed at the thought. "I took her to a banquet at school and we showed those ol' crudmudgeons how it's done. That was the night the girl of my dreams stood me up." He stopped talking and looked at Maggie. "Thank the good Lord!" He smiled and nearly laughed. "That was also the night I had to hoist Liddy through a bathroom window. Now THAT was a fun night!"

Kurtis recognized the sound of Jesse's truck and warned Maggie. She tossed the rest of the clothes into the basket and hauled them upstairs to her room. Kurtis walked outside and began helping Ben set up the sound system. As much as he loved his own little make-shift family with Lydia and Shawn he realized that this one was something very special.

Ben sang as Jesse and Lydia walked toward the house.

"We'll wake up all the neighbors, make the whole block hate us, til the cops show up, try to shut us down!"

Jesse laughed. "I think they already hate us."

Kurtis warned Lydia, "Ben's workin' up a very special playlist just for you." He grinned at her and she rolled her eyes. "Careful Kurtis. You might have outgrown me but I'm still your mama!"

When Jesse and Lydia couldn't find their laundry Jesse had a feeling his sister was up to no good. He shook his head and informed Lydia of his suspicions. "I just hope it's not in the pool. But I have to say, you look awfully nice in my sister's clothes. I feel like I'm dating a college girl." He smiled at her with the warmth she'd grown to love.

"Thanks, I think. Maybe she and I can go shopping before we head back home. Or better still, I'll just send her for me. I know you get tired of seeing me in worn out jeans and t-shirts."

Jesse stopped her. "That's not what I meant. See that's how we end up feeling bad." He looked up to see the eyes of his brothers on them. "Step in here with me."

She laughed when he pulled her into the little bathroom.

He shut the door behind them and sat on the closed toilet. Taking her hands in his he looked up at her. "Darlin' I think both of us worry too much about what the other is thinking. I LOVE how you look. In fact that's part of the problem. You are so beautiful I wonder if I'm too old for you. But remember, today is the day we decided, no more doubting."

She nodded, "You're right. No more doubting. I promised. But just so you know, I have never once thought of you as old. C'mon, let's get out of here. I can't believe you pulled me into the bathroom."

Jesse laughed, "Around here you've got to take what you can get so far as privacy is concerned." As he stood he flushed the toilet with his elbow out of habit.

Lydia covered her mouth and laughed louder than she wished. Jesse turned red and laughed with her. "I guess that will raise a few questions but hey, we're a couple now so they can think what they want to."

Lydia opened the door and nearly bumped into Sam. "Sorry Darlin'. I was looking for Jesse. Oh. There you are. Someone called from a church for you on the house phone. Here's the number. I told them you'd get back to them."

The toilet sucked the water down loudly as Jesse took the note from his father's hand. "Thanks Dad." He glanced at Lydia who was doing her best to act like nothing was unusual about the two of them leaving the bathroom together.

Sam spoke as she walked toward the den. "Yep, around here we share everything: the good, the bad, the ugly... the bathroom."

She glanced back at him smiling as Squeeze asked, "What's wrong Jesse? Is it too hot in here? You look a little flushed."

Ben and Adam joined him laughing but Pete warned them not to wake the baby. Jesse walked outside still smiling at his brothers. One thing for sure, they all approved of his girl. Nobody had ever dared to tease him about Kenya. Not once.

Chapter 27

Jesse walked away from the house trying to hear above the sound checks Ben was doing on his deejay equipment. An unfamiliar voice answered, identified himself as the Lead Pastor Chuck Jacobs and began speaking to him as though he knew him. Apparently there had been an explosion of growth at the church and they were considering opening a new campus. He wondered if he and Jesse might speak about the possibility of being a part of the new church plant.

"I know it's Christmas Day but I wanted to speak to you in person while you're still in town. If this is going to happen I've got to get the ball rolling pretty fast. Let's meet for dinner around six. That'll give me an excuse to skip the in-laws!" He laughed a hearty laugh.

Jesse paused and offered. "Tomorrow would be better for me. What time is good for you?"

After a significant pause came the reply. "I'll treat you to breakfast, eight o'clock."

Jesse noted the place then walked back toward the house. He'd not considered pastoring since Kenya left. The passage in 1st Timothy about properly leading his own household had warned his tender heart not to pursue the role of a pastor. But God had definitely given him a desire to serve. And now God had brought a woman into his life who also loved the Lord. He prayed as he walked and wondered what Lydia would think of the possibility.

Right on cue, Lydia called from an upper window. "Your sister's a harlot, even worse than me." Maggie laughed behind her. "It was Kurt's idea."

Kurtis stepped away from the house so he could see them from the patio. "It was the wicked woman Liddy warned me about. She batted her eyelashes and I couldn't resist."

Jesse shook his head and laughed to himself.

Yep. I'd make a GREAT pastor.

~~~~~~~

Ice cream and toppings were lined up on the kitchen counters. Apparently this was a Christmas tradition with each family being in charge of something different. There were strawberries, bananas, pecans and crumbled cookies; syrups of all flavors and of course ice cream. Cans of whipped cream beckoned at the end of the line along with long stemmed candied cherries.

Lydia was happy to be given the task of holding baby Jesse while Jesse scooped up baby Micah. Mamas and daddies helped little ones choose their toppings then escorted them outside to picnic tables. Eventually everyone was served. Jesse and Lydia happily held onto the little ones. Together in the swing the four of them alternated bites of banana and ice cream laughing at the look on Micah's face. All he could think about was getting into Lydia's hair. He squirmed and reached his sticky little hands as she did her best to stay out of his reach.

Jesse spoke low so only Lydia could hear. "I understand Micah. I feel the same way. I can hardly leave the poor girl alone when she has her hair down."

Lydia looked at him surprised. Jesse wasn't one to say things like that often. But since their talk he seemed more comfortable. It felt really good to know that he was attracted to her. She'd never had to wonder with Jack as he'd often made it abundantly clear.

She caught herself and rewarded Jesse with a smile as she asked God to protect her heart from memories of Jack.

Nora walked toward them with a dish. "I forgot to get out the brownies. Better grab one before I make my rounds. I know you're a chocolate fan like me." She served up one into Lydia's bowl. Jesse shook his head no and Lydia remembered the pie she'd promised him for his birthday. At some point she'd need to go somewhere to buy apples.

Jesse broke into her thoughts as his mom walked away. "Honey I need you to pray about something."

Micah opened his mouth and waited as Jesse held the bite on his spoon. "I got a call from a pastor in the area. He and I are meeting in the morning for breakfast to talk over ministry opportunities. So be praying about that and especially for wisdom."

Lydia laughed at Micah and fed him a bite of banana. "Sorry sweet boy. Better stay away from the chocolate. Your mama might snatch a knot in me if I feed you brownies." She watched as he sucked the fruit from the spoon. Then she asked Jesse, "Did he say what he had in mind?"

Jesse nodded. "He mentioned the role of pastor but I'd really have to pray about that." He looked at Lydia wondering what she thought. She tried not to look at him when she asked, "Does he know you're dating a harlot?"

Jesse laughed. "I haven't mentioned it just yet."

Lydia laughed with him and wondered at the peace in her heart. "I'll sure be praying for you. God knows what's next. You're really a great speaker and such a Godly man. I'm surprised it hasn't come up sooner."

He looked at her encouraged. "Wow! That's not the reaction I expected. Thanks Darlin'." He leaned over and kissed her head snatching Micah's sticky fingers back just in time. "But don't worry. Whatever he offers, we'll pray about it and make the decision together. I sure won't do anything without you."

Her heart leaped with joy at his words. She nearly teared up and had to whisper. "Jesse honey I'm with you no matter what."

To Jesse it was the confirmation he needed that God could still use him, especially with her by his side. He leaned over to kiss her in front of everyone and Micah finally got his wish.

Chapter 28

Faces and hands and white picnic tables were wiped clean. The patio was cleared of furniture then children gathered at the newly located tables around the perimeter. Abby, Maggie and Kelly helped the kids fashion invitations while the others put away the sundae toppings. Parents walked the children through the neighborhood knocking on doors and handing out homemade cards. Several neighbors mentioned that they'd looked forward to it all year.

Folks started dropping in bringing snacks and yard chairs. Ben cranked up the music and made note of requests. Some wanted to hear *White Christmas* while Randall, a neighbor from the block behind them requested *Play that Funky Music White Boy*. Variety was the one thing the Mills family could always count on. Since the sun was officially due to set at 5:37pm, party lights were plugged up and the tree out front was lit.

Lydia shivered and decided to change out of the shorts Maggie had loaned her. Bounding up the stairs not wanting to miss anything she found Jesse there trying to sort their laundry.

"Have you seen my white jeans?" she asked.

Jesse jumped at the sound of her voice and they both laughed.

Lydia noticed he'd made piles of clothes on the bed and had just gotten down to the underwear.

"Here, let me take care of the rest. That way if that pastor asks if you've seen my underwear you won't have to lie."

Jesse shook his head. "Those Goobers. Here are your jeans I think. They look awfully small." Lydia stopped to look at him.

"What are you saying dear? Awfully small for such an ample woman?"

He laughed. "No... see... this is why we can't do laundry together. I knew it would get me in trouble. I'm goin' downstairs."

She laughed again at his discomfort and sorted the clothes glad he wasn't there to witness her ragged undies. Purchasing new ones must indeed become a priority no matter how bad she hated shopping.

Quickly she changed into the white jeans and added her black Converses. She checked the mirror and touched up her make up. Thankfully the pretty black top had stood the test of sticky baby fingers. Suddenly she thought she heard the sound of a familiar truck.

Surely not… she thought and tried to see out the window. The sound of the diesel being turned off rose from somewhere outside but she couldn't see. Saying a quick prayer she hurried downstairs to see if it was indeed who she thought.

Striding confidently toward the house was a tall handsome man in a black cowboy hat. His blue eyes sparkled as he reached for her and hugged her tight.

"Merry Christmas Coppercurls! I sure have missed you."

Tearfully she gazed back into those eyes she found so hard to resist.

"Merry Christmas to you too Daddy." She smiled and added truthfully, "I've missed you too."

Jesse walked toward him smiling. "Hey Lynerd. It's been a while! Merry Christmas!" He shook his hand and slapped him on the back. "Come meet my parents."

Sam and Nora shook his hand and smiled warmly as Sam asked, "Did you have any trouble finding us?"

Lynerd replied with a graciousness that surprised Lydia, "Nah, you gave perfect directions. Thanks for the invite."

She wondered what had come over the man. She also wondered what had possessed Sam to invite him. But the good thing about her dad was that he never stayed anywhere long. She was sure he'd be gone before morning. And he loved music. Maybe they could have an evening together without coming to blows.

If only he could forgive her.

Ben cranked up the music and kicked it off with *House Party* by Sam Hunt. A couple Zac Brown songs later and the brothers were ready for their routine. With fedoras in hand Pete, Adam, Ben, Squeeze, and Jonathan lined up and danced to *Play that Funky Music White Boy*. Everyone cheered and Lydia suddenly understood why several of the neighbors had requested it. Apparently it had become a Christmas tradition.

She laughed at their craziness and asked Jesse, "Why aren't you up there with your brothers?" He shook his head. "Are you kiddin'? I can't keep up with all that. Besides, that's just what I want; people looking at me while I make a fool of myself."

Lydia nodded with understanding. "Yeah, me too, only I lost a bet with Kurtis last summer. So don't be surprised when you get to see me perform something special with him in a minute."

Jesse laughed at the look on her face. "Uh-oh. Sounds serious. What happened?"

She sighed. "Kurtis heard me griping one day about gaining weight and all of it landing in my rear end. He had the nerve to make the comment, 'Liddy you can't drive by Cook-Out's without stopping for a milkshake.'" She made a face and tried to imitate his voice.

"So I bet him that I could go the whole month of June without one. But he caught me driving down the road one day slurping down a chocolate fudge. So now, every time that song *Crash and Burn* comes on I have to dance with him this crazy routine he made up. Be warned, you have never seen anything quite like it."

They laughed and looked across the patio to where Kurtis grinned and pointed at her. She shook her head and pointed back at him with a warning look. Maggie laughed as apparently Kurtis had just revealed the same story to her.

A deep voice behind Lydia asked, "Whatcha sittin' here waistin' all this good music for? Come on Darlin' and dance with your daddy." He pulled her to her feet and immediately she was transported back to the tiny kitchen in their trailer. Only this time she didn't need to stand on his boots to keep time. He had taught her well through the years and it had been her favorite part of growing up.

Jesse watched and part of him was glad that her daddy was there while the other part wished it was he who held her. In his heart he prayed that the two would somehow be reconciled. He knew they loved each other. But Lydia had hidden a terrible secret from her father for years and it had caused him to hate Blue. Maybe a Christmas miracle could still occur. He prayed for it and smiled as Lynerd moved his only daughter to the strains of *White Christmas*.

He was surprised when Ben played *Blue Christmas* by Elvis even though Jesse had specifically asked him not to. Lydia took her father's hand and pulled him away from the crowd.

"Walk with me, talk with me daddy." She smiled up at him and tried her best not to cry. Jesse went inside to the little bathroom where he shut the door and took the only seat. There he prayed.

Lord, if it's time, please give her strength. Help Lynerd react well. Make this a turning point so that Lydia can heal. Oh God, I love her so much.

Chapter 29

Her face flushed and her throat seemed to close when she tried to speak. Her daddy's silence was a welcome relief. Though they no longer held hands he walked with her without protest. They found a bench on the beach and her daddy took out a handkerchief and wiped the moisture from it. She smiled at his ever present hanky. It was another thing she loved about him. Praying a quick prayer she tried to begin.

"Daddy... I need to tell you something very hard." Immediately the tears came and she hated herself for it. Thankfully her father didn't reprimand her for being weak. Finally he spoke in that deep voice that normally scared the life out of her. But this time there was a hint of gentleness.

"Spill it Copper. It's time we buried the hatchet."

His words gave her the courage she needed to continue.

"After mama died, and you needed to leave for work and stuff, I know it was something you had to do. So don't think I blamed you." She paused and tried to find the words.

He looked at her sorrowfully. Leaving his teenage daughter alone had been one of his biggest regrets. But his grief was unbearable and being around her while he drank was a worse option. After all this time would she finally be honest about allowing her boyfriend in the house? His blood still boiled at the thought of Blue taking advantage of her grief.

Lydia tried to say the words she'd rehearsed a thousand times. How skillful she'd become at lying to her father. Hopefully he'd be able to recognize the truth if she finally spoke it.

"Daddy... there was a man that I trusted... someone you knew well..." She paused reminding herself to give as few details as possible.

"He always seemed to know when you were away." She swallowed hard and pushed herself to say the rest.

"Daddy... I had no idea when I let him in that..."

The tears poured and she could hardly continue. Her daddy put his arm about her shoulders and stroked her head. When he swiped at a tear she knew he believed her so she tried to finish telling the awful secret. "It wasn't my fault but I was so ashamed... so afraid. I began having terrible nightmares. He would knock on the door and I would hide just hoping he'd leave." She shivered from the memory and for a moment wondered if she might be sick. A few deep breaths later she was able to say the rest.

"Daddy, Blue began staying with me as my protector. The night you caught us on the couch, we weren't doing anything but watching football. But he did spend the night there often and I knew it was against the rules. I'm sorry I lied to you. But you need to know that Blue was watching after me."

Lynerd pulled her to his side and wiped away another tear. "Copper why didn't you tell me? I would've killed the S.O.B."

She sighed. "I knew that daddy. That's why I couldn't tell you. But if it makes you feel any better, Blue caught him near the trailer one night and beat the crap out of him. That was the last time he ever tried coming there that I know of."

Lynerd sighed heavily then finally spoke.

"All these years I've hated Blue for taking advantage of you. Who was it Copper? I ain't afraid of prison. I need to know. Who was it?"

His tone was filled with anger and she knew he meant business.

"Daddy, I will never say his name, so please don't bring it up. I've only told Blue and then finally years later I told Jesse in counseling. He's the one who's finally helped me know how to get over it. But every time it comes up or I rehash it, it's like reliving that terrible time all over again. So for my sake, let it go. And for Blue's sake, please forgive me for asking him to stay at the house when you were gone. Daddy he loved me with all his heart. And as embarrassing as it is for me to say out loud, our first time was on our wedding night. He had to deal with my fears the whole time we were married. But he loved me through it."

Lynerd took his arm away and leaned forward with his elbows on his knees and his head in his hands. Finally he leaned back and looked at her.

He stammered out the words she'd never heard before. "Honey I'm sorry. I owe big ol' Blue an apology. But you're right. It does feel good to know he put a hurtin' on the S.O.B. One thing about him, he could throw a punch. My jaw still aches sometimes when it rains." He rubbed his face and chuckled. "From now on instead of cursing your former husband I'll ask God to shake his hand for protecting you."

Lydia recalled the awful night her daddy had caught Blue in the house with her. He'd hit Blue hard but Blue had knocked him on his butt with one solid punch to the chin.

Her daddy spoke revealing the sudden tenderness of his heart. "I'm sorry I didn't walk you down the aisle at y'all's wedding. I'll do better next time if you want me."

She smiled at him tearing up again. "Well don't hold your breath. Jesse is as slow as Christmas in the matters of the heart. I guess he and Blue are opposite in that regard."

Lynerd smiled at her. "But Christmas does eventually get here don't it?" He hugged her and laughed. "Let's get back to the party honey. And if anything ever happens like that again, it's my turn to be your protector. All it takes is one shot to the head and you'll never be bothered again. Or a butcher knife through the heart. You done good girl." He gave her another squeeze and kissed her cheek.

She shook her head and sighed. Finally it seemed her father was proud of her and it was for killing a man. His words confirmed what she often suspected. As they walked back to the house she thought again about his crazy travel, large amounts of cash, and expensive gifts to her at random times. Though she didn't know it for sure, she was likely the daughter of a hit man.

Yep. She thought. *I would make an awesome pastor's wife.*

~~~~~~~

Lydia and her father joined the group on the patio. The song Ben MEANT to play instead of *Blue Christmas* began as Jesse walked out to greet her. One look at her told him she'd finally spoken the hard truth to her father. He pulled her into his arms away from the others. Slowly they danced to Elvis singing *I Can't Help Falling in Love with You.*

"Are you okay Darlin'?" Jesse whispered into her hair.

She nodded a weak yes and leaned heavily on him. "Thank you for praying. I could feel it honey. Finally it's done. Maybe now he can forgive me, and Blue too."

Jesse pulled her closer and stroked her back tenderly. She relaxed feeling the warmth of his strong arms about her. The stress of the earlier moments melted away in their embrace.

Kurtis gently held Maggie not caring what her brothers thought. Her smile gave him all the courage he needed to ask her to dance. Besides, Jesse had made his approval known so at least one out of six of her brothers endorsed them as a couple. The song ended and Kurtis kissed her hand. "Gotta go. Time to make Liddy suffer."

Maggie laughed as he took Lydia front and center and began twirling her like a prom date from the fifties. *Crash and Burn* played as Kurtis flipped her over his shoulder and back through his legs. She did her best to keep up but could hardly stop laughing. The sting of what she'd revealed to her father was suddenly a distant memory. The crazy routine Kurtis dreamed up for them in June had erased many a pain during the months of pining away for Jack. Even at the banquet where Kurtis was honored they performed a slightly less vigorous version. Though that night had included several levels of aggravation, they'd been able to have fun because of that silly dance. Breathlessly they finished and hugged each other.

Jesse stood and applauded for his crazy chick. She might be a lot younger but she was his girl. He made a mental note to take dance lessons even if they only danced in the house. Anything that brought that much joy to her should definitely become part of their lives together.

Lynerd spoke to Jesse quietly as Lydia searched for a drink of water. "Thanks Jesse for all you've done for my girl." He extended his hand and Jesse shook it firmly.

"My pleasure Lynerd. But you will always be her first love." Jesse smiled at him glad that Lydia had finally revealed the truth.

The tough old guy softened at the words. "Tell her I left something for her in the dash of your truck. Good luck to you two." He walked away but Lydia caught up to him.

She tried to match strides as she spoke. "Daddy don't go. Stick around and sing *Simple Man* for me. It's my favorite."

He stopped and looked at her surprised at the invitation. "That was your mama's favorite too. Do you think they could work me in? I've got a guitar in the truck."

"Yes Daddy, please get it. I'll go ask Ben if you can be next."

Something by Santana played as apparently Sam and Nora and some of their neighbors had taken salsa lessons. A few songs later Lynerd returned and plugged up his guitar to the amp. Sitting on a stool and leaning toward the mic he spoke. "My name's Lynerd like Skynyrd. See that pretty redhead over there? She's the love of my life. Honey this is for you and Jesse."

He played the guitar with ease and sang the words in his deep silky voice.

"Oh take your time... Don't live too fast. Troubles will come... they will pass.
Go find a woman... you'll find love. Don't forget son... there is Someone up above
Be a simple kind of man, be something you'll love and understand
Be a simple kind of man, won't you do this for me son... if you can."

They held hands and watched her father play the song for them knowing it was his way of giving his blessing. They were surprised when he finished and added, "That kid Thomas Rhett who does the song Kurtis and Copper entertained us with also does this one. See if you like it."

He smiled at Jesse and played "Die a Happy Man." They couldn't help but notice that Kurtis and Maggie enjoyed it too as well as several other couples. Jesse whispered to Lydia as they danced, "It's true Darlin'. All I need is you."

She smiled up at him and thought,

Yep and about five years to make it happen.

When he finished Lynerd came over for another hug before he left. Lydia was taken aback as her father was not the hugging type. But it felt really good. Suddenly she knew she was accepted and loved though her daddy never said it. He'd come closer to saying it than ever before when he called her the 'love of his life.' It seemed another turning point had occurred in her soul and she wondered if perhaps it was the feeling of forgiveness. As they walked him to his truck she found herself wishing he would stay.

She dared to hug him again and whispered, "Merry Christmas Daddy. I sure do love you!" He hugged her but couldn't find his voice. So he just continued to hold her for a long moment. Finally he whispered back, "Bye Coppercurls. Merry Christmas."

She stood at the road with Jesse's arm about her and watched as her daddy rolled out of sight.

Maggie took the mic as Pete, Ben and Jonathan brought out guitars to accompany her. She smiled at their neighbors and introduced her song. "This one by Lauren Daigle sums up the reason we do this party every year." In a strong voice she sang,

"You plead my cause… You right my wrongs… You break my chains… You overcome…. You gave Your life to give me mine… You say that I am free. How can it be?

Though I fall You can make me new… from this death I will rise with You, Oh the grace reaching out for me… how can it be? How can it be?"

She finished strong then added, "Without Him we are nothing. The good news is simply this: Jesus was born for the purpose of dying in our place. He rose from the dead to prove He paid for our sin. We have eternal life when we trust Him. So trust Him tonight dear friends! Welcome to the family! We love you!"

Kurtis couldn't take his eyes off her. Silently he prayed that God would turn their friendship into something very special.

Sam and Nora walked around speaking to their neighbors and friends while children were gathered in from their late night fun. Jesse and Lydia emptied trash and moved furniture back in place while Jonathan and Squeeze helped Ben put away the sound system. Kurtis was happy to find Maggie cleaning up the kitchen and even happier to have an excuse to be with her alone. He said a quick prayer then dared to broach the subject.

"You did an amazing job on that song. Have you ever thought about being a worship leader? They've started a course at my college to train people in that field." He dried a snack tray and placed it on top of the refrigerator where he'd seen it earlier.

She was quiet for a moment then looked at him. "I don't know that my voice is strong enough but I might make a good doo-wop girl."

Kurtis laughed at her words but knew what she meant. "I think you'd be great either way. Your voice is plenty strong. And it's low enough that even guys could sing with you. I really like it." He washed another platter and tried not to look at her. But his heart beat fast at the thought of her moving to North Carolina and attending his school.

She dried the platter and handed it back to him so he could put it away. "I'll pray about that. I've got a few weeks before the next semester starts." She too was careful not to look at him lest she give away her feelings. The guy beside her had definitely gotten her attention. But North Carolina? A thousand miles from home would be an awful place to go and get dumped. She knew it could happen. But on the other hand, Jesse would let her stay with him. He'd invited her many times and it would save her a lot of money. She decided that she would indeed pray about it.

Kurtis finally glanced at her and then around the den. Still holding the tray he slowly leaned in and kissed her lightly. He smiled at her surprised look and whispered. "Sorry. I couldn't help myself since your brothers are not here to give me the stink-eye."

She laughed and glanced down at his lips. "I promise not to tell them," she whispered.

Jesse came through the back door looking for the trash can under the sink. Kurt and Maggie stepped apart so he could pull the can out of the cabinet. Kurt made a fearful face and Maggie laughed. Jesse continued to pull the bag from the can and tie it shut.

Jesse mumbled under his breath in fake aggravation. "Okay back to the courting. You're standing in front of an open window you know."

The two of them glanced up and realized he was kidding. Not only was the window closed but so were the blinds. Maggie wound her dishtowel and popped Jesse on the leg as he walked the trash outside. He turned and grinned at her and she knew he'd be an easy man to live with if the occasion presented itself.

"G'nite Unka Kurtis. I wuv you." JoJo came from the guest bath all clean and dressed for bed. She hugged his leg so he picked her up and kissed her little face. "I love you too JoJo." He held her over for Maggie to do the same as she added, "Love you honey!"

The little girl ran to her room with curls bouncing and Maggie's heart did another happy leap at the sight of Kurtis' kindness. He reminded her so much of Jesse with his gentle ways. Though they'd had only one day together it had been quite special.

Chapter 30

Lydia was next to come through the back door. "Kurtis honey, do you know where you're sleeping tonight?"

He looked toward the den and asked just as Jesse walked in. "Will anyone be on the couch?"

Jesse spoke before Lydia had a chance to offer it to him. "Lydia's sleeping there. But we can either put an air mattress in the boys' room or you can crash in my truck. It sleeps pretty good."

Kurtis nodded. "That's what I'll do. It's so warm I'll be fine out there."

Maggie went upstairs to find covers and a pillow. Lydia noticed Jesse wanted her near and it made her happy. Maybe they'd have a few minutes alone to talk.

Sure enough, sooner than she expected everyone had turned in for the night. She changed into a tee shirt and pajama pants and headed to the sofa. Jesse came with blankets and pillows tossing it on the large sectional. He took her hand and pulled her to kneel with him there. It seemed like the most natural thing in the world and she realized they'd missed their normal time in Scripture together. He prayed softly as he held her hand.

Lord, I think You've answered a prayer that I've prayed for Lydia for a long time. Thank You for her courage to speak to her father. Give them forgiveness and heal their wounded hearts. Bless her Lord and give her rest in this matter. Thank You for bringing us together… for this time in mama and daddy's home… that Kurtis could be with us… for him and Maggie. And that all the rest of my family was able to come again this year.

Lord I ask for wisdom for us as I speak to the pastor in the morning. May all we do honor and please You dear Father. Bless and keep my beloved Lydia. Thank You that I can finally tell her what You have known for years. We love You Lord. In Jesus' Name… Amen.

Jesse leaned over, kissed her tenderly and whispered. "Good night girl. Wake me up if you need me. I'll be right here beside you."

She could tell he was embarrassed that it was hard to get off his knees so she took her time getting up as well. Trying to distract from his discomfort she asked, "Can you be my counselor for a minute before we turn off the lamp?"

"Sure honey. I was hoping you could talk to me about it." He sat on the sofa beside her instead of moving to the recliner end. "How did it go with your dad?"

She nodded. "Better than I thought it would. I'm sure I should've told him years ago. He even spoke of shaking Blue's hand. But I still need to be really careful. It wouldn't take much for him to figure out who..."

She swallowed hard and felt the fear rising as she said the words. "It wouldn't take much and he'll know who the man was. Hopefully he'll let it go. I guess that will have to be on the list of things I can't worry about."

She sighed and leaned into Jesse. He added as she sat quietly, "That's wise Darlin'. Put it on the list with Jack's baby, and Kenya, and Cook Out's closing. There's nothing you can do about it."

She looked up startled. "They're closing Cook Out's?"

He laughed. "No but that would be terrible wouldn't it?" She smacked his arm glad for a reason to laugh.

"Anyway... I know that the few times I've talked about being abused it has triggered nightmares. I'm scared to death to go to sleep tonight. But I'm so tired. Maybe I should trade places with Kurtis just in case."

Jesse put his arm around her. "Nah. You're done with nightmares. I'm here now and it's over. Once we get situated slide this way and put your feet in my lap. Then you can feel how close I am. Nothing can hurt you when I'm near."

She looked at him skeptically but did as he asked. He reached up and turned off the lamp as he settled into the recliner. Holding her feet in his big hands she rested so well that she hardly moved all night. For the first time in a very long time an alarm woke her instead of an internal clock. Jesse had a job interview.

Chapter 31

Pastor Jacobs was an impressive man. His clothes were stylish for a pastor in his mid-fifties. Apparently he worked out regularly as he was in great shape. He spoke to Jesse as a friend and admitted to being a fan.

"I followed your career as a Panther. You had some moves back in the day! I always loved to watch you run." He held his hand up and motioned for Jesse to do the same. "You've got some massive mitts too! It was a rare occasion for you to drop a pass. If memory serves correctly you never fumbled your entire career. Am I right?" He gulped his coffee and motioned for the waitress to bring more.

Jesse smiled at his mannerisms. The man seemed to have a lot of nervous energy and continued to speak without waiting for replies.

"You know Jesse, you've got a lot of influence as a former NFL player and it's wise not to let that go to waste. We're about to open another campus in the Corpus area and I know you have ties here. The starting salary won't be much to speak of but the opportunity is one that won't come along very often. I'll be honest with you. It would be a boost to have your picture on our billboards."

Jesse listened as the man continued to speak. The possibility of pastoring a new church was very attractive and it really didn't matter about the money. Though he would love to live near his parents he wondered how Lydia would feel. Pastor Jacobs asked but seemed to know already. "You're divorced aren't you?"

Jesse nodded yes. "I am."

Jacobs continued, "Well don't worry about it. That will actually be rather attractive in today's market. At least you were honest enough to walk away unlike most men in this field who hang on for dear life trying to keep a woman happy. In fact being single will probably bring in plenty of hopeful candidates. Believe me, you'll have your pick." He laughed and dug into his breakfast. "They never bring enough fruit for these waffles," he complained and motioned for the waitress again.

Jesse waited then began eating as he assumed the man was too excited about the new church to ask the blessing. Silently he asked the Lord for wisdom again and tried to calm his heart. It all seemed so attractive. Corpus Christi was a beautiful coastal city on the move. With a military base and Texas A&M University of Corpus many young adults could be mentored and influenced for Christ.

"I'm going to need an answer soon as my leadership team has another candidate in mind. Think about it and call me tonight. I'd love to make an announcement in church tomorrow."

Jesse was caught off-guard. "Sorry Pastor. That can't happen. A decision of this magnitude will take more than a few hours to pray about."

Jacobs was taken aback. "Well don't be surprised if I have to withdraw my offer. Like I said, timing is everything. Our church is used to things happening fast. No need letting grass grow under our feet when the flock is restless." He held up his empty cup for the waitress to come refill.

"And of course the other guy we've spoken to is excited too. So it's only fair to let him know something as soon as possible. But I'm telling you, you're the best man for the job. I heard the podcast of your message at the Panthers' banquet. Your presence is commanding and you have such a way of drawing people into the emotional side of things. It wouldn't surprise me at all for you to have a thousand people attending within a few months. People are glad to lend their support to a young talented man such as yourself!" He slapped Jesse on the back as he rose. "I've got this. I'll put the tip on my card too so don't leave anything."

Jesse rose and Pastor Jacobs shook his hand. "Call me tonight. I may drop a hint to my congregation tomorrow just to encourage them."

Jesse laughed. "I wouldn't do that if I were you." But Jacobs was already at the register swiping his card. Jesse sat back down and finished his breakfast. The waitress noticed his coffee cup was empty and stopped to refill it.

"Thank you ma'am." He smiled up at her and went back to eating. When he finished he left her a twenty dollar bill and a roll of Lifesavers. Thinking of Lydia he smiled at her story of being a waitress and hating church people most of all. They always tended to demand more and tip less. She'd told him of the elderly pastor who'd left her candy every time he came. It had been part of the reason she gave God another chance in her life.

As Jesse pushed the door open to leave, a voice came behind him. "Thanks Mister! You made my day!" A young lady smiled and waved.

He had a feeling he'd love being a pastor in Corpus Christi, Texas.

~~~~~~~

He carefully mulled things over on the way back to his parents. If he talked to Lydia about the offer he might worry her. But she'd expressed support for him the day before when he'd spoken briefly of it. He sighed at the thought of ruining their week-end, and especially his birthday. If she had a phone he would go ahead and call and give her the short version. He called his dad instead. It went to voicemail so he called his mom.

"Hey son. Finished already?"

"Yep." He answered. "Do you know where Lydia is?"

"She's right here. We're at the produce market. Want to speak to her?"

"Nah, I'll meet you there in a bit." Jesse hung up and left the little restaurant. He suddenly felt young especially compared to Pastor Jacobs. Of the gifts God had given him, public speaking was one of his favorites because he knew the ability came straight from the Lord. As shy as he had always been somehow speaking came easy when he stood before a crowd. In his thinking it was definitely a modern day miracle. Plus all the things that came with pastoring were right up his alley. He loved counseling, visiting, teaching and studying Scripture. Excitement began to build as he thought about the possibility. Perhaps Maggie and some of his brothers would be willing to help with the music ministry.

Though his mom and dad had been part of a small congregation for the five years they'd lived there, maybe they'd support him as well.

He smiled at the thought of his dad being proud of him and imagined his mom starting a Zumba class for the ladies.

He parked and looked for Lydia at the market. Happily he spotted her across the way. She stood with one hand on a hip and a finger pointing with the other. Though she smiled he had a feeling a negotiation was being made over something he couldn't see. She counted out money and handed it to the man in the booth. He wrapped the object in newspaper and handed her the change. Spotting Jesse striding toward her she held a hand up for him to stop then pointed a finger at him in mock anger.

He stopped dead in his tracks and laughed at her. Apparently the humidity had worked its magic as her hair was piled on top of her head and loose curls fell around her face. She had on a cute little blouse that fell close showing off her tiny waist. Even in her regular uniform of soft faded jeans his heart beat fast at the sight of her. She could sigh all she wanted over her ample hips. Jesse couldn't help but love her curves. She smiled happily at the man in the booth, shook his hand, placed the wrapped object in a larger bag then walked toward Jesse.

"When one has a birthday one should not just show up all willy-nilly." She smiled and led him a different way lest he peer into the booth where she'd just completed her transaction.

"Sorry ma'am. Do we still have a date tomorrow?" He watched as she fumbled with the heavy bag.

"Well I sure hope so! If we do supper I can wear my red dress." She smiled up at him with a definite sparkle in her eye.

He gazed at her mischievously. "Then by all means let's do supper. Happy birthday to ME!"

She laughed glad that she had found something to give him that he could unwrap.

"Where's mama?" he asked.

She looked around then admitted. "I have no idea. I get so turned around I don't even know where I am. As soon as we get back I'm gonna have to buy a phone if for no other reason in case I get lost. You know how I am."

He took the bag from her hand as she had stopped to shift it once again. "I won't look. Just let me carry it for you. I bet they went to get tamales."

"Yep. That's what she said." Lydia shook her head at her own forgetfulness. Jesse turned and headed in the opposite direction.

"Have you had breakfast?"

"If you want to count a bowl of cereal as breakfast I have. I might need a tamale since I've never had one."

Jesse nodded. "Yep. You definitely want a couple tamales and a breakfast burrito as well."

They sat at a small table and he ordered for them. He could always eat again. He wondered if she'd ask about the meeting and she finally did.

"So how did it go?" She bit into the tamale surprised at the flavor. "Wow! I like this. If I lived here I'd be big as a barn." She licked her fingers and looked up at him wondering about the meeting.

Jesse smiled and she thought maybe he'd already made his decision. She continued to eat as he tried to decide how much to say.

"Well, he's interested in me being the pastor of a new church plant. He wanted an answer right away but I told him I'd get back to him." He bit into his own tamale. "Mmm! I never get tired of these. So fresh!"

Lydia tipped her head and asked, "How does he know you? Through your parents or a brother?" She finished her tamale and started in on the burrito. "Mercy! I like this even better. I love that white cheese sauce. Good gracious. I could eat these every day."

Jesse smiled at the words but he had to be careful not to get the cart before the horse. There was certainly no need broaching the subject of moving. "I'm sorry. What was the question? I was busy looking at that drop of sauce on your mouth."

She licked her lips and asked, "How does he know you? What made him offer you the job so fast?" Wiping her face with a paper napkin she tried to slow down as she realized she was nearly inhaling the wonderful authentic food.

Jesse thought then answered. "He listened to the message I gave at the Panther banquet. And he said I have a commanding stage presence. He also called me young and it wasn't an issue that I'm divorced."

Lydia listened then asked, "How did he treat the waitress?"

Jesse laughed. "You'll be happy to know that I left her a nice tip even though he put one on his card at the register. AND I left her a whole roll of Lifesavers, never even been opened." He smiled at his funny chick.

She smiled back. "It's not you I'm concerned about Jesse. You're always generous. I asked about him. Did he treat her with respect or did he wave his coffee cup at her impatiently? You can tell a lot about a man by the way he treats those who serve."

Jesse thought a bit then smiled. "He did fine. He wasn't rude, but I could tell he was in a hurry. I guess everyone can't take life in slow motion like I do."

Lydia nearly snorted water through her nose.

"Ya reckon?" She couldn't help but laugh at his admission. "So did he ask about your doctrine or schooling or where you stand on salvation by faith? Or is he a 'work to earn God's favor' kind of guy?"

Jesse suddenly realized the man had said lots of flattering things that he apparently longed to hear. But neither of them had asked the important. In his defense the meal had been really rushed. Lydia interrupted his thoughts.

"And why does he have to have an answer from you so fast? You've told me to watch out for people who push us into quick decisions.

What's that you always say?" She was trying to quote him correctly so he answered for her.

"If it's wise today, it will be wise tomorrow and a year from now as well." He sat back in his chair and pondered. Why DID the man want to tell his congregation so soon? Surely the leadership team would want to properly vet him.

"Girl… when did you get to be so wise?" He smiled at her, took her hand and kissed it.

She smiled back at him. "Must be all this salt air! I have to say it's gonna be hard to go back to good ol' cold North Carolina!"

Her look turned sympathetic. "I'm not saying you shouldn't take the job Jesse. He's right in thinking you'd be a great asset to his team. But you'll be a great leader wherever God takes you. I feel like the Lord has some very special things in store for your future. You're such a Godly tenderhearted man."

She paused and added gently, "Just be sure his interest in you is not because of your status as a pro football player instead of in you personally. There are still lots of Kenya's in this world and I don't like the idea of you being used."

He brushed a curl from her eyes and stroked her face. How far they had come! How many times had he heard his mom give his dad similar wisdom?

"Will you pray with me about it?" Jesse still looked into her eyes. He could tell by her response that the decision had nothing to do with his moving. Her reply gave him the peace he needed.

"I sure will honey. And even if God works this out and it means you moving here, I've got a feeling Kurtis will be glad to help me drive down for visits. Just think of how happy your mama and daddy would be to have you near them."

Jesse gazed at her wondering how he could ever do life without her near. She finished up her burrito with gusto and licked the sauce from her fingers never knowing she'd been the voice of the Lord that morning.

Chapter 32

Sam and Nora found them as they finished up. He placed a large box on the table and Nora exclaimed excitedly, "Look what we found." She pulled the contraption out and Lydia clapped like a little girl.

"Yay! That's gonna come in handy after while!" She cranked the handle.

Jesse asked, "What in the world?"

Sam showed him. "It's an apple peeler. The apple goes here, you turn the handle, and it cores and peels it lickety split."

Nora added, "We already took the apples to the car. When we came back to look for you we saw this. Girl you've got to get a phone. But we should've known Jesse would have you here eating. He loves this food. We had some earlier. I hope it doesn't make you hurt."

Lydia shook her head. "It probably won't. It tasted so real I doubt there's anything in there that would set off my crazy mystery pain. In fact, I haven't hurt at all while I've been here. Must be all the salty air, and of course the good company."

Nora laughed. "Yeah right. Most of that 'good company' will be leaving tomorrow after lunch. I always hate to see them go, but it's kinda nice to get back to normal, whatever the heck that is."

Jesse nodded. "A hot shower wouldn't hurt my feelings any. Hopefully I can get one at some point. I've got a hot date tomorrow night!"

Sam smiled knowingly. "Yep. A shower never hurts when you're trying to impress a girl. We've taught you well son."

Nora shook her head at the men and smiled. Lydia asked, "Is everyone leaving but us?" She wondered about Maggie and Kurtis.

Sam spoke up but looked at Nora for confirmation. "I think they all have to be back at work Monday except for Maggie. She lost her job right before she came home. But that was the Lord's doing. Now maybe she and Kurtis will have more time together."

Nora nodded, "He seems like such a good boy." She laughed at the recollection of the night before. "Who taught him to dance?"

Lydia shook her head, "I'm afraid that's my doing. But he's certainly made it his own… the crazy Goober." She sighed and added, "Oh my goodness I love that kid. I've got a bigger version of him at home only he's more…" She looked at Jesse and thought. "He's more reserved but such a good young man. I can't believe how much I miss him. Too bad you don't have another daughter. We could fix them up."

Jesse glanced up at his parents and wondered if they would say anything. On cue Sam bent over and kissed the top of Lydia's head. "I think we gained another daughter for Christmas. But she's already taken."

Lydia smiled up at him. "You guys have been so kind. Thank you for everything. We'll be out of your hair soon though. I know it's time." Suddenly it occurred to her that she might be leaving without Jesse. Her heart took a nosedive as she wondered if that's why the Lord had sent Kurtis to Texas, so she wouldn't have to make her way home by herself.

She looked away doing her best not to tear up as they headed from the market. Jesse carried the bag and held her hand. Inwardly she made it top priority not to hold him back from something he obviously wanted. With a forced smile she prayed as they walked.

Thy will be done Lord. He was Your man first. But You know how much I love him.

~~~~~~~

The ride toward the house was quiet and Jesse knew it had suddenly hit her. She was surprised when he pulled into the home improvement store parking lot.

"Want to wait here or run inside with me? It'll only take a minute." Jesse asked knowing she probably needed some time alone.

"I'll wait here. The sun feels really good coming through the windshield." She answered trying not to give away how suddenly weary she felt.

Jesse locked the doors, headed in, then turned around before he got there. "I forgot. Your dad left you something in the glove compartment." He left again before she could look to see what it was.

A large envelope with a wad of cash waited for her there. Lynerd had scribbled a note on the outside.

Use this for anything you need. An extra land payment never hurts. Wish I had known you were in the hospital. Norma didn't call me til after the fact and Jackass had already moved in. I'm sorry for thinking the worst Copper. I should've known better, about everything. Don't know why it's so damn hard to say. But I love you girl. Always have-- always will.

Lydia was glad that Jesse had forgotten to tell her about the gift. She could sit in the truck and cry in peace with no one to witness her broken heart. At least now it made sense why her daddy had not even contacted her during the awful ordeal. Just like the situation when she was a young girl, her daddy couldn't fix what he didn't know was broken.

She held the envelope to her chest treasuring the words. He loved her. He always had and he always would. Though the truth was so much more valuable than the money she still pulled the cash out and counted it. She laughed at the amount. $7737. 77. Between the two of them when she was growing up, if there was ever a question involving a number her daddy would say without fail. "Seven is the answer, but if you have to use another number three is the next best thing." Often he'd hand her 77 cents for milk money when a carton of milk at school was only 50 cents. But this time good grief! Seven THOUSAND dollars? She would've been thrilled with seven hundred. She shook her head at her crazy daddy. Several other times just when she needed it most she'd found money in her old truck with a note from him. The notes had never been so kind and the amount had never been so generous. She sighed and really hoped he wasn't into something illegal. But this sure took the sting out of the possible move by Jesse. At least she could afford a plane ticket home.

Jesse returned to the truck smiling and handed her a bag. "I thought you might need this. I think mama has one but you need one at your house. I think yours is on its last lap."

She peered inside the bag at a fancy new food processor. "Ooh… nice! This really will help. Thanks sweet Jesse-man!" She leaned over and kissed him. He pulled her close and kissed her again.

He still held her as he whispered, "Remember when I bought you the mixer and you kissed me right there in the parking lot? That's one of my all-time favorite moments. You caught me by complete surprise girl!"

She smiled at him glad that she could think about something besides the possibility of his move to Texas. "I told you Cowboy, I've got my own love language. If you never bought me another thing I'd be happy just to be in your arms."

He hugged her tight. "You have no idea how happy you make me." Letting go they buckled seat belts and he started the truck. "I see you found your daddy's gift. Sorry I forgot about it til now."

She wondered whether to say it but decided he needed to know. "Hey Jesse if you take that job and need to stay here, daddy gave me plenty of money to get a plane ticket. Maybe God sent Kurtis down so I wouldn't have to fly home alone."

Jesse never missed a beat. He pulled over at the next parking lot and took her hand. "No Darlin'. Whatever we do, we'll do together. Just like Jesus, I will never leave you nor forsake you."

Her heart leaped again as he kissed her tenderly. A horn behind them sounded and a guy ran up to the door. Jesse saw who it was and opened his window.

"It must be God ordained for you to take the position!" His voice was cheerful and he beamed with excitement. "Come in here and I'll show you what we have in mind for the church."

Jesse and Lydia got out of the truck and followed Pastor Jacobs inside the abandoned mega-mart.

Jesse stopped the tour before it got started. "Pastor, this is my girl Lydia. She'll be helping me pray about the decision."

The man smiled a charming smile. "Nice to meet you. What do you think?" He waved his hand over the expanse of concrete floors and metal beamed ceilings. Lydia looked around wondering.

"Well, I'm all for making something out of nothing. And I personally choose old over new any day. This seems like a prime location too."

Jesse smiled at her words and wondered if he was part of the 'old' she spoke of.

Jacobs was impressed. "Exactly! For a fraction of the cost we can up-fit this place into a huge auditorium. That back area could be a nice industrial kitchen. There's plumbing already in place. It's really perfect! We just need the right man to cast the vision. That's where this guy comes in. People love athletes especially young good looking men like Jesse. Now what's your name again?"

She repeated it for him but he'd moved on to show them where the potential offices would be. They followed him around for a bit then he offered.

"Let's go grab a bite to eat and see what it will take to get you on board." He smiled broadly and headed to his car. "Lydia you ride with me so I can get to know you. Jesse stay on my bumper as I tend to lose people when they lag behind."

Jesse saw the look on her face and took her hand. "We're going to have to decline Pastor. My brothers are only in town today and tomorrow and mom's expecting us back at the house. I'll call you tonight."

Jacobs was disappointed. "It won't take that long. I promise. Lydia has questions. I can tell to look at her. Come on! Don't make me second guess my offer."

She was surprised that he actually remembered her name and she was even more surprised that his invitation sounded somewhat like a threat. But she was really surprised that Jesse didn't give in. She knew he wanted to know more and even as skeptical as she was, the building definitely had potential. How nice it would be to see a church there instead of a rundown strip mall.

Jesse spoke more firmly the second time. "Can't meet with you now. But I tell you what I will do. I'll fast and pray until breakfast tomorrow. The Lord will give us wisdom in this. There's no need to rush into anything."

Jacobs' demeanor changed and his face flushed a bit. Lydia looked at him wondering if it was embarrassment or anger. When he spoke she sensed it was the later. "You may not be in a hurry to make things happen but I've got a job to do. My head is on the chopping block in certain circles right now and I could use your help. Fasting and praying are fine when there's an emergency but today there is just no time. But suit yourself. You may not be the guy I'm looking for anyway."

He nearly leaped into his very shiny car then rolled the window down. "Why don't you at least come to church in the morning? The leadership team will be happy to see that I've got a solution in the works. Can you do that for me?" He started the car and put it in gear.

Jesse looked down at Lydia then back at the pastor. "I'll pray about it. What time?"

Jacobs sighed again and shook his head laughing. "Some things are awfully small to be bothering the Almighty about. The first service starts at 8:30. If you come around eight I can introduce you to my people and have you on stage before the second song. Bring Strawberry Shortcake too. She looks good beside you for those who may question your stability. But dress to impress. You look like you've been slumming at the flea market." He added as he pulled away. "See you in the morning. Eight o'clock sharp!"

Lydia looked at Jesse and laughed. "Yep. Been slummin' at the flea market. Bought my man something real NICE for his birthday."

Jesse shook his head and laughed too. His gut told him something was amiss.

When Lydia spoke he realized at least part of the problem. "He didn't mention the Lord except to tell you not to bother Him."

Jesse thought and prayed as they started for home. Though he never liked missing a meal, this seemed to be the perfect occasion to do so.

Chapter 33

Nora and Sam were showing the grandkids how to use the apple peeler. After each apple Nora would let one of them toss the long peel over their shoulder to see what letter it would make. The boys all hoped for an 'S' to indicate they were Superman while JoJo hoped for a 'K' for Kurtis. Maggie took a turn and exclaimed happily, "Look! I think I got a 'K'!" JoJo stepped down from the stool where she watched her Grammy with the new toy. Leaning over to examine the pile of unbroken peeling she said with authority. "Nope. That's a 'X'. So you get nobody.

Maggie made a pouty face and laughed. "I was afraid of that." Kurtis offered, "There's a Xavier in my school. If you play your cards right I could introduce you."

Nora laughed at him then picked up on his subtle hint. Sam did as well and called from the kitchen table where he sliced apples. "Nobody's changing schools at this point, not even for Xavier." Nora shot him a look so he added, "Unless of course one were to pray diligently and discover God had a plan that seemed rather foolish."

Maggie smiled at the look on Kurtis' face. They were both surprised at her father's words.

With bag in hand Jesse entered the house with Lydia. "Wow! Y'all are smokin'!" Jesse exclaimed regarding the progress in the apple department. "I got Lydia a new food processor to make the crusts. I wasn't sure if you had one or not mama." He opened the box and washed the parts.

Lydia stopped by the table where Sam sat slicing apples. "Thanks Sam! It's gonna take a bunch of apples to feed this crowd."

He looked up at her smiling. "Anything for apple pie. I can't wait! You're making these today right?"

She glanced at Jesse. "I had planned to, but I think we'll wait til tomorrow for somebody's birthday."

Jesse offered not thinking, "Why wait Darlin'? We can always save me a slice so I can blow out a candle tomorrow."

She smiled at him thinking it was probably the first time she'd ever heard him utter the words "Why wait?" Now it was to his detriment.

"Because sweet man, I thought you were going to fast this afternoon. It seems a terrible shame to bake your favorite on a day when you can't have it."

He suddenly remembered and sighed heavily. "Oh man. I forgot about that. Maybe I'll save fasting for tomorrow."

She cocked an eyebrow and asked, "Did you forget about our date? And your mama will not be pleased if you fast through your birthday lunch."

Jesse frowned and made a pouty face similar to Maggie's. "Bummer. Oh well. Like my favorite verse says, 'I will not sacrifice to the Lord that which costs me nothing.' Just be sure to save me a slice for tomorrow."

Lydia laughed and shook her head. "Stupid Jacobs."

Jesse laughed too though he wondered if it was appropriate. Yep. She'd make an awesome pastor's wife someday. He walked outside as she began making dough in her new food processor.

Nora was impressed. "Wow! That was easy. Now what?"

Lydia formed the dough into discs and wrapped them in plastic wrap. Four pounds of butter later she had enough for eight crusts or four pies. Stacking them in the refrigerator to chill she asked Nora, "Is it okay if we bake these tomorrow after church? I can't stand the thought of Jesse smelling this all afternoon when he's trying to fast."

Nora nodded. "I thought the same thing. We'll put the apples in cold water in the fridge. I think they'll be fine. So what are you thinking about his opportunity?"

Lydia sighed more than she meant to. "He'd be a great pastor. But I've got a bad feeling about the guy offering the job. I don't want to say too much because it needs to be Jesse's decision. I know you'd love to have him here in Texas with you though." She tried not to look at Nora lest she give away her own fear of being separated from Jesse.

Nora surprised her with a hug. "Don't worry Darlin'. Jesse's not gonna do anything without you. It'll all work out."

Lydia laughed. "That's what I keep hearing! Did Jesse go down to the beach?"

Nora looked out the window but couldn't see him. "I think so. He's probably trying to avoid the aroma he thinks will be wafting from the kitchen. Good call on waiting til tomorrow."

Lydia smiled at the woman she'd grown close to so quickly. She was definitely going to miss her when the time came to leave.

Chapter 34

She found Jesse on the beach throwing a football with his brothers. She spread a towel by Maggie and sat with her watching.

"Can I do your hair tomorrow?" Maggie looked at the pile of curls on top of Lydia's head.

Lydia looked at her and sighed, "Sure. Why not? It's such a mess in this humidity. I have no idea what to do with it. I'm starting to really love Nora's hairstyle; short and easy! It shows off her pretty face."

Maggie shook her head and twirled one of Lydia's escaped ringlets. "Don't you dare. Let me do it for you before you and Jesse go out. I never use shampoo. We'll wash it with conditioner instead. It's a trick us curly girls use to keep the curls defined. I'll show you."

"Thanks Maggie. I've never had a sister before." Lydia thought a bit then asked, "If I show you a dress I'm planning to wear will you be honest with me about it? I don't want to look like a harlot."

Maggie laughed. "Are you kidding? You're so funny with your beautiful figure and your grandmaw underwear. We need to go shopping so when you and Jesse..." She stopped.

Lydia felt her face turn red. "Yep. We need to go shopping. But I don't think there's any rush."

Maggie laughed and shook her head. "Sorry... but yeah. We need to get you some decent underwear and something pretty to sleep in besides that godawful Panther jersey." She looked at Lydia and laughed again as she added. "But you're right. This is Jesse we're talking about. So no hurry."

Kurtis came over and pulled Maggie to her feet. "What are you two cooking up? Looks like mischief to me don't you think Jesse?"

Jesse plunked down beside Lydia on Maggie's towel. "Don't let my sister ruin you Chickadee. She's been known to drag people into all sorts of debauchery."

Lydia smiled at his words. She wondered what he'd say if he actually knew what his sister was up to.

Maggie shot back at him. "Already using those big preacher words. What is debauchery anyway?" She drug Kurtis toward the house but winked at Lydia before they left. "Soon sister soon!"

Lydia smiled and wondered if she referred to the shopping or needing decent underwear. Apparently the girl didn't know her very Godly brother.

Squeeze and Jonathan dropped the football at Jesse's feet and picked Lydia up by the ankles and wrists. "Gotta get one more splash in before we leave. Come on girl, you're goin' in!"

"NO guys NOOOO! Please don't!" She tried to wriggle free.

They swung her over the waves counting backward. "Five, four, three, two…"

Jesse whistled. "Put her down guys and not in the water! She's had enough fun for one Christmas."

"Awww man!" Jonathan dropped her feet and Squeeze held one of her arms until she stood upright. "You're really gonna miss us when we leave tomorrow."

Lydia stumbled trying to get her balance. Jesse had stood and started toward her. "You okay? Or do I need to deliver a butt whooping to one or more of my siblings?"

She laughed at the look on their faces. "I kinda like option B."

His two youngest brothers ran in mock terror toward the house as Jesse glared at them. Lydia sighed. "Thank you so much. I'm not in the mood for a swim at this point."

Jesse sat by her on the towel. "Especially not in that white blouse. You look so pretty today. I don't know what that crazy pastor was thinking when he said that about how we're dressed. I didn't much appreciate it."

Lydia laughed glad he'd noticed. "I wonder how he'd feel if I showed up in my Strawberry Shortcake t-shirt."

Jesse tipped his head. "Strawberry Shortcake has always been my favorite. Do you really have one?"

Lydia nodded. "Yep. Not sure that I can still get into it but it's in a drawer. It's one of those things I can't bear to part with." She smiled and loved how close he sat to her. He slipped his arm around her waist and leaned his head on her head.

"Tell me what you're thinking girl. What's your take on things?"

She sat silent, glad for the interest in her opinion but not sure whether to say what she really thought.

"I'll fast with you today and pray. God will show you." She kissed his head and stroked his back. "Just don't let it ruin your birthday. We're gonna have fun. I'm saving the pie baking til tomorrow."

He sat up and looked at her. "THANK YOU! Oh I was so tempted! In one fell swoop you've gone from Rahab to Ruth again. I shall rise up and call you blessed among all women."

She laughed at his funny words and hoped she wouldn't be demoted back to Rahab when he saw her in the red dress. She wondered if she should ask Kurtis instead of Maggie. He would definitely be honest.

They threw the football on the beach while the rest of the family stuffed themselves with pizza. Eventually the little ones joined them there where they played foursquare and Frisbee keep away. Lydia's tummy gnawed and she realized she'd never actually fasted before. Once some other adults joined them she and Jesse walked down the beach as he prayed out loud for wisdom and guidance. He invited Lydia to pray and she gave it a try even though it felt weird not to close her eyes. But she'd grown accustomed to praying as she drove so it was similar. It was nice having Jesse hold her hand as the two of them walked and talked with the Lord as friends. When finally they returned the sun was getting low. Jesse had her stand still while he clicked a picture of the sinking sun behind her. Her face was too dark so he switched positions and took a shot of them together.

"I like it!" she smiled. "Send me a copy." She sighed. "Oh. Never mind. Hey when I get a new phone should I keep my old number? I've had it for years and I hate to change it. But if I get a new number maybe Jack won't be able to call me."

Jesse shook his head. "Keep your old number. Jack's gonna find a way to call you even if he has to go through me." He sighed.

"Maybe not," she added thoughtfully. "He'll find somebody new and move on. It wouldn't surprise me one bit if he hasn't already. With all the women swarming over him like they do, I can't imagine why he's bothered with me this long. I think it's only because somebody finally told him no. He's probably never heard that word in his whole life." She laughed then changed the subject.

"I never got a chance to tell you, daddy left me over seven thousand dollars. Crazy man. I might check on Shawn's school bill and see if I can help him out. Do you have any ideas on how to best use that money? I can stick it in savings but that's not always the wisest option."

Jesse thought for a bit then answered. "I'll pray with you about that too. You probably need to go shopping with some of it." He caught himself. "Not that there's anything wrong with what you wear. I'm just saying that while you're here with my sister and my mama it might be more fun than if you have to go alone. I know how much you hate to shop."

She smiled mischievously as she replied. "Your sister and I were just talking about that. Maybe Monday."

He looked at her wondering then smiled mischievously as well. He too had a secret.

Chapter 35

Jesse felt at peace about skipping the invitation to meet the leadership in the church where he'd been invited on staff. Pastor Jacobs was very surprised that Jesse declined his offer. He wasn't used to being told no and he surely wasn't used to being turned down so firmly. He made one last effort.

"If this is about rumors floating around over finances I'll be happy to get our accountant to discuss the particulars with you. Most of it was a misunderstanding. You know how church people can be; very high maintenance when it comes to money but stingy as all get out when there's a need for expansion."

Jesse sighed into the phone. "No, actually I might have given your offer more consideration had you been a little nicer to the waitress. A wise friend told me I could tell the heart of a man by how he treats those who serve. Take care Pastor Jacobs."

Lydia was so happy to hear his decision. But she was even happier to know she'd not guilted him into declining.

They both wished they had time for more than just cereal and toast for breakfast Sunday morning. But they couldn't very well break out the bacon and eggs with everyone else scurrying around trying to keep little faces and shirts clean.

Getting twenty four people including ten children ready for church was no small task. But everyone knew this was Nora's one Christmas request each year. Others could ask for shiny baubles all they liked. All she wanted was to see her kids together in church. Easily they would fill three rows and it made her happy knowing that it didn't take a funeral to bring them all to church. However it did nearly take an act of God to get them there clothed and in their right minds.

The message was especially good as the pastor continued a study in the book of Luke. Jesse put his arm about Lydia's shoulders and sat close stealing glances often. It was almost embarrassing to her. She was glad for the opportunity to help Abigail by holding baby Jesse. She thought maybe that's what her Jesse was so enthralled by. The boy was such a cuddle bug and seemed to love nuzzling Lydia's neck.

Lydia whispered to Jesse during a song, "Is everything okay? My blouse is not unbuttoned or something is it?"

Jesse smiled at her and whispered, "No. I'm just jealous of my namesake. I'd love to be where he is right now."

She nearly laughed out loud at his sudden lack of shyness. Instead she whispered back, "I think you need to pay attention!"

He gave her shoulder a squeeze. "Oh I am Darlin'. I can hardly take my eyes off you." Lydia had no idea what the rest of the message was about. At that point it didn't even matter. The man was in love with her and he wasn't moving to Texas.

On the way home she asked him why he'd turned down the offer. He thought for a moment then kissed her hand. "I was still praying about it last night just before I called him. It seemed the Lord asked me whose kingdom I'd be building. It was the question I needed to ask myself to make things clear." He looked at her and smiled. "We're so good together! I hope you know that. I appreciate you being open to the opportunity but being honest too. You really didn't like the guy did you?"

She shook her head. "Not one little bit."

Jesse laughed at her admission. "Women usually have an intuition about people." He glanced back at her. "Well… most of the time."

She nodded in agreement. "Yep. But sometimes the devil can look PRETTY GOOD." She laughed and hoped her words didn't come across wrong since she was obviously referring to Jack.

When they parked at the house she pulled his gift from the back seat through the console. "Happy birthday Jesse-man! I wanted you to open this without everyone around."

He pulled the metal object from the bag and unwrapped it. His reaction was exactly what she needed to assure that he liked her choice.

"Oh wow! This is beautiful! You know how much I love trees! How perfect. Thank you honey." He leaned over to kiss her.

"You're welcome. The guy who made it said that each leaf is a drop of metal that splashed down while it was hot to form those unique shapes. He hammered and formed the trunk himself. I couldn't believe how beautiful the craftsmanship is for, you know… an artist in the slums."

Jesse laughed remembering Jacobs' words. He eyed the piece carefully turning it in his hands. "You'll have to help me hang this and create a gallery wall with my mission kids all around it. Honey you couldn't have given me anything I'd like more. I really love it!"

She beamed with happiness and wondered if gift giving was one of her love languages too.

They moved inside where Jesse showed off his birthday present. Lydia went upstairs to change and was surprised to hear Jesse knock on the door.

"Come take a walk with me before you get comfortable."

She opened the door. "I was just going to put on my jeans and a t-shirt. You okay with that Master?" She teased him. Everyone else had already ditched their church clothes so she knew it wasn't about taking another family picture.

"Sure. I'll change too then." He walked toward the boys' room as she called behind him. "But not too much 'cause you know… I love you just the way you are!"

He laughed at her. "Hurry up girl. I want to take a nice walk before daddy gets the chicken fried."

"Yes dear." She closed the door and jumped into her uniform as he called it. Soft worn out jeans with a Carolina t-shirt was the norm. As she glanced in the mirror she thought of Maggie's words about wearing stuff up to her neck. Quickly she changed back into the blouse she'd worn to church that Jesse seemed to love. Maggie had given it to her and it fit closer than her normal attire. Though she'd never worn pink it looked good with her slight tan. Stepping back in front of the mirror she decided to change her jeans too. Her black ones would be a better choice. After all, it was Jesse's birthday. She might as well look as nice as possible for the man. The thought of him made her heart leap so she hurried out the door to find him waiting downstairs.

He smiled up at her as she came down. He'd changed into black jeans as well and a gray golf shirt. She smiled back at him glad that she'd opted out of her uniform.

"Good gracious birthday boy. You are just too handsome!"

His mom came from the kitchen where the family was busy preparing side items to go with the chicken Sam fried outdoors.

"Did y'all plan to co-ordinate your outfits?" She laughed as they looked at themselves. "Here, let your old mother get a picture. I haven't seen both of you dressed up since…"

Jesse asked, "This morning at church?" He laughed at her but gathered Lydia to his side.

Nora snapped a few then told Lydia to stand on the steps behind him. She obliged and hugged around Jesse's shoulders. He turned and kissed her glad that his mom caught the moment.

Nora shooed them out of the house. "All right you two. Go get your walk in. Lydia you're off duty today since you'll be slaving over pies after while. Lunch will be ready in about thirty minutes."

As she turned Lydia thought she saw her brush a tear. It was kind of weird since Nora was not a weeper like herself. Hopefully she wasn't too disappointed that Jesse wouldn't be moving near because of the job.

Jesse held Lydia's hand as they jogged across the road. Together they walked down to the surf where he took another picture.

"I have GOT to get a phone just so I can have these pictures of us." Lydia looked at the screen and wondered what he was fiddling with. He put his phone back in his pocket and brought something else out. Suddenly he was down on one knee looking up at her. She covered her mouth with her hand as her heart nearly beat out of her chest.

He tried to speak but couldn't. Finally he swallowed hard and began. "Lydia... honey... I want to take you home and love you forever. Will you please marry me?"

He opened the ring box and held it waiting as he looked up at her with tears in his eyes.

She caught her breath and hugged his neck. "Yes Jesse yes! A thousand times yes! I'll love you forever too!"

He stood and pushed the ring onto her finger. "Wow. I can't believe it's a perfect fit. Do you like it?"

She looked at it through tear filled eyes. "Oh Jesse it's gorgeous! So classic! My heart is pounding!"

He kissed her tenderly and turned toward the house. Throwing his hands in the air like a victorious gymnast, he laughed as they heard the hearty cheers of his family.

She laughed too and hugged him again. "How long have you had this planned? I see the ring is from Barnhardt Jewelers at home."

He smiled at her with sparkling eyes. "Yep. Today is 'Gotcha Day' remember? But I've wanted to ask you for much longer than I can say. I was so afraid you'd turn me down." He held her trying not to tear up again.

"Oh Jesse. I thought we'd still be dating next Christmas." She stopped and backtracked. "So... when would you like to get married? Do you want a long engagement?" She held her breath waiting for his answer.

He started with his normal. "Well... honestly I just want to be married to you. I don't care where or when we do the wedding. We'll do anything you want. But if I get to choose, I prefer sooner rather than later." He looked at her wondering if she'd need time to process everything. It always took her a while to warm up to things.

She nearly knocked him off his feet when she hugged him excitedly and shouted, "YES! The sooner the better! Oh Jesse! I can't wait!"

Things were going so well that he tossed something else out to her. "You know I'm the sentimental type. Mama and daddy got married on Valentine's Day. Is that too soon?" He asked expecting to get shot down.

She laughed. "That sounds absolutely perfect. I thought you were going to suggest this afternoon since your family's here. But I need a dress and some new underwear!"

Her hand flew to her mouth. "I'm sorry. But you might as well get used to it. I tend to speak freely around the one I love. So yes! I plan to buy new underwear and knock your socks off on your wedding night." She laughed again. "Did your sister know you were proposing?" Lydia thought of her earlier conversation with Maggie.

Jesse was still smiling from ear to ear. "The whole family knew. They've been praying for us since last Christmas. There have been quite a few little slip ups if you think back over our time here. Probably the first one was JoJo saying she hoped you'd fix your hair better when you married Uncle Jesse. Apparently she heard Pete and Abigail talking."

Lydia smiled. "I never picked up on it. Bless your heart. And then for Jack to call… oh honey. No wonder you were in such a funk." She grew serious as she thought about it. "You need to know that I never once considered leaving you for him. Like your daddy said, we were in a very strong spiritual battle."

She looked up at him and they stopped their trek toward the house. "Jesse honey I love you with all my heart. I will do everything I can to make you happy. Valentine's Day can't come soon enough!"

Her heart nearly melted when he leaned down to kiss her again. Another cheer went up from across the road.

"Okay girl. You've got seven weeks to find a dress. I don't care where we have the wedding, or really anything else. I'd love for daddy to do the ceremony if that's okay. I'll plan the honeymoon but let's have fun putting things together. Like I said, I just want to be married to you." He kissed her again for good measure and whispered, "Happy Birthday to me!"

She laughed and they ran across the road together to show off her ring to the waiting family.

Everyone came outside to greet them with hugs and cheers. Lydia was still in shock over Jesse's proposal and the gorgeous ring. Maggie whispered, "Guess we'd better go shopping." She and Lydia shared a private laugh. Kurtis stood in the background taking it all in happily. Once Jesse had been hugged by all his family he stepped toward him.

"Congratulations man." Kurtis hugged him tight. "I'm so happy for both of you. Honestly, I'd almost given up on y'all getting together. And I need to apologize for something."

Jesse leaned close to listen as Kurtis spoke quietly. "I kept pushing her, every time she and Jack would have a fight, I'd keep on at her til they'd make up. I'm sorry Jesse. But I have to say, once you finally asked her out I've been pulling for you ever since. She is so happy when she's with you."

Jesse hugged him again. "I know Kurtis. You're a good man. You've always wanted what's best for her, just like me." He sighed, "Those were some rough times but finally, she's MY girl!"

Kurtis laughed and nodded. "Yes she is! I'm so happy for both of you! So when's the wedding?"

Jesse noticed Lydia looking at him so he stepped over and took her hand to make the announcement. "Okay family. Here's the scoop. In honor of mama and daddy's anniversary," he smiled at his mom, "Lydia and I want to get married on Valentine's Day."

Abigail asked, "THIS Valentine's Day? Like in a couple weeks?"

Everyone laughed and Jesse looked at Lydia for confirmation.

She nodded firmly. "Yep. THIS Valentine's Day."

Jesse picked the conversation back up. "So you have seven weeks to figure out if you can get to North Carolina." He looked again at Lydia and whispered the question, "North Carolina okay?" She laughed and whispered back. "Sounds good."

Jesse looked up at everyone and tried again. "Of course we don't know all the logistics yet. But Valentine's Day lands on Sunday this year so we'll all go to church together then we'll have a wedding before the sun goes down."

His mama laughed. "That sounds easy enough."

Lydia couldn't quit smiling. She honestly didn't care. Her first wedding had been after church. There were no attendants. She'd walked down the aisle by herself with a bouquet of daisies that Blue had picked for her the day before. His face had lit up at the sight of her in the pretty white dress she'd found in a thrift store. Her face had hurt from smiling so much. Nobody had fussed over her hair or make up and Blue had loved how she looked. Their honeymoon was beautiful in the cool North Carolina Mountains and they were thoroughly married by the time they got back to work a week later.

The wedding plans were not that important to her. Being married to her beautiful gentle man was all she really cared about.

Maggie asked, "Where will y'all live after the wedding?" She'd been doing some planning too.

Jesse and Lydia looked at each other and Jesse answered, "North Carolina. I didn't take that position."

Lydia knew what Maggie was asking and she wondered also which house they'd live in. She thought about Shawn and Kurtis. If she and Jesse lived in his house the boys could have hers. Maybe she could still bake from her own kitchen though.

Sam interrupted by announcing, "The chicken is ready. Gather 'round sheeps and lambs." Everyone smiled especially Nora who was tearing up again. Her man had made that same call to his family for nearly forty years. She took his hand and the brood made a circle as he prayed.

Dear Lord, we are so thankful on this special day, Jesse's day. Thirty years ago today he became ours legally though he had been in our home and hearts for seven already. Oh how we bless the day that You trusted us with this very special boy. Our lives were forever changed. Today You've given us another. Lydia is ours as well through our son. We ask Your greatest blessings on their marriage. If it be Your will we ask for children no matter how they come. You are wise and You direct each path. Thank You so much for our family. Keep us safe and strong against the evil one. If it be Your will we ask that everyone would be able to be at the wedding in February. That's an awful lot to work out but You are God and we are not. So we trust You. Thank You for Your precious Son Jesus Who made it possible to be adopted into Your family. Oh how we love You! Amen.

"And thanks for the food," added Nora as she kissed her husband.

Sam smiled and added, "Amen!"

Chapter 36

A chorus of Happy Birthday ensued as Jesse was pushed to the front of the line. All his favorite foods were there except for apple pie which would come later. His mom had baked a ham with an orange glaze plus she'd made gravy from the drippings. A ladle of that over Kelly's hot baked potato salad was Jesse's favorite side. Adam's avocado salsa with black beans, Abigail's sweet potato casserole and Maggie's corn soufflé finished off the beautiful buffet. Of course his daddy's wonderful fried chicken was his absolute favorite.

Nora called to Jonathan and Squeeze, "Did you boys bring dinner rolls like I asked?"

They looked at each other. Jonathan finally answered. "No. We decided bread is fattening."

Nora shook her head. "No problem. Since you're watching your calories I guess you won't care for any pie later."

Kurtis laughed at Maggie's youngest brothers. They reminded him of Shawn and himself and he actually missed his friend. He found Lydia and asked, "Want to use my phone to call Shawn?"

She looked up from her place on the swing by Jesse and happily took his cell. "Thanks Kurtis! Is that okay with you Jesse-man? Is there anyone else we need to tell besides Shawn? Word travels fast."

"Shawn first, then probably Norma. I think everybody else is here." He thought of Jack and went back to eating. Maybe he'd give him a courtesy call later.

Shawn was happy for them as best Lydia could tell. As usual he wasn't great at telephone conversations. He sounded odd so she left her plate and walked around to the front of the house. When she was alone she asked, "Honey, are you okay? You sound worried."

After a long pause he stammered, "I need prayer Liddy. I miss y'all."

Her heart nearly broke at the sound of his sadness. "Did you and Tessa have a fight?" She waited for his answer and was surprised when he finally spoke. "No, but we're not doing good. I gotta go Liddy. When are y'all comin' home?"

She thought then realized, "We haven't talked about it but it takes two solid days to get there. Do you need us to leave right away?"

He laughed a weird laugh. "No… I don't want to spoil your visit. Hey, put Kurt on the phone."

It worried her that he was so vague so she asked, "Shawn are you in some kind of trouble? Do you need to talk to Jesse?"

He finally broke down. "I'm worried about Tessa. I don't think she's in a good place but she's got nowhere to go. I might have to kill somebody if anything happens to her." He stopped speaking and she could tell he was close to tears.

"Honey take her to the house."

Shawn interrupted her. "Liddy I CAN'T! We can't be here alone like that."

She interrupted him. "But you could stay at Jesse's. Let me get him. Tell him everything. He'll know what to do."

His silence was killing her and she hurried to Jesse. Before she handed over the phone she added, "Shawn honey, I'm proud of you. I love you so much. Stay strong son. Here's Jesse."

Jesse walked to the front steps and Lydia sat beside him praying. She wondered if she'd advised correctly and she listened as Jesse talked to Shawn.

"No son. Go right now and get her. Help her pack up her things and take her straight to Lydia's. If you think she's in danger you probably don't know the half of it. From what you noticed I think you're right. You've got my spare keys so take one of the rooms upstairs and make yourself at home. But be careful. She's very vulnerable right now and once the dust settles you don't want her to feel like you've taken advantage. Call me after while and check in. Just know I'll be asking hard questions. It's part of accountability. I love you son."

He hung up and looked at Lydia. "I think we need to go home before next week-end. Shawn noticed bruises on Tessa's arm that looked like someone had grabbed her."

Lydia caught her breath and fear gripped her heart. Jesse tried to continue without giving too many details.

"Let's spend tomorrow with mama and daddy then get on the road early Tuesday. We'll be home by Wednesday night." He noticed Lydia's worried look and hugged her shoulders. "It's okay honey. I'm glad Kurtis had you call. God's watching over them but let's pray for his and Tessa's safety."

He bowed and prayed for all of it. They walked back to the swing and finished lunch. Lydia could hardly swallow because of the fear she had for both Shawn and Tessa. What if there was an altercation when he went to get her? What if someone hurt Tessa before Shawn could move her? A familiar worry nearly overwhelmed her as memories of her own past flooded her soul. She left Jesse's side and headed to the kitchen. Thankfully she found herself alone. A rolling pin became her weapon of choice as she worked the stiff dough into submission. A stack of pie pans in the drawer below the stove were discovered. She drained the apples and spread them on a clean towel to dry. A short while later four crusts were filled with apples, sprinkled with sugar, and dotted with butter. Side by side they waited to be covered as Lydia beat out the next stiff disc.

Jesse's voice startled her so much that she jumped and dropped the rolling pin onto the counter. Instead of laughing he circled her waist from behind and tenderly kissed her neck. She leaned backward into his embrace and rested in his strong arms as he whispered. "I've been wanting to do that all day."

Reaching up she stroked his face against her and relaxed. His deep voice and gentle touch cured what ailed her.

"Honey I need you to do something for me." He whispered.

She sighed softly as she replied, "Mercy Cowboy. Anything." She turned and smiled at him. "Need cinnamon in the pie because I can totally do that."

He laughed at her words then pushed a curl from her face. "This is something serious."

Waiting to make sure he had her attention he continued. "When you get afraid… when those ol' demons pound at your heart… instead of hiding I need you to draw closer to me than ever. Can you try that for me?"

She turned back to the pie crust and brushed excess flour from the top as she folded it into fourths. Her heart hurt and she wasn't sure why. Once she had the crust on top of its designated bottom she brushed her hands and turned back to him where he waited. "I can sure try. But tell me this. How do you know what's going on in my heart so many times? I mean… I can hardly figure it out myself." She could tell the tears were coming so she turned back to the crust.

He drew close and whispered into her hair. "Because it's my job to take care of you, so I've spent a great deal of time praying and listening with you in mind." He kissed her cheek and hugged around her waist. "Darlin' I know you well enough to know that when things come up about abuse it triggers fear. You sympathize so much with Tessa right now that it's almost like going through it again yourself. So draw close to me and rest in my protection. I'll help you through it."

She turned and put her arms around his neck. "You're a little bit wonderful Jesse. Thank you. I might have to be reminded but it's only because I usually deal with things by making myself as busy as possible. I guess it's my way of running." She smiled up at him loving his gentle embrace.

He kissed her tenderly then added, "And a sprinkle of cinnamon wouldn't hurt, but just a tiny hint." He smiled and went back outside without realizing he had flour on the back of his collar.

Squeeze noticed it first. "Mmm-hmmm… got a little somethin' somethin' on the back of your neck there lover boy."

Jonathan happily joined in. "Yep. Been checkin' on the fiancée! Bakin' pies up in the house!"

Jesse laughed at his brothers and took it all in stride as he brushed the back of his neck. Kurtis came to help get the rest of it off his shoulder. "Good grief. Don't be distractin' Liddy. No tellin' what those pies will taste like now." He smiled at Jesse and asked, "Can I talk to you somewhere? I've got a situation."

Jesse walked with him to the front porch steps where he'd just talked to Shawn. He thought to himself that he'd always wanted kids. Now he'd inherited two already.

"So you've got a situation?"

Kurt explained. "It's about your sister." He looked at Jesse sheepishly. "I'm hoping she might transfer to Catawba next semester. I mentioned it to her and she's actually thinking about it. They've got a good music course for worship leaders. I think she'd make a great one. Don't you?" Kurtis presented his case for her move with gusto and Jesse tried not to smile.

"So no ulterior motives? This would be for educational opportunities only?" Jesse was able to ask with a straight face but had to look away when Kurt fidgeted.

Kurtis sighed. "I'm not gonna lie. I'd love to have her close by." He surprised even himself when he added. "I guess we need to get to know each other if I'm gonna marry the girl."

Jesse and Kurtis laughed together at that. "Well all righty then! So what's the question? She'll be the one to make that call. But if you're asking for my blessing you've got it!"

Kurtis paused then asked, "Could she live with you at first? Then by the time you and Liddy get married we can work out something else."

Jesse realized Kurtis would likely need to move in with him due to the Tessa issue.

So he asked, "Actually how about if you and Shawn move in with me and we ask Lydia if Maggie can move in with her. There's another situation we're dealing with. In fact, be praying for Shawn. He's probably in process right now of helping Tessa out of a bad place. Call him later and see if he wants to talk about it."

Kurtis couldn't believe things might work out. Plus he'd love to live at Jesse's house where all the cool man toys were. But he sure would miss Liddy. However, he'd feel right at home going over to her house to see Maggie. Everything swirled in his brain so he stopped Jesse and asked for one more thing.

"So if Maggie agrees could we take your truck to Waco to get her stuff? Her little truck will only hold so much. Then we could follow you and Liddy home so when we have to stay overnight we could share rooms."

Jesse nodded knowing what he meant. "Kurtis, you're a good man! Good luck convincing my sister to get on board with your big plan. And I have to say, if she agrees to all that, she must really think a lot of you. So don't take it for granted once she gets there." He looked at Kurtis sternly then laughed. Hugging him he admitted, "I think you two might deserve each other."

Chapter 37

The pies came out pretty good considering the oven was hotter than hers at home. Sam brought a huge tub of vanilla ice cream from a chest freezer in the pool house. He ended up microwaving it for a bit so it would be soft enough to scoop.

Jesse was in heaven. "My favorite girl, my favorite pie, my family, all this love and ice cream too. Happy birthday to me!" Everyone laughed as he blew out the candle on his piece of pie.

Lydia teased, "So I'm your FAVORITE girl but apparently there are plenty of others. At least I get to be your favorite. Thank the good Lord I can bake a pie or I might find myself farther down on the list."

Jesse busied himself with his pie but laughed when she exclaimed out of the blue.

"Oh my goodness! I need to call my daddy!"

Jesse handed her his phone and she looked for his number. Glancing up at Jesse she smiled, "You told him you were going to ask didn't you? That's why he came and was so sweet to me the other night."

Jesse swallowed another bite and nodded. "Yep. I called and asked for his blessing. It's the southern thing to do."

Lydia laughed. "Well I'm glad he gave you the right answer." She stopped and looked at Jesse. "He gave you the right answer didn't he?"

Everyone laughed including Jesse. "Yep but it wasn't easy. Believe me. The man knows the art of intimidation."

Lydia nodded. "Don't I know it!" She refrained from adding that her father had told Blue no when he asked to marry her. In fact it had been one of their biggest fights.

"Hey daddy." She walked outside to talk but again sat in a patio chair under an open window. "Jesse proposed to me. But I told him no. I was afraid you wouldn't approve."

She laughed into the phone. "I'm kidding. Please don't swear. He told me he asked for your blessing. So does this mean you'll walk me down the aisle?" Her voice grew softer. "I'd love that daddy. Thank you. Oh and thank you for the money. Now I can shop for a wedding dress."

She paused then answered, "Valentine's Day. Yep… seven weeks…. I do too. Yep… his idea. That's his parents' anniversary…. We don't know yet, probably his house. I'm not worried about it. All right. Hey daddy… I sure do love you. Thanks for your note… Okay. Take care."

She hung up and started to walk across the street to the shore when she thought of Jesse's words. So instead she sat tight for a moment trying to gather herself. Just as she stood to go back inside Jesse came out to her.

"Need to take a walk?" he asked.

She nodded trying her best not to cry. They walked for a while then returned to sit on the bench. Jesse put his arm around her shoulders and they rested there for a moment. Across the road a flurry of activity began as his siblings packed to leave.

Lydia looked across the road and offered, "We probably should go help them gather things or hold a kid or something."

Jesse nodded. "Yep."

But he didn't move so Lydia rested against his chest.

"I hope Shawn's okay… and Tessa."

Jesse stroked her hair from her face and kissed her head. "Yep. Kurtis is gonna call him in a bit. Then I'll check on him later."

She sighed and wondered, "Do you still want to go out tonight? We've had a big day already."

He nodded and hugged her to him. "Yep. We'll take a nap once all the kiddos are gone."

She looked at him and laughed. "We're already like an old married couple. No worries and nothing a nap won't cure."

He smiled at her observation. "Yep. Only 'nap' will take on a whole new meaning in a few weeks."

She laughed again surprised at his candor. "Yep," she agreed happily.

He pulled her to her feet. "Let's go help with the mayhem."

Chapter 38

Vehicles were loaded. Goodbyes were said. Hugs were distributed and a few tears were shed, mostly by Sam. Kurtis was happy that each brother shook his hand or slapped his back and gave him a hug. All the little boys did too. JoJo however wouldn't look at him. He found her sitting in her car seat waiting to be buckled.

Kurt leaned inside the minivan. "Bye JoJo. It was sure nice meeting you."

She busied herself with her favorite stuffed puppy.

He tried again. "Will you write me a letter when you get home?"

She thought about it. "I don't know where you live or nothin'. So how will the mail lady know how to find you?"

Kurtis smiled. "You can send it to Uncle Jesse's house. I live close to him so he can give it to me."

She brightened and crawled out of her seat to give him a hug. "Someday I will grow taller and you can be my boyfrin' then. Daddy said I'm too short now."

Kurtis nodded. "Always listen to your daddy. He's very wise. But we'll be very good friends, like me and Aunt Liddy. Next time I see you might be at Uncle Jesse's wedding and we can dance together."

She smiled at him happily. "Like Bell in the *Beauty and the Beast*?"

Kurtis nodded, "Just like that. I'll see you then!" He gave her a hug as Abigail situated baby Jesse in. JoJo returned to her car seat and pulled the harness over her shoulders. Kurtis stepped back and Pete fastened his little princess in. Shaking Kurtis' hand again he added, "Thanks. The girl has moped all morning and the only thing I came up with was that she was too short for you." He laughed and added, "You're gonna be an awesome dad someday. I'm glad we got to meet you. And as one of her brothers I have to say, Maggie has always been a handful for mom and dad. But she has a tender heart. Please treat her well. I'd hate to have to kill you."

Kurtis was surprised. Pete was actually the last brother he would expect to hear that from. But he understood. "I think you'd have to get in line." He laughed and waved at JoJo through the window.

~~~~~~~

Micah giggled and sucked his breath in for another belly laugh as Lydia tickled his face with her hair. She played with him on the swing taking in every moment. She could only imagine how sad she would've felt if they wouldn't be seeing everyone again soon. As she gathered the baby up for snuggles little Toby ran to give her something.

"I brang you a she shell Ain't Liddy. If you get stung by a jellyfish you can scrape out the stingers with it. Then Unka Jesse can pee on it and it will feel better."

She hugged him and took the present from his little boy hand. "Thank you Toby. Does your leg feel better?"

He twisted his leg around and showed her the welt. "It's aww rite. Jes part of growin' up to be a man."

She laughed as he ran away. Calling behind him she asked, "Can I have kisses?"

He ran back to her and puckered up kissing her right on the lips. His big brothers Marcus and Peyton were on his heels and kissed her as well. "See you soon Ain't Liddy." The boys ran together to their daddy Ben who began buckling everyone in.

Eva came to fetch Micah. "I knew I was forgetting something," she teased as she reached for the baby.

Lydia handed him over and laughed. "I'd be calling you as soon as he needed to be nursed. Or else he would. That could get frustrating for a little fellow." Eva agreed as she added, "He'll be screaming before we get home. Hopefully Adam will pull over before he gets too hungry. If I wasn't afraid of tossing him through the windshield I'd feed him going down the road."

Lydia shuddered at the thought. "It's hard to know what to do sometimes."

Micah craned his little head around for a drink and Eva sighed. "Look at him. He's already hungry and we haven't even gotten started. Oh well. I'd better see what Adam wants to do. We really need to get going."

Lydia stood to hug her. "I hope y'all can come to the wedding. I miss you already, especially this little guy."

Eva hugged her and shifted Micah for a hug from his new favorite aunt. "Tell her bye bye." She waved his little hand and Lydia's heart melted. Watching them walk to their van she even allowed herself to hope. Jesse joined her there as Ben and Kelly navigated their camper around the Christmas tree. Under Sam's supervision they finally pulled out of the yard.

Next came Adam's brood and Lydia noticed Micah in the front with his mom. She prayed for their safety again as she thought of the crazy wonderful life they lived with five little boys.

Jonathan and Squeeze pulled out behind them. Though they hated traveling so slowly behind their brothers, Sam had asked that they do so in case there was an emergency. Their music was cranked up loud and the windows were down. Honking the horn as they left was mandatory and Jesse laughed as they paused long enough to call out to him. "Got a little somethin' somethin' on your collar." They brushed the back of their necks mocking him. Jonathan stopped in the middle of the road so Squeeze could ask Lydia, "Need one more swim before we leave?"

She laughed at her crazy new brothers. "No thanks. I'm good!"

Maggie came running with a nasty blanket. "Asher left his cuddles." She and Kurtis hopped into her truck to chase down the caravan. Sam laughed but Nora called behind them. "Don't have a wreck trying to catch them!" The two of them held hands and walked inside.

Jesse smiled at Lydia. "No telling what else they'll find. Makes me tired just watching everybody leave."

Lydia said without thinking. "I think I need a nap!"

Jesse laughed and smiled at her mischievously. "I know I sure do."

Chapter 39

He took her hand and walked to the bench across the road. "There's a situation you need to be aware of."

She looked at him and laughed, "Another one?"

He explained what Kurtis had shared about Maggie possibly switching schools. Lydia was thrilled. "Then I won't have to live with boys in the house! Woohoo!"

Jesse tipped his head and looked at her. "You know you're gonna have to live with me at some point right?"

She smiled and whispered. "I long for the day. What in the world will we do then?"

He laughed. "I plan on lots and lots of naps."

She shook her head at him but smiled. "I mean about our four kids."

"Oh that. Well, let's get through the next few weeks then I'm sure something will work out. They can always move to the dorms. Do you care which house we live in?"

She shook her head. "Not really. I'm sure I can get your kitchen approved for my business if you want to live there. Or we can take the small house and the kids can live at your place." She stopped. "No wait… that won't work. Oh well. For now, like you said, let's just get through the next month. It'll all shake out in the wash. Hopefully Maggie and Tessa will get along if they both end up at my place. I think it will be really good for Tessa. She has a hard time trusting people, and rightfully so. I see myself in her so much."

Jesse nodded. "Yep. I do too. Only she's the old Lydia that used to scare me half to death."

Lydia looked at him surprised. "That's funny Jesse. When did I scare you?"

He sighed. "Every single time I saw you. You had that 'don't mess with me look.' You think your dad is intimidating. Why do you think it took me so long to ask you out?"

She threw her head back and laughed. "I cannot imagine you being afraid of me. Oh how funny!" Looking at him sympathetically she added, "I'm really sorry about that. Thank you for not giving up on me."

He hugged her to his side. "I couldn't. I knew you were the only girl for me."

She dared to bring it up. "I'm sorry for all the things I put you through when Jack was in my life. That must've been really hard. But thank you for loving me in spite of all of it." She stroked his face and gazed at him tenderly. "Jesse honey, I owe you everything. I love you so much."

He looked into her eyes thanking God for getting them through it. "I love you too girl. And even if you never bake another pie, you will always be my favorite."

~~~~~~~

Jesse was happy to find that Lydia had hidden the extra pie in the oven for him. Nora had already disappeared into the master and Sam was on his way.

"Naptime!" He smiled happily at his eldest son. "Get some rest this afternoon. We'll clean up the mess tomorrow."

Jesse smiled at his father then heated a piece of pie. Lydia stretched and yawned. "If it's okay with you I'm gonna go to Maggie's room and rest. I'm whooped!" She hugged his neck and turned to go. He pulled her back for another hug and whispered, "Rest well girl. Our dinner reservation is at seven and it's just past three now, so you've got plenty of time."

Upstairs she slid into the extra bed and sank into the cool sheets. Though she was exhausted and fearful memories had been unearthed earlier in the day, rest came easily as she remembered again Jesse's words.

Draw close to me and rest in my protection. I'll help you through it.

And even though he wasn't in the bed beside her, he would be soon. Only seven weeks and she'd no longer be sleeping alone wondering if there was someone in her closet. Just the thought of having Jesse near, being within his circle of protection gave such comfort that her dreams were sweet.

Chapter 40

About six o'clock Maggie came bursting through the door. Lydia forced her eyes to open as her new sister exclaimed too loudly.

"Get up you crazy chick! You've got a hot date tonight!" Maggie plunked on the bed as if it were the most natural thing in the world. Lydia tried to sit up and pretend she wasn't annoyed.

"What time is it?" she murmured as she stretched.

Maggie bounced on the bed like a puppy and nearly shouted. "It's almost six o'clock! Kurtis and I just got home and I thought you'd be ready for me to do your hair by now!"

Lydia looked around and realized the sun was already down. How had she slept nearly three hours in the middle of the day? She hopped from the bed and ran to the bathroom bumping into Kurtis as he came out. How in the world would she ever get her hair dry by seven? But it had to be washed. She could not go on their special date with grungy hair.

Maggie was right behind her. "Jump in and wash it with this conditioner. Just saturate your hair like you would with shampoo then leave it in while you bathe. Don't rinse it til you're ready to get out. Hurry hurry!"

Lydia stood looking at the girl who'd followed her into the bathroom. "Uh… you need to leave. I'm not used to all this… sharing."

Maggie laughed as she left. "HOLY COW! You and Jesse are just alike. I'm LEAVING for crying out loud."

She shut the door behind her then returned with Jesse's bathrobe. "Here! Hurry up. Y'all need to leave in approximately forty three minutes. Where's your dress?'

Lydia spoke through the shower curtain and Maggie went to retrieve it. Back into the bathroom she came. "I'm hanging it on the back of the door so the wrinkles will fall out in the steam."

Lydia reached for a towel and dried behind the shower curtain. Maggie pushed Jesse's robe in to her. "Put this on then wrap your hair in the towel. Squeeze out all the moisture you can but don't rub it… squeeeezeee it! Hurry girl hurry."

Lydia finally laughed. She wondered if Jesse could hear them downstairs. "Hey Maggie, hand me another towel."

Maggie tossed one back to her and Lydia wrapped herself in it handing the robe out. "I forgot to shave my legs." She pushed the shower curtain back to discover the bathroom door open.

"Mind closing the door?" She peered from the shower.

Maggie nearly shouted. "Nobody's comin' up here! Just sit on the side of the tub and shave while I comb out your hair! Good grief! How do you ever get anywhere woman?"

Lydia complied and wondered if she needed to rethink the decision about Maggie moving in with her. How had their roles so quickly reversed? Lydia was used to being in charge of herself. But she'd also been on her own for a very long time. It was kinda nice having someone help her know how to do stuff.

But when Maggie turned on the blow dryer Lydia reached behind her and jerked the plug out of the wall.

"No darlin'. I don't blow dry my hair. It will look like a big ol' wad of cotton candy."

Maggie jumped up from the closed toilet where she sat and plugged the dryer back in. "We're doin' this Missy! Tonight you're gonna look fabulous. We have the same hair and I dry mine all the time. Believe me this is gonna rock your world!"

She turned the dryer on high and advised Lydia to flip her head over. Reddish blonde curls flew all over the bathroom until finally it was dry. When she was allowed to stand upright Maggie quickly rubbed her favorite product between her hands and scrunched it into Lydia's mane.

"Sit!" Maggie ordered and Lydia complied. Her younger sister twirled and worked the strands with her fingers until she was satisfied. "See what you think!"

Lydia looked in the mirror and smiled. "I LIKE it! Good gracious. How'd you do that?" She tipped her head and noticed Maggie had kept it as natural as possible but somehow she had tamed the frizz."

"Step over here." Maggie moved the door which had a mirror so that she could see the reflection of the back of her head. "This is the prettiest part. Look at that!" She smiled happily at the results. A mass of light copper curls fell down Lydia's back. "Now shake your head. See how it moves and springs right back into place? I love it!"

Lydia stood gazing with surprise at her reflection. "My hair has never looked this good. Thank you so much! What time is it?" Again she missed her phone.

Maggie checked. "Six thirty seven. Move it woman! We still need to do your make-up!"

"I got it. Get out of here so I can get dressed." Lydia reached for the bathrobe.

"Nope. Sit! I'm doin' your face. You have no idea how pretty your eyes could be with more mascara. SIT!" Maggie nearly shoved Lydia onto the closed toilet.

As she worked her magic Lydia warned. "Don't go for the hoochie mama look. I'm already worried about my dress."

Maggie shook her head. "Relax Rahab. You're gonna look fantastic. Stop squinting." She stepped back to admire her work. With more hair product on her fingers she worked on the curls falling across Lydia's face. "Perfect!"

Lydia looked and worried a little. At least Jesse would know his sister had been in charge of her appearance. Hopefully he wouldn't regret asking her to marry him.

Maggie was holding up lipstick to match the dress. Lydia spoke firmly. "Nope. I'm not wearing lipstick. It looks fake on me. Besides, there's enough going on with the top half of my face. Good grief."

Maggie started to insist and Lydia held up a hand. "Get out of here and let me brush my teeth." She heard how she sounded and added,

"Please. And thank you for doing my hair. It looks really nice. Do you think I should wear it like this for the wedding?" She turned and glanced at the back again.

Maggie was glad she liked it. "Oh yeah! Unless you find a dress with a really pretty back. Then I can give you an up-do if you like. But I know Jesse loves how long it is."

Lydia finished up in the bathroom and scurried to find underwear. There was Maggie again holding out what she needed. "Where are your shoes?"

Lydia caught her breath. "Dag nabbit. I forgot my shoes!"

Maggie actually laughed at her. "Dag nabbit?"

Lydia decided not to reveal that the word was quite an upgrade from her former language. Maggie was busy looking through the shoes in a hanging bag on the back of her closet door. "Try on these. We might be close to the same size." She tossed them toward Lydia who stood in Jesse's robe and tried them on.

"These shoes are weird. Do they even match?" Lydia was having a hard time picturing them with the red dress.

Maggie was clearly exasperated. "YES! Trust me! Now get dressed!" She left the room and Lydia hurried into her clothes. Thankfully the shoes fit but she still wasn't sure about the dress. She thought about calling down for Kurtis to come up but she didn't want to hurt Maggie's feelings. Maggie burst through the door.

She stopped in her tracks.

"Merciful heavens woman. Where did you find that dress?" The look on Maggie's face did not give away what she was thinking. Lydia stepped back from the mirror, smoothed the dress then pulled at the deep neckline.

"Do you have something else I can wear? This is too…"

Maggie smacked her on the arm. "Lydia! It's gorgeous! What are you worried about? Looking too hot for your fiancé? If Jesse hadn't already proposed I'm sure he would tonight!"

Lydia still peered into the mirror with uncertainty. "Maggie are you sure? When I wore this to Kurt's banquet I got fussed at. I really don't want Jesse to be disappointed in me." Her fear nearly brought tears.

Maggie spoke kindly. "Honey please trust me. You are beautiful. Jesse is going to love it. And stand up tall like you ARE somebody. Here's a smaller purse. And do me a favor. At least wear some lip gloss."

Lydia complied then gave her a hug. "Thank you Maggie. I'll be calling on you again February 14th!" She walked down the stairs like a prom date and Jesse stood up. His heart beat fast at the sight of her and he had a hard time finding his voice. Taking her hand he led her toward the door. Finally he turned and spoke to his family. "Don't wait up!"

Sam and Nora stood together and Maggie took Kurtis' hand as the door closed behind their favorite couple. Maggie high fived her mom and Kurtis laughed as Maggie proclaimed. "My work here is done!"

The four of them heated up leftovers and Maggie thought to ask Kurtis, "Who had the nerve to reprimand Lydia at your banquet? She almost wouldn't wear that dress and she looks fantastic in it."

Kurt downed a bite of his ham sandwich before he answered. "It was an old guy in charge of the scholarship fund." He laughed at the memory but was surprised when Sam asked, "Well I hope you put him in his place."

Kurtis tried to swallow. "I didn't get a chance. Liddy…" He thought twice about telling everything. "Liddy asked him what was the hardest he'd ever been slapped."

The four of them laughed heartily at that. Kurtis added, "She's a lot nicer since she's going with Jesse. He always brings out the best in her."

Nora and Sam smiled at each other and Nora commented. "That sounds familiar. I completely understand."

Chapter 41

The restaurant was beautiful and Lydia was glad she had dressed up. Jesse looked particularly handsome and she told him so. He seemed unusually quiet and for just a moment the memory of the date with Jack that had turned out so bad gave Lydia pause. What if she'd made a mistake by wearing the dress?

With menus in hand she smiled at Jesse warmly. "This is my treat. Order anything you want birthday boy. Surely seven thousand seven hundred and thirty seven dollars and seventy seven cents will be enough."

He laughed and kissed her hand. "I have no idea what to order. I can't think for looking at you. Honey I'm not kidding." He looked into her eyes and teared up.

She tipped her head and looked at him wondering. He leaned over and kissed her lightly. "Darlin' I've always known you were pretty, but tonight…" He cleared his throat and whispered. "Happy birthday to ME!"

They laughed together as the waiter came.

Jesse ordered wine while Lydia scanned the menu trying not to think about the prices. She really needed tires for the truck. Closing the menu she asked, "Jesse will you order for me? You know me better than I know myself."

He smiled and answered. "It would be my pleasure."

They dined by candlelight then danced slowly and loved soaking in each other's presence. Jesse couldn't think of a thing to say. But for some reason it didn't bother Lydia at all. His gentle embrace gave her all the assurance she needed that everything was okay.

At one point she noticed he moved rather tentatively as they danced. She started to ask if he planned to have knee surgery before the wedding but realized it might make him feel old again. There was certainly no need to risk that so she just held him closer.

She wondered what he thought of her dress and started to ask. But clearly he loved the way she looked so she left that question unasked too. With her head on his shoulder she realized that they were the only ones dancing. Many eyes were on them but she was so in love that she hardly cared.

~~~~~~~

Jesse's heart pounded when she looked at him and smiled. It seemed the whole world faded to the background just knowing that she loved him. He wondered for a moment what he would've been feeling had he not proposed earlier. His first plan had been to ask her to marry him after their date. But his brothers wanted to be a part of the joy. So with a great deal of fear in his heart he'd decided to ask her while they were still at his parents' house. He praised God again that she said yes.

His knee reminded him that indeed he needed surgery. He started to ask her what she thought about him trying to have it done before the wedding. But he had a lot to do before they moved in together. His heart leaped at the thought and right on cue she pulled him closer. Apparently she hadn't noticed that they were the only ones dancing. Or maybe she had decided not to let it bother her. Either way he tried not to care that so many eyes were on them. Suddenly he wondered if he had toilet paper on his shoe.

The song ended and he led her back to the table. Several folks clapped and the waiter made his way to them. "Can I get you two some dessert tonight? We have a wonderful chocolate mousse that's to die for."

Lydia found her voice first. "I'd love that and a cup of coffee please. How about you sweet man?" She looked at Jesse who thought a moment. "Key lime pie for me and coffee."

The waiter added before he left. "The two of you are lovely together. I hope you don't mind. A photographer from the *Caller-Times* took your picture while you were dancing. He asked me to give you his card."

Jesse looked at Lydia who smiled back at him with approval. "Would you ask him to send me a copy? Here's my number." Jesse handed the waiter his card knowing that he'd love to have a memento of their special night. He'd never seen Lydia quite so stunning. The waiter complied and moments later Jesse's phone received the picture he'd treasure forever. Of course it included a waiver for him to return so the photographer could use it in an ad he was compiling for the restaurant. Jesse happily sent him the info he needed being careful to use the word fiancée as it had such a wonderful meaning. Soon he would be married to the love of his life.

~~~~~~~

She tried to ignore it but it wouldn't go away. Determined to finish the silky chocolate cloud she unintentionally put her hand over her heart and sucked in her breath. Quickly she placed her hand back in her lap hoping Jesse hadn't noticed.

He looked up from his pie and waited. She was careful not to look at him.

"Honey…" He took her hand.

She sighed. "Let's finish our dessert then head on home."

It hit her again and she placed her spoon in the dish and leaned back a bit. A few deep breaths later she knew they needed to leave as quickly as possible. Fumbling with her purse she could hardly think. The pain was unbearable and ran down her arm. Her jaw began to ache and terrible shocks of pain radiated from the center of her back. She was afraid to stand.

Jesse motioned to the waiter who took his debit card. Lydia tried to sip the coffee but couldn't bear to hold her cup. She found it hard to speak and her vision blurred.

"Jesse honey…" She clutched her chest in pain. It was getting hard to breathe. He checked his phone for the nearest E.R. then took her arm. The waiter brought back his card and tried to help. "Let me walk you out." He moved to the other side and held her arm. "Should we call for an ambulance?" The waiter was really concerned.

Lydia was able to say 'no' very firmly but for a minute wondered if she was about to die.

A valet brought the truck around and Jesse helped her in. She winced in pain and cried into his chest. Finally he was able to fasten her in then ran to the driver's side and screeched out of the parking lot. It was then that the waiter realized he still held her purse.

Jesse drove as quickly as possible to get her to the nearest E.R.

A short while later she sighed deeply and calmly informed him. "I'm okay now. It was just one of those attacks I have. I'm sorry honey."

He slowed down and looked at her. She reached across the console but was careful not to move. He took her hand and looked at her trying to decide what to do. A few blocks later he pulled into the emergency room parking lot. Once they were parked he got out and walked around to the passenger side. Holding her for a moment he asked, "Want to get checked out just in case? They can at least listen to your heart."

She shook her head no. "It's something I ate, I'm sure of it. I'm still hurting but the pain is easing off."

He looked at her tearfully. "Maybe you're allergic to me. This happened the last time we tried to have a nice date."

She smiled. "No honey, I think you're the CURE, not the problem. Let's go home." He closed her door and returned to the driver's side.

She asked, "Did you happen to pick up my purse? I think I might have left it at the restaurant."

Jesse turned around and headed back to where they'd just been. "You didn't really have all that money in your purse did you?"

"No. The money's still locked in your glove compartment. I just pulled this little stunt so you'd have to pick up the tab."

He was glad that she was returning to normal. The waiter met him with her purse when he came through the door. "Is she okay?" he asked genuinely concerned.

Jesse answered kindly though he was in a hurry to get back to her. "We think so. Apparently she ate something she's allergic to."

He called behind Jesse as he left. "Some people can't have wine because they're allergic to sulfites."

Jesse stopped. "Thanks man. Will you check to see if there was MSG in the dish she had?"

The waiter covertly inquired and returned to confirm. "Yes, but if this turns into a lawsuit I have never seen you before in my life!" He laughed nervously.

Jesse shook his hand and tipped him well. "Thanks again."

Chapter 42

The house was dark when they returned. Apparently the other four family members had gone to a movie. The note by the coffee pot read, "Don't wait up."

Lydia wondered what to do. She was still in a lot of pain but at least she was breathing easier. Jesse noticed the look on her face and asked, "What can I do to help you?"

She sighed looking at the stairs. "I really hate to ask you to go up the steps for me but I don't think I can climb them just yet." She swallowed hard. "Honey... I need help but I don't want to embarrass you."

He held her for a moment. "Darlin'..." He shook his head. "I'm not embarrassed, I'm just being respectful. I always want you to know that I love you for who you are, not for any other reason." He kissed the top of her head. "Now what can I do for you?"

She sighed again and looked up at him wondering. The man was certainly a mystery but somehow he continually had a way of assuring her she was loved.

"Could you please fetch my snowman pajamas? They're in my bag in Maggie's room."

He helped her make her way to the guest room where he removed her shoes. She felt like Cinderella watching him down on his knees before her looking like Prince Charming.

"I'll be right back." He smiled up at her then returned shortly with her pajamas. "Can you manage the rest? Want me to..."

He looked at her and laughed. "I'm sorry. I started to say 'Happy Birthday to me!' again but somehow it just didn't seem right. Here..."

He reached around her, moved her hair and unfastened her bra through her dress. She looked at him surprised. "Whoa! You kinda did that like a pro." She laughed as he walked out of the room.

"Still got it Darlin'!" He laughed too and closed the door behind him.

Just having her bra unfastened helped her breathe more normally. Finally she managed to dress in the flannel pajamas thanking the Lord that the weather had turned much cooler. She joined him on the sofa where he waited in his own flannel pajamas. She couldn't help but laugh.

"We are such a couple of old geezers." Slowly she walked trying not to give in to the pain.

He stood and invited, "Can you sit in the recliner with me? Maybe you can get comfy and we can be close. I don't like cutting our date short."

She teared up at his sweetness and sat with him there. He carefully pulled the lever and the footstool popped out. "How's this honey?"

She rested next to his side comfortably. One of his arms was around her so she nestled her head on his chest. "Perfect. Mercy Jesse. You're so good for what ails me."

He opened his Bible with his free hand and read to her from Psalm 91.

Those who live in the shelter of the Most High will find rest in the shadow of the Almighty.
This I declare about the LORD: He alone is my refuge, my place of safety;
He is my God, and I trust Him;
For He will rescue you from every trap and protect you from deadly disease;
He will cover you with His feathers. He will shelter you with His wings.
His faithful promises are your armor and protection.
Do not dread the disease that stalks in darkness nor the disaster that strikes at midday.

He paused then skipped to the end.

The LORD says, 'I will rescue those who love me.
I will protect those who trust in My Name.
When they call on Me I will answer.
I will be with them in trouble.
I will rescue and honor them.

He hugged her to his side. "Honey I know this stuff is bound to scare you. And it may be something we deal with for the rest of our lives. But we'll get through it together. The Lord will help us figure it out. In fact,

I think the reason we left your purse was so God could give me a chance to find out there was MSG in your food. The waiter checked for me."

She looked up at him surprised. "But you told him specifically when you ordered that I was allergic to it."

Jesse shook his head. "I'll have to be more firm about it next time. And if I were to guess I'd say our waiter will probably speak to someone in the kitchen since he saw how much pain you were in. He also mentioned that some people are allergic to wine but I've never heard of that before."

She thought for a minute then remembered. "You know… the last time we ended up rushing to a clinic I had wine; but only a little. Tonight I had a whole glass. Maybe I'll stay away from it til I know for sure."

Jesse agreed. "That's how we'll approach this. But you've got to be honest with me and not try to hide the pain. We'll take notes together." He hugged her again and she realized that she always had to be reminded to be truthful. It was definitely something she needed to work on.

As if on cue he asked, "Now talk to me woman. Honestly, what is your idea of home? Where is your happy place? I like dreaming of where we'll live."

She smiled up at him. "I think I'm there! Just being in your arms IS my happy place."

Chapter 43

"Tessa, are you okay in there?" Shawn asked through the bathroom door.

She wiped tears away and called back to him. "I'm fine. Go do whatever you do and leave me alone." The hot bath helped but she could hardly relax in the strange place, especially with him talking to her though the door.

His phone lit up and he was glad to see it was Jesse. Walking outside so she couldn't hear he answered. "Hey man. Thanks for calling."

Jesse heard the tremor in his voice and asked, "How'd it go? Were you able to get her to leave with you?"

Shawn paused to pull himself together. "It was bad. She'd locked herself in the bathroom because her uncle was still in the house. He tried to run me off so we had a big fight. But I got her. She's pretty banged up so she's soaking in the tub here at Liddy's. I don't know what to do to help her."

Jesse was glad Lydia had left to go to the bathroom. He could feel the rage building in his own heart. "Shawn, do either of you need to go to the emergency room tonight?"

Shawn answered, "I'm fine but I don't know about her. He was pretty drunk. If he hit her half as hard as he hit me then she's bound to be hurting. I thought about going back over there once I get her settled and just blow his brains out."

Jesse understood his anger and told him so. "Listen to me son. You won't be much good to her dead. She doesn't need to be left alone tonight anyway. I'll help you know what to do about her uncle when I get back."

Shawn asked, "Liddy's not listening is she?"

Jesse answered, "No but she'll be back in a minute."

Shawn sighed, "I'm gonna stay here tonight and move my stuff to your house tomorrow. But don't worry. She won't let me near her. It's like she's scared of me or something."

Jesse sighed. "She is very afraid right now Shawn. She expects you to use her like every other man in her life. Instead give her plenty of space. Don't be surprised if she lashes out or pushes you away. Do your best to be very patient."

Shawn was silent and Jesse could tell he was really upset. "Stay strong son. You'll get through this. We'll be home Wednesday night good Lord willing. Did Kurtis call you?"

Shawn sighed, "Yep but I couldn't pick up. I was too busy getting my brains beat out."

Jesse tried not to let his anger show. "I'm sorry I'm not there, though I don't know what I could do that you're not already doing. Remember what I said. Give her plenty of space. Pray for her and ask God for wisdom in dealing with her pain. You're a good man Shawn. I love you."

Shawn nearly teared up at the words and tried to reply. Finally he was able to stammer out, "Thanks Jesse. And thanks for praying."

Chapter 44

Remembering Jesse's advice to give her lots of space Shawn went to his recliner in the den to watch Sunday Night Football. But before he did, he turned back the daybed and slipped a note under the bathroom door.

Soup in the fridge if you want some.
Daybed in the sunroom is ready for you.
Call me if you need anything.
Praying for you.

Jesse was right to warn Shawn that Tessa might lash out at him. When finally she dared to venture from the bathroom she unlocked the door and stepped tentatively into the hall.

He muted the television and heard her using the microwave. With any luck at all she'd join him in the den. He prayed for her and asked God for wisdom. His gut told him to stay put. So he did.

She peered around the doorway to where he sat and scolded him. "Just like a man. If a ballgame is on you can't hear nothing else!"

He looked up at her and she noticed his black-eye for the first time. "Just trying to give you some space. Have you taken anything for pain?"

She was startled at the look of concern on his face. No man had ever cared for her before except maybe her grandfather.

"No. I don't have nothing. I ain't gonna go diggin' through Liddy's stuff to find anything either."

Shawn rose but made a wide berth around her to check the bathroom medicine cabinet. He brought out the Advil, took a couple then handed her the bottle. "I hope this will help. There's an extra blanket on the daybed in case you get cold. It's turning cooler all of a sudden."

He headed back to his chair then invited. "You can eat that soup in here if you want. Liddy doesn't mind us eatin' in the den."

She turned and went back to sit at the kitchen table. Shawn laughed but was careful to do so quietly. Next to Liddy she was the stubbornest woman he'd ever met.

He heard the microwave again and was glad that she was having seconds. No telling how long it had been since she'd eaten. Her voice came from the kitchen. "You saving this bread for anything special?"

He smiled and called back. "Saved it special for you. It sure is good but I'm not worthy."

She looked through to the den where he sat. He glanced up at her with a smile but she didn't smile back. A few minutes later she came to him with a piece warmed and buttered.

"There's plenty for both of us." A smile played at her lips but she thought better and returned to the kitchen. At the table she sat and ate alone. Though her back was to him he could tell she shivered. They'd grabbed her few clothes quickly and stuffed them into a couple Walmart bags. He wondered if she had anything warmer to wear. From his room he fetched a hoodie jacket and placed it on the kitchen chair beside her.

"It might get chilly in here tonight. Here's a jacket you can use. Just so you know, I'll move to Jesse's house tomorrow and you can stay here. He and Liddy will be home Wednesday night."

She looked up but he quickly moved back to the den. Silently she finished her supper then washed the dishes thankful to have the time alone. As she dried and put them away she noticed the mismatched stacks of bowls and plates in the cupboards.

She rinsed the soap from the sink and recalled something she'd heard about the house. Again she shivered. She dried her hands and put on Shawn's jacket. It smelled like smoke but she liked it. In fact she remembered him wearing it at a bonfire the church had for the college kids. She had let him drag her along just to get out of being alone with her uncle after her sister's family moved out.

She brought the arm of the jacket near her nose and sniffed again. It reminded her of the fun night with the cute country boy who never even tried to kiss her. He was definitely a rare bird.

Venturing into the den she sat on the purple sofa. He pulled a quilt from the rack and tossed it to her.

"Want me to build a fire?" Shawn stood waiting on her reply.

She sneered at him. "Don't think you're gonna get all cozy with me. Stay over there in your big-ass recliner and watch your stupid football game."

Shawn laughed back at her. "Well don't think you're gettin' all cozy with me neither. That's why I tossed you the stinkin' quilt. Do you want a fire or not? I'm plenty warm."

Taken aback she replied, "I don't need nothin' from you white boy. Leave me alone."

He shook his head and sat down. Except for the game the room was silent for a while. Finally he stood again and set about building a fire.

She watched as it came up to a warm even blaze then asked, "Is it true she murdered a man in this house?"

Shawn was surprised at the question. He wondered if 'murder' was the right word. It seemed wrong to call Lydia a murderer.

"Yep. She killed a man who was attacking her. But it wasn't murder."

The frail young woman nearly spat back at him. "You know what I mean. So he died in this house?"

Shawn looked from the television to where she sat huddled on the sofa. "Yep. Bled out on the kitchen floor. She nearly did too but Jack found her."

He turned back to the game and reminded himself not to hate Jack too much. A part of him wanted to keep the conversation going but another part felt almost as if he were divulging private information on the woman he cared most about in the world.

Tessa's tone seemed accusing. "So the same guy I made her talk to in the truck is the same one who saved her life?" She thought for a bit. "He really made her cry. I thought she was gonna have a nervous breakdown. It was weird."

Shawn looked at her and his expression changed. "She's a good person and sometimes bad things happen to the best people. So what is it that you really want to know?"

Her tone softened and she asked, "Do you think the dead guy's ghost is still in this house? I mean, what if he ran Jack off? It seems weird that he just up and left."

Shawn turned to look at her trying not to get angry. "Jack left because he's a womanizer and he chose to do his own thing no matter how bad it hurt Liddy. There is no ghost in this house because when we're absent from the body we are present with the Lord."

She wasn't buying it. "There ain't no way that creep is in heaven."

Shawn realized it was a valid point and answered well. "I didn't say he was in heaven. He's probably burning in Hell right now. But the second he died he stood before God Almighty and answered for what he'd done. There ain't no second chances after death. That's why it's pretty important to pick sides now."

She thought on his words then asked. "You believe that?"

He answered with certainty. "Yep. Scripture spells it out plain and clear. 'Believe on the Lord Jesus Christ and you will be saved.' Have you ever done that?"

She laughed. "You trying to make me a good girl? It's too late for that white boy."

He shook his head and looked at her kindly. "It's not about you Tessa. It's all about Him. Jesus didn't come to save good people. He came to pay for everybody's sin. We just have to trust that He is God and we are not."

The room warmed up and she relaxed thinking about his words. A spiritual battle raged that she couldn't see, but she felt it and Shawn did too. Suddenly she patted the sofa beside her.

"Maybe you need to come over here and explain things to me." She smiled for the first time since he'd rescued her. Flipping the blanket back she invited him. "Come to mama white boy."

Shawn gazed at her tenderly and surprised her by saying, "No Tessa. You won't believe this but I actually care for you an awful lot. That's why I came to get you today. I was worried about you. So don't get your feelings hurt. The Lord happens to think you're worth saving, and so do I."

He turned back to the game and hoped she wouldn't cuss him. Silently he prayed for strength. He knew it could get worse so he asked the Lord if he should just get in his truck and go to Jesse's. Though he already cared a great deal for her, mostly they'd been fishing and hanging out together. He'd never even tried to kiss her.

She fell silent so he stole a glance trying to read her mood. Tears slipped down her face and she pulled the covers around herself.

He turned off the television and sat down beside her. When her tears began pouring full force he put his arm around her shoulders and hugged her to his side. "You mean a lot to me Little Bird. And no matter what you've been through, you mean a lot to the Lord too. Trust Him. He's got a good plan even for the worst of us."

She wouldn't speak or look at him so eventually he fetched a pillow from the daybed and placed it on the sofa.

"I'm headed to bed. It'll be nice and warm in here if you'd like to sleep on the sofa. Here's the remote if you wanta watch the game." He smiled at her and wished she'd smile back. Though she didn't at least her tears had stopped.

"I'll be leaving for work in the morning about 7:30 if you want me to take you somewhere. Or you can sleep in and hang out here. I get off around five and then I've got to go get some groceries. There's nothing left in this house to eat except soup and I can't handle another bite of that."

She actually laughed. "So what're you gettin' at the grocery store? I could cook us some supper."

He thought a minute. "I have no idea. Tell me whatcha want and I'll pick it up."

She brightened and asked, "Do you like chicken and dumplins?"

Shawn nodded happily. "I love me some chicken and dumplins! You know how to make 'em?"

She looked away from him still not sure about her current situation. "Oh yeah. It's easy. Get a whole fresh chicken. It takes a bit to stew but it'll be good. And I'll need flour but she probably has that; and a couple eggs."

Shawn was so excited at the prospect that he started to hug her. Instead he said, "Thanks. If you think of anything else just text me."

She watched as he walked away. Her heart grew fearful as he turned around and came back into the room. He added a couple logs on the fire then smiled at her. "Sleep well Little Bird."

Chapter 45

Jesse retrieved his gift and waited in the recliner. He leaned forward with elbows on his knees and prayed diligently for his young friend and the girl. Lydia eventually met him there and they reclined again to their happy place. Jesse gave his fears for Shawn and Tessa to the Lord and asked Him to help him as well when he gave his gift to Lydia. Suddenly it didn't seem like a very wise idea and he wondered what had come over him when he bought it.

Together they rested a bit then he finally spoke. "Okay... I've got something for you but I don't want you to take it wrong."

She lifted her head from his chest and looked up at him. "UH-oh. Is it a book on how to be a decent woman? Because I could totally use that since I'm going to be your wife."

He laughed at her funny words then realized she'd revealed part of her heart. "No actually it's kind of the opposite." He held something small in his hand but she couldn't see what it was.

"You know I gave you your pajamas in the Victoria Secret bag? Well... I stepped into the store and asked if I could buy a bag and the girl at the register suggested a gift card. So... I got you one hoping you were going to say yes when I proposed."

She smiled at him happily then he added. "But you need to know, the only reason I want you to have things from there is so you feel good about yourself."

She laughed and leaned up so she could look at his face. "UM-hum... that's the only reason huh? Apparently you've put some thought into this."

He couldn't help but laugh. "Well... maybe just a little. I actually learned that in a marriage class." He handed her the card. "And I have to say, I'm glad you're not into long engagements."

She kissed him sweetly and laughed. "Thank you Cowboy. It's a great gift."

~~~~~~~

Sam and Nora and Kurt and Maggie had a very interesting discussion over coffee after the movie. Maggie had decided to transfer. Her grades were excellent so she had no worries about getting in. Plus she'd been unhappy with her roommates' lifestyles and had been praying about what to do. And her love interest at Baylor had dumped her just before Christmas, so when the option came up to move to North Carolina it seemed the perfect choice.

Nervously Kurtis tossed out one more option. "I spoke to Jesse about this, so he and Liddy are aware of the situation. He offered for me and my roommate Shawn to move in with him, and Maggie move in with Liddy. Shawn has just rescued a girl from a bad place and she has nowhere to go. So I'm hoping Maggie, that we can switch places."

Maggie looked at him surprised. "Why didn't you talk to me about this?" Kurtis was immediately worried. She seemed pretty miffed.

"It just came up. Shawn texted me while we were in the movie that he was able to get her to Liddy's house." He waited anxiously as all eyes seemed to be upon him. Finally Sam spoke.

"Actually that would be better all the way around if Lydia is willing to put up with your domineering personality. You've always loved being in the kitchen and she mentioned she needs help with her bakery."

Maggie looked at her father indignantly. "I do NOT have a domineering personality! I just feel like if something needs to be done then DO it for crying out loud. Lydia would still be gazing in the mirror trying to figure out which dress to wear if I hadn't shoved her out the door!"

Kurtis tried to make himself busy with his coffee. Suddenly he was afraid the whole deal might go up in smoke.

Nora saved the day when she mentioned almost as an afterthought. "That's why it will be good to have someone like you around when she goes to plan the wedding."

The thought of coordinating her brother's wedding completely tipped the scales in favor of moving to North Carolina no matter where she lived. Maggie actually smiled.

Sam had to add. "But you'll have to remember that it's not your wedding. Lydia may not want all the insight you have to offer. So try your best to reign in your helpfulness Miz Bossy Britches."

Maggie smacked her daddy's arm and looked to Kurtis for support. The poor guy stammered out, "So how about those Panthers?"

Nora laughed then smiled knowingly. "Or Maggie you could still move in with your brother and Kurtis could stay at Lydia's with the new girl. I feel sure there's plenty of room and she could use a friend."

Maggie didn't like the idea of that at all. Kurtis didn't say a word even though he knew there was no chance Lydia would let him or Shawn stay in the house with Tessa.

Maggie frowned. She did not like being told what to do and was very used to being in charge. "Maybe I'll just stay here." She sighed sadly.

Nora laughed, "You are so full of it! Tomorrow we'll go to Waco and pack up your apartment. Depending on what will fit on your truck you can ask Jesse if he wants you to bring any of your furniture with you or if we need to find a place to store it."

It was finally Kurtis' chance to be the good guy. "I asked Jesse already and he said we could use his truck too to get your stuff. In fact he's got a rec room in his basement if you want to set up a place of your own. Lydia's house is pretty small."

Maggie hugged him and kissed his cheek right there in front of her parents. "Kurtis you're the best! Thank you!"

Chapter 46

Lydia hurt all night and could not get comfortable on the sofa. As quietly as possible she moved to the second recliner on the other end from where Jesse slept. He stirred and asked softly, "Honey, is there anything I can do for you?"

"Nah…" she whispered trying not to wake him all the way. "I'm just gonna see if this works better. Go back to sleep." She settled into the large chair then reclined it halfway back.

A few minutes later he asked, "What's the top five things you love about your house?"

She laughed softly. "Go to sleep you crazy man."

He answered just above a whisper. "Right after you tell me your favorite things about living where you live."

She thought as she situated the covers around her bare feet. "I love my sunroom but I can't sleep out there anymore. I used to love my outdoor shower. But I don't care as much for it since I'm not coming home filthy every day and there seems to be people in and out all the time. I love the view out the back looking down to the pond. I love the swing and the front porch because that's where you and I first got to know each other. So maybe my swing is number one. The new kitchen table you built is so perfect. I really love the farmhouse style of it. I love that crazy work island on wheels that me and the boys put together. It was kind of the first time I knew I was going to make it without Jack. I like my new kitchen and that stove like yours. It makes baking so much better." She thought a minute more then asked, "How many is that?"

He answered glad that she was talking with him. He'd been awake for hours just thinking of the two of them starting their lives together. "That's six. So give me one more and we'll have seven."

She smiled that he remembered her silly story about her favorite number. "Well… I like how clean and white it is, except for that crazy purple sofa."

He asked truly wondering, "What about the kitchen appliances? I know you loved them though Jack picked them out."

She sighed. "I don't want to like them for that reason. But I kinda do. They give just enough color that the kitchen is cheerful. But if I had it to do over again, I'd order all the same color as the refrigerator. I still can't get used to having a blue fridge and a green dishwasher and a yellow microwave." She laughed and asked, "So what about you? What do you like most about your house?"

He was quiet for a moment. His answer surprised her. "The only time I love my house is when it's full of people. Like at Thanksgiving when there's plenty of room at the table, and lots of places to sit. Or when my whole family comes to visit, I like it then. But normally when I come home from work it's just too big and empty."

She heard the loneliness in his voice and understood. Loneliness had made it easy for her to let Jack move in.

He asked another question as he still dreamed of their future. "So what do you NOT like about your house besides the purple sofa?" He laughed quietly.

She sighed as she wondered how much to say. A bit later she was able to speak the truth.

"I don't like the memories there. Before I let Jack move in, I could think of Blue and the happy times we had. But then the bedroom became Jack's room so now I just lay in there by myself and wonder if someone's in the closet. The sunroom daybed freaks me out knowing that man was watching me from the woods. The kitchen reminds me of Jack and the floor still has a dark place where the bloodstain won't come out. So in an effort to speak honestly with you, sometimes I just want to burn the whole place down and start from scratch. So maybe we should live at your house and try our best to fill all those rooms up." Even as she said it her heart hurt knowing she was not likely to have children.

In the darkness she heard Jesse get up and move toward her. He brought his pillow and nestled it on her lap as he settled into the sofa with his covers. She loved having him near and stroked his hair from his face. He whispered softly, "We'll make our own memories wherever we live. I love you girl." He took her hand and kissed it as he was finally able to go to sleep.

"I love you too sweet Jesse-man. It's gonna be good just to be together." Finally she too was able to relax and drift off.

Chapter 47

It aggravated Shawn when he got up early and Tessa was in the bathroom again with the door shut. He gathered his clothes and went to the outdoor shower. The winter wind hit him full force and he shivered in the cold. Steaming hot water warmed him through and through as he checked his wounds in the dim morning light. His eye looked bad but his side hurt the worst. Apparently he'd landed some good punches as his knuckles were bruised and painful. He hoped he could hold a wrench on the job as his boss was a stickler for good character. Maybe he wouldn't notice the clear evidence that Shawn had been in a fight.

He dried off and dressed while the steam had the small space at least a little warm. Fumbling in the dampness he dropped his shirt onto the wet floor.

"Crap," he murmured still annoyed that he couldn't get ready inside. Dressed only in his pants he entered the back door drying his hair with the towel. He stopped by the laundry closet and spread his wet shirt over the washer. Digging through the dryer he found another shirt and gingerly pulled it over his sore body. As he turned toward the kitchen, there stood Tessa looking at him.

"Your side looks awful! Did Gerald do that to you?"

Shawn finished pulling the shirt down. "Yep. But I bet he's not moving too swift today either."

She sighed and went back to the stove. "I'm cookin' you some grits before you head out."

He stopped. "Thanks. How about you? Are you hurtin' today?"

She stirred the grits then banged the spoon on the side of the pot. "Nothin' I can't handle." She wouldn't look at him.

He stood there wondering. "Tessa, do I need to get you to a doctor?"

The look she gave him shot a barb through his soul. "Stay out of my business Shawn." She turned back to the grits so he headed to the bathroom. He prayed for her there and wished he could help.

A flush later he remembered. He had intended to get the exhaust fan installed before Liddy got home. Maybe he still could. He reached over the tub and opened the window. At least before the day was over there would be something in the house to eat besides bean soup.

Chapter 48

Maggie chatted excitedly as she cooked rice, bacon and eggs for breakfast. Kurtis smiled at her happy mood and bouncing curls as he sipped coffee at the kitchen bar. In a day they would be making a road trip back to North Carolina. He looked forward to the two of them in her little truck and wouldn't mind if she talked all the way. Something about her enthusiasm for adventure made him hopeful.

Sam and Nora returned from their walk and Sam exclaimed, "It's getting cold out there, especially with the wind picking up. I'm glad we had such warm weather while the family was here!" Nora checked her phone. "They're calling for a big ice storm out your way Lydia, probably around New Year's Day. So it's good that y'all planned to leave tomorrow. Hopefully you'll be home before it hits."

Lydia looked up from the recliner where she sat reading her Bible. Jesse instinctively tossed her his phone. She called Shawn and could tell he was flustered.

"Hey Shawn honey. I won't keep you but a minute. Before you leave, go in my room and get some cash from my dresser drawer. You know where I keep it. Yep… take enough to stock up on groceries. I feel sure you're out of food by now. I'll text you a list. There's supposed to be an ice storm moving in about the time we get home and I don't want to be stuck in a house full of hungry kids with no food."

Shawn was in no mood to visit so she asked, "Are you okay?"

"Has Jesse told you about yesterday?"

She replied that he had not.

"He'll fill you in. I gotta go right now Liddy. Thanks for the grocery money. Pray for me. I miss you." His tone had softened and he sounded odd.

Lydia was taken aback at his words. Shawn seldom expressed his care for her. "I miss you too Shawn. We'll be home soon." She hung up and looked at Jesse. "Did something happen with him and Tessa?"

Jesse nodded. "I'll tell you about it in a little while. I'm surprised he hasn't left for work yet. It's almost eight o'clock there."

Lydia looked at his phone for the time. "Hmmm... I wonder why he was still at the house. That's not like him at all." She glanced up at Jesse glad that Sam and Nora were no longer in the room and that Maggie was not paying attention. Kurtis however looked at them very concerned.

~~~~~~~

Shawn nearly flew down the back road toward the garage where he worked. His boss had generously scheduled him for extra hours over Christmas break and now he was running late. But he couldn't leave Tessa there alone throwing her guts up. When finally she'd emerged from the bathroom she was surprised he was still there and had reprimanded him again.

He couldn't win.

Still, he felt so sorry for her.

"Little Bird" was the name he'd assigned her the first day they'd met at Jesse's and it was so appropriate. Such a tiny thing she'd captured his attention with those beautiful green eyes. Her light brown skin and pretty wavy hair made his heart skip. She loved fishing and being outdoors with him. But ever since her sister's family had moved into their own place Tessa had become withdrawn. At first he thought she was trying to get rid of him. But then she'd call and they'd talk half the night. They laughed over the craziest stuff and he would dread hanging up. He tried to figure out why he was so drawn to her then one day it dawned on him. She reminded him of Lydia back when Blue was alive. So feisty and tough she was always ready for a fight. How many times had Liddy pointed a finger at him and told him exactly how he would behave, then turn around and do something kind; like bake cupcakes for him to take to school for no apparent reason.

Tessa was the same. He recalled the warm buttered yeast roll she'd brought him the night before without a smile. What in the world was going on with the girl?

His boss met him as he parked his truck. The giant man looked at his watch and glared Shawn's way. As Shawn walked toward him he could tell his boss noticed his swollen eye. For some reason his demeanor changed and he asked, "What happened to you boy? I've never known you to be late before."

He looked Shawn over waiting for an answer.

"Sorry Mr. Hedrick. I'll be glad to work through lunch if you need me too."

Tim Hedrick sighed. Shawn's character had been evident in the few months he'd worked for him. He knew he came from a rough background but the kid had never been disrespectful. In fact Hedrick had often given him assignments that required him to lock up behind himself knowing he could be trusted. So when he noticed his bruised knuckles and other wounds he wondered.

"Did your ol' man do that to you? I know he's usually around for Christmas."

Shawn quickly spoke in defense of his father. "No sir. I picked this fight myself. There was a girl that needed help. But I can't talk about it. Can I still work today?" He waited fearing the worst and wondered if he was about to lose his job.

Hedrick smacked him on the shoulder and noticed that he winced. "Sure. In fact, come look at the diagnostics on the Nissan."

Shawn sighed with relief and hoped he could figure out the problem with the Altima. He liked making Mr. Hedrick proud of him.

~~~~~~~

Tessa had found the cash the night before once she was sure Shawn was sleeping soundly. Though she'd placed it back in the drawer she had thought all night about how far she could get with a couple hundred dollars. As she rested on the purple sofa thinking of her options the warm fire comforted her and she realized she had not felt that safe since her grandfather passed. She wondered why Shawn had welcomed her into the home so kindly. He knew a part of her story but not the worst of it.

As the product of two people having an affair, she'd been ignored by her white mother and raised by her black grandparents. Though her father had brought her into his parents' home, he never acknowledged that she was his. It had been hers to discover by process of elimination. His legitimate daughter Windy was the black sister that Lydia had met. Tessa referred to her as 'the good sister.' She and her husband Eddie were trying their best to overcome a history of sickness and unemployment.

On the other side, the legitimate daughter of her white mother was the 'bad sister.' She had found Tessa in high school and revealed what she knew about their mother's affair. Often she'd taken her to parties as the boys were always attracted to Tessa. Then she'd ditch her while she took off with some loser. That's how Tessa had wound up alone at Jesse's house on Thanksgiving.

Shawn's words from the night before haunted her. If anybody ever needed God Almighty it was definitely her. But she had no idea what to do about it. He made it seem so easy but Tessa was pretty sure that God hated her. How could He not?

She was the cast-off girl that nobody wanted. Often she wondered why her mother had not aborted her. Now that she carried a child of her own she understood. As much as she regretted getting pregnant, the baby was not to blame.

Staring at the fire she blamed God again. Right before she met Shawn she'd fallen for a guy her sister hooked her up with. He obviously wanted her. But he hadn't called her back since she'd told him about the baby. Apparently the 'love at first sight' he spoke of was very short lived.

Now she could hardly be near Shawn knowing that soon she'd be discovered and he would hate her. If only he had listened to her the night before she might have convinced him that the baby was his.

Instead he had to be noble and push her away.

She rose and checked the envelope in the drawer. He'd taken it all. Pilfering through the other drawers she found the scrapbook and sat on the bed looking at the pictures. Lydia had been tiny in high school but she looked rather rough. Her boyfriend was cute, and big. The wedding picture of them made her smile. But she barely recognized the woman by the motorcycle and was surprised when she realized it was also Lydia. It was hard to imagine what had taken her down such a dark path. A happy picture fell from the book and Tessa smiled at the joy of the pregnant woman in the pretty white gown. Obviously Lydia was close to giving birth but Tessa had never heard anything about a baby. She wondered what happened. As she finished looking through the drawer she carefully tucked everything back as she had found it.

She ran her hand between the mattress and boxsprings just in case there was more hidden cash and was surprised to find a small handgun. Checking to see if it was loaded she was glad that it was. Maybe that was her way out.

She sat on the bed with the gun in her hand and wondered if it were true what Shawn said. Something about dying and standing in front of God. She shuddered at the thought and knew she wasn't ready.

Even so, the prospect of bearing a child and trying to raise it herself with nowhere to go was just as scary. Maybe God would understand.

The cold steel of the barrel in her mouth made her sad. She removed it and cocked the gun so she could pull the trigger easily. Just as she turned the gun toward herself again the phone in her pocket made her jump.

She answered it as if nothing were amiss.

"Hey Shawn. What do you want?" Her tone was cold and she was mad to be interrupted.

Shawn sighed into the phone. "I just wanted to check on you. Feeling any better?"

She wasn't sure how to answer. "I haven't thrown up since you left. How's your side?"

He was surprised she asked. "It's okay. Like you said, nothing I can't handle. Hey... I know this will sound weird, but I felt like God wanted me to call you. You keep saying you're okay, but I've got sense enough to know that something's wrong. So hang on Little Bird. I'll bring you a chocolate milkshake after work. That always makes Liddy feel better."

She laughed at the funny boy. But somehow it made her feel good that he cared enough to call her. Sure, he'd change his mind once he knew her secret, but it would be a while before she started showing. Maybe she'd just wait and end things later.

"Thanks White Boy. Don't forget to stop by the store for stuff to make dumplins."

Shawn was glad for her laugh even though it seemed hollow. "Yes ma'am. I can't wait for dumplins. There might be a chicken in the big freezer by the washer if you want to start before I get home. I don't know how late I'll be. And there's dry wood on the front porch if you get cold."

For a moment she allowed herself to imagine living with the man. She tried to stall.

"Hey White Boy…"

Shawn noticed a smile in her voice so he answered, "Yes Dear?"

She actually laughed. "Hurry home with that milkshake."

Shawn wasn't sure what to make of her words so he replied his usual.

"Yes ma'am. See you soon."

He hung up and for some reason she was sad he was gone. She sat on the bed looking at the gun wondering what had changed.

Something in her heart told her she wanted to live at least until after she saw him again… and had that milkshake.

Chapter 49

Shawn worked through lunch since he'd shown up late. Mr. Hedrick noticed and told him to knock off early. "Go take care of that girl." He smiled at Shawn then asked, "Did you kick his butt?"

"Sort of. It was more of a mutual butt kicking."

Mr. Hedrick laughed and added, "He'd be a fool to mess with you boy. You're a hoss! But be careful."

"Yes sir." Shawn answered glad to be leaving early. He thought of Tessa and hurried by *Cook-Out's*. Then on to the grocery store he went. It was packed and he looked at the list Lydia had sent him.

"Good grief!" He sighed. He hurried through the store clueless as to most of the stuff he was looking for. Tossing things into the buggy as fast as he could, all he could think about was chicken and dumplings. He hoped she'd found a chicken in the freezer or else it would still be a couple hours til supper. At least he had milkshakes waiting in his truck.

Finally he was on his way home. He turned off the radio and prayed. Thinking of his conversation with Tessa earlier that morning, he realized he'd never felt such an urgency to call someone before. It seemed to be part of the rescue somehow. He'd also never spoken to anyone so directly about the Lord. He wondered if he might be in love. She sure wasn't making it easy. He sucked down his banana milkshake and hoped the chocolate one he bought for her would make her feel better.

Remembering Jesse's words he decided to try to give her as much space as he could. He also decided to tell her when he needed to be in the bathroom in the morning. He sure couldn't risk being late again.

Pulling up to the back door he brought her milkshake in one hand and a couple bags of groceries in the other. Liddy would just have to deal with the fact that he'd not used her recycled cloth bags but had indeed brought groceries home in the plastic bags from hell. He shook his head at her craziness and realized again how much he missed her.

Tessa opened the door for him and even smiled. "Hey White Boy. You must've gotten off early. Is that for me?" She took the shake from his hand. "Thanks!"

He looked at her surprised. "You're welcome. It smells good in here. You must've found a chicken."

She sipped her treat then answered. "I did. I'll drop the dumplins after we get the groceries put up. You hungry?"

"Starvin' Darlin'!" He realized he used Lydia's words and smiled as he returned to the truck for more groceries. Tessa started putting things away and was happy that Shawn did as well.

"She keeps her canned goods over here." He opened a cabinet. "And the bakery type stuff goes in this pantry." He stepped around Tessa and pulled out an empty sugar canister. "I picked up some frozen yeast rolls. They're not as good as homemade but they're the next best thing. I know you liked those last night."

She looked at him wondering. "Why you wanta be so nice to me all the time?" Her tone was softer than he'd heard in a while and it gave him hope.

He smiled and teased. "I have no idea. You're kind of a pain in the butt."

She put her hand on her hip and tried to act angry but laughed instead. "You got that right!"

He thought about kissing her. She was so cute standing there with his big gray jacket hanging down past her hips and the sleeves rolled up to her elbows. Her green eyes smiled back at him with a sparkle.

Instead he gathered up the plastic grocery bags into a ball and took them to the laundry room. A cloth bag held the other banned bags so he crammed them together.

"Wow. Did you do my laundry today?" Shawn looked in the dryer and found it empty. On top were stacks of clean folded shirts and jeans. "Thanks!"

She finally took her eyes off him and began dropping the thin pastry into boiling chicken broth. Inside she wondered why her heart beat fast at the sight of him. Behind her he stood watching and then dared to step closer.

"So how do you know when to drop the next noodle?" He peered over the top of the large pot.

She added a long one. "Watch. When it comes back up, that's when you drop the next one. That way they don't stick together and the broth doesn't cool off too quick. See how it's still bubbling?"

He looked at her as she worked. "I see that. Is the chicken already in there?" He loved hearing her talk when she wasn't angry.

"Yeah but we don't need all of it. I put part in the refrigerator and I'll make us something else tomorrow. Do you like chicken pie?"

Shawn patted his tummy. "I LOVE me some chicken pie."

She laughed. "You just love food in general don't you?"

He nodded. "Yep."

She continued to drop the noodles in one by one. "You've probably never had chicken pie like mine. I use boiled eggs and then make biscuits for on top. Did you buy cooking oil?"

He nodded. "I did. Liddy sent me a list. I have no idea if I bought the right stuff. The place was packed. They're calling for an ice storm this week end."

She dropped the last in and watched til they came to the top and rolled back down. "The biscuits will be done in about three minutes." She opened the oven to check. "Go wash up and we'll be ready to eat."

He headed outside and washed in the sink he was used to using when he worked at the garage. Tessa put bowls on the table at the chairs next to each other on the front side of the table. As Shawn came back in she pulled biscuits from the oven. She dipped fat noodles into the bowls with shredded chicken and broth. A basket of steaming hot biscuits waited by the butter and jelly Shawn had retrieved from the refrigerator.

"Man! I haven't eat this good since I can't remember." He pulled her chair out then sat down beside her. Reaching for her hand she looked at him a little startled.

He laughed. "I'm sorry. We always hold hands when we ask the blessing. That way you don't get a belly ache. That's probably why you got sick this morning."

Tessa laughed and let him hold her hand. He bowed but she looked at him while he prayed.

"Lord, thank you for this food and the tiny little bird that prepared it. Watch over her for me. She's such a pretty little thing."

He could feel her looking at him so he spoke a loud AMEN right in her face. She jumped but laughed really big.

It made him incredibly happy.

And so did the dumplings.

And the biscuits with butter and homemade Muscadine jelly.

Chapter 50

It was obvious that Lydia needed to opt out of Maggie's moving adventure in anticipation of their trip home. Though the pain from the night before was less, she still had a hard time moving.

"But you can go Jesse. I'll be fine here by myself." She offered honestly. "I plan to park in front of HGTV all day."

Jesse shook his head. "Nope. My first concern is you Darlin'. You might as well get used to having me under foot."

He tossed his keys to his mom. Nora was happy to drive Jesse's truck to Waco and Sam was happy riding shotgun. Kurtis was not as relaxed with Maggie driving her little Frontier. She talked happily as she navigated the busy highway. Several times he caught himself holding the overhead handle near the passenger door. He hoped she wouldn't notice his death grip or the look of sheer terror on his face. Even Lydia didn't drive that bad.

Four and a half terrifying hours later he nearly kissed the ground at her apartment. The four of them loaded the two trucks with her eclectic mishmash of furniture and other household items. She hugged her roommates good-bye as they eyed Kurtis and took a few parting shots.

One of her friends whispered with the hug. "I'll make sure Terrance gets a copy of this." She showed her the picture of Kurtis smiling at Maggie as his blonde wavy hair framed his tanned face. Maggie smiled. "That's the plan!"

After a quick bite of lunch they were on their way back to Corpus. Kurtis had covertly suggested that he switch places with Sam to give Maggie some time with her dad before she moved. Sam was sufficiently impressed with Kurtis' thoughtfulness. As Kurt climbed into Jesse's Tundra Nora smiled at him knowingly.

He looked at her and asked. "Too obvious?" She shook her head. "Only to me. I've ridden with the girl so I completely understand." She and Kurtis shared a laugh but it ended when Nora added, "It's a long way to North Carolina son. Bless your heart."

Chapter 51

"So where do you want to get married?" Lydia decided she might as well ask Jesse since she really didn't care.

He looked up from the book he was reading on the sofa beside her. "I was thinking North Carolina." He wondered if she had something else in mind.

She smiled and added. "I mean where in North Carolina?"

He thought for a bit. "If the weather wasn't so unpredictable in February we could have an outdoor wedding. I know how much you'd love that. But I hate for you to have to walk down the aisle in your Army jacket and brogans."

She sighed, "Aw man, that's what I had picked out already."

He was still thinking. "We could get married at my place. You could get ready upstairs and walk down the steps with your attendants coming first. Then we could say the vows in front of the fireplace."

She tipped her head and wondered. "I'm having attendants?"

He thought for a minute. "Not if you don't want to. But I know Maggie would love to be a part if you don't kill her before the wedding. Really whatever you want is fine with me."

She tried to visualize how that would be. "Are your stairs wide enough for two people side-by-side? I already asked daddy to walk me down the aisle. Or I guess he could walk me from the bottom of the steps to the fireplace."

Jesse thought. "I believe they're wide enough." He smiled as he imagined. "I know how my heart felt last night when you came down these steps. It's something I'll never forget." The love in his eyes nearly melted her soul.

"Then that's what we'll do." She answered and was glad the decision was made.

~~~~~~~

By the time the four weary road warriors returned to Corpus they were thoroughly tired but Jesse and Lydia were thoroughly rested. So the two of them had supper ready then rearranged and repacked the trucks for an early start on Tuesday. Maggie could hardly sleep she was so excited but Kurtis lay awake praying most of the night. He was more than a little worried. The girl was as cute as she could be but he was not used to all the chatter. He wondered if he'd rushed things. He wished he had a way to talk to Lydia alone but the opportunity had not presented itself.

Jesse and Lydia rested well after working to get the trucks road ready. When they kissed good night each mentioned how much they'd miss their nights together.

Sam and Nora slept especially well just looking forward to getting all the sheets and towels washed and their home back in order. Sam commented as he turned out their lamp. "Sometimes tail lights are a beautiful thing."

Chapter 52

Tessa was up very early again throwing up. Though Shawn had informed her that he had to be ready and out of the house by seven thirty he found the door closed and heard her retching in the only bathroom. Again he headed outside in the cold to shower. As he prayed for her it dawned on him.

He nearly cried as he talked to the Lord. A gentle voice spoke to his soul and seemed to whisper, *"Take your time. She needs you."*

A short while later he was dried, dressed and in the kitchen starting the grits. She met him there bleary eyed and shivering. "Let me finish that." She took the spoon from his hand and stirred as the pot came to a boil. Lowering the heat she returned the lid and asked, "Did you add salt?"

Shawn nodded and took her hand. Walking her to the table he sat facing her still holding her hand. "Talk to me Little Bird."

She glanced at the clock on the microwave and rose to leave. "You ain't got time to talk. I've already run you late again. Get your ass movin' White Boy!" She swiped at a tear and thought of the gun that waited for him to leave.

He stood and gently pulled her back to the chair. "I'm not leaving til you talk to me. I don't care if I lose my job. But I do care about you. Now talk."

The tears poured. All her life she'd been able to keep a stone cold façade. Now suddenly she couldn't stop crying. But she refused to talk.

Shawn pulled her onto his lap and wrapped his big arms around her. She was too weak to resist his embrace and found she really didn't want to. Her sobs nearly broke his heart. He had no idea what to say. So he just waited til her tears turned to deep sorrowful breathing. Finally she rested her head on his chest. He felt her tiny little body relax so he patted her shoulder.

She lifted her head. "My grandfather used to hold me on his lap and pat me just like that." She laughed a hollow laugh trying to hide the pain.

Shawn looked at her with tear filled eyes. "I'll help you through this if you'll let me."

She sprang from his lap and stirred the grits. "There's nothing you can do Shawn. Nothing. I have messed up everything and there's no way out."

He wondered what to say so he tossed up a quick prayer and asked, "So will it be white or black?"

She turned in a huff and nearly spat the words. "What does it matter?"

She took the pot from the burner and dipped some onto a plate for him. "I can't stand to look at eggs this morning. But the grits are ready. If you hurry you can still get to work on time."

Shawn stepped close and pulled her into his arms. "Tessa, is the baby going to be white enough to pass for mine?"

She looked up at him with complete surprise. With a trembling hand she patted his chest and leaned onto him hard. Her legs were weak so he helped her back to the chair. Resting her head on the table in her folded arms she heard Shawn make a call.

"Mr. Hedrick? I'm sorry I won't be in today. I've got a family emergency. Yes sir. I understand. Yes sir. It can't be helped. This is something I need to take care of. I know… well… whatever you think is best."

Apparently Mr. Hedrick was through talking because the call ended.

Shawn slid his chair as close as he could to her and rubbed her back. "How far along are you?"

She tried to lift her head but the room was spinning. "Are there crackers somewhere?"

Shawn fetched them plus a glass of milk. "I think you're supposed to drink like a gallon of milk a day."

She heaved and he jumped out of the way though nothing came.

"Or not!" He brought the mop bucket from outside just as she tried to move back to the bathroom. When the cool air came through the backdoor she stopped and let it hit her. "Oh… that helps."

Shawn took her arm and led her to the deck. "How's that?"

She sighed. "How did you know? I haven't told anyone."

Shawn wondered why he'd been so sure. "God put you on my heart Little Bird. I've been prayin' for you night and day since the first time we met. I knew something happened when Windy and Eddie moved out. I was afraid it was your Uncle Gerald. Was I right?"

She shook her head no. "He's bad to get drunk and I'm used to staying out of his way. No, I met this guy before Thanksgiving, so I'm not that far along. But I found out for sure the same day my sister left." She finally looked at him glad her secret was out.

Shawn asked. "Does the father know?"

She nodded. "He does but he won't return my calls. But I haven't told anyone else, not even Windy." She shivered so Shawn took her arm again and moved her toward the door. "Let's sit in the sunroom. It's cooler than the kitchen."

He sat with her on the wicker love seat. "So could I pass for the father?"

She still wondered at his words. "Shawn you don't owe me nothin'. This is my problem. I ain't lookin' to get married. So don't feel sorry for me. I ain't used to it."

Shawn put his arm about her shoulders. "But what if I want to take care of you? What if I find us a place to live and made sure you're safe?" He tipped her chin up so he could look in her eyes. "What if I love you?"

She laughed. "You can't love me. I'm not a good person. And I know you can't take care of me cause you just lost your job!"

Shawn wasn't giving up. "If you're only a few weeks along and if the father is white, nobody would have to know it wasn't mine. The baby could grow up with a real daddy in her life."

Tearfully she looked up. "Shawn you don't know what you're doin'. Why you wanta be so good? And what makes you think it's a girl?"

"I just have a feeling." He hugged her to his side and remembered Jesse's words about giving her space. "How about this? Pray all day. I'm gonna see if I can still get to work if you'll be okay here by yourself. While I'm gone, ask God for wisdom. It's the prayer that saved Liddy from the wrong man. If God wants the baby's father to be the daddy then He'll show you and I'll never bother you again."

He added as he rose to leave. "Be careful today and don't do too much." He kissed her head and left to fetch his work boots. A few minutes later he was out the door. She watched as he hurried to his truck so he called behind him, "Need another milkshake?"

She gagged and he hollered back. "I'll take that as a no."

Chapter 53

Mr. Hedrick was glad to see Shawn pull in to work but didn't want to let him know. "You're late again boy! This better be the last time!"

Shawn was so glad he didn't send him packing that he replied humbly. "Yes sir. Let's finish up these last few repairs before New Year's Day!" He smiled at his boss and noticed that he nearly smiled back.

A co-worker came around the rack as he looked at his cell phone and nearly bowled Shawn over. The wound on his side throbbed and Shawn cringed with pain.

"Sorry man." The guy walked away absent-mindedly.

Shawn shook his head and tried to catch his breath as he began his work. Liddy and Jesse should be on the road for home. "Kurtis and Maggie too," he thought happily. He wondered what they'd think of him if he took Tessa under his wing permanently. No matter what, he'd protect her as long as she'd let him.

He prayed for her again and asked God for wisdom for both of them. With each turn of the wrench he felt the urging of the Lord to pray for her safety. "The baby girl too Lord. Keep her safe."

~~~~~~~

The two couples were on the road very early Tuesday morning. Jesse led the caravan in his Tundra which was packed to the gills. He'd surrounded Lydia with pillows trying to help her manage the pain. Maggie was at the wheel with Kurtis again riding shotgun. With coffee in hand he tried his best to lean back and not look as she tailgated her brother's truck or any other vehicle that dared separate them. A smile crossed his lips as he realized he'd definitely be prayed up by the time they reached home.

"So what's Lydia's house like?" Maggie asked as she changed lanes without checking her rearview mirror.

Kurtis thought for a moment but before he could reply Maggie asked more. "Is it big like Jesse's? I know they're neighbors. Every house on mama and daddy's street was built at the same time so they're all pretty much the same. Except my parents added the second story then some of the neighbors did the same after they saw how nice it turned out. I can't imagine how we'd get through the holidays without the extra bathrooms. And the outdoor shower really helped this year with all those nasty little boys running back and forth to the beach. Lydia has an extra bathroom outside doesn't she?"

Kurtis wondered which question to answer first. But it didn't matter. She'd moved on to another topic; something about setting up her furniture in Jesse's basement. "There's a bathroom down there so really, if he wasn't so proper I could live there. That girl that Shawn is dating... is she pretty?"

Maggie wondered if Kurt liked her and how close they were.

Kurtis shook his head. "She's very pretty." He wondered why Maggie went silent. He glanced at her and added, "But not as pretty as you." He smiled and was glad she smiled back. "You two are like opposites."

Maggie was suddenly interested. "How's that?" She sped up when she noticed Jesse was topping the next bridge without her.

Kurtis thought about the two girls and for the first time worried about Lydia in the new arrangement.

"She's tiny. And she has the prettiest green eyes I've ever seen; very light like looking through a glass bottle. And her skin is sort of eternally tanned and smooth. I think she had a white mother and a black father so that always makes for a pretty baby. Her hair is curly but not like yours. It's wavy like mine but longer." Kurtis gazed out the side window trying not to look at how she drove. Maggie was still quiet so he tried to make small talk.

"She has a way about her that's interesting. You just want to draw her out because she says so little, kind of like Liddy. She's feisty but seems to always have something funny to say. I like her."

Maggie had an odd look on her face. "Obviously..."

Kurt was surprised and tried to clean up whatever mess he'd made. "I mean I like her better than anyone else Shawn has dated. They're good together."

Maggie still wasn't looking at him and she sped up again to catch up with her brother. It felt like anger so Kurtis looked at her trying to think of something else to talk about.

"Have you signed up for the music auditions in February? As good as your voice is I think you could win a nice scholarship."

She glanced at him knowing he was trying to flatter her. "I have. And I've sent in my application and the first fees. Orientation for transfer students is in two weeks and then classes start in three."

Kurtis noticed the chattering had stopped and he was glad. But then she added, "So Tessa's the opposite of me. Quiet, pretty, and best of all tiny. So what does that make me Kurtis?" She whipped around a vehicle that slowed in front of her and nearly caused a wreck.

He grabbed the handle at the top of his door frame and hung on for dear life wondering what to say.

"Please don't wreck us Maggie. You're scaring the crap out of me."

She glared at him and sped up. "You didn't answer me Kurtis. Since I am the opposite of quiet, pretty and tiny I'd love to know why you invited me to North Carolina. And apparently I'm a terrible driver as well. You might have mentioned these things instead of encouraging me to drop everything so we could be together!"

He wondered when he'd committed his life to her well-being and was beginning to feel boxed in. But he really hadn't meant to hurt her feelings. He reached over to take her hand but she pushed him away.

"Maggie you're pretty too... just different. Different is good! It's why I came all the way to Texas to see you."

She glanced at him hoping he'd tell her how much he liked her eyes and how she wasn't as fat as she felt when she looked in the mirror. Instead he was still quiet. She sighed and wanted to push him from the truck.

Kurtis tried. "Tessa doesn't know the Lord but Shawn is working on it. She gets hateful and kind of mean when she's angry. She's been through a lot and she doesn't know that she's worth anything yet. Me and Shawn have both been through that so we get it.

But you're so beautiful with how excited you are about everything you do. You jump in with both feet just sure it will all work out. I like that about you. It makes me feel like we could do anything together."

She was warming up and Kurtis could tell he was making headway.

"And I love how your curls bounce like a little girl when you talk. And your eyes kind of sparkle when you smile. But when you're mad they flash like gunshot and it's pretty scary."

She actually laughed but caught herself. She wasn't quite ready to let him off the hook. "But I'm still the opposite of tiny." She sighed and he realized that was the real issue.

Kurtis smiled and reached for her hand again. "Who said tiny is a good thing? I'd rather have curvy like Marilyn Monroe any day."

She smiled and even teared up slightly. "Awww... okay... you totally just made up for everything. So you don't think I'm fat?"

He laughed. "No! You're like the OPPOSITE of fat!"

She laughed big at that. "And my driving isn't really that bad?"

Kurt sighed. "Actually your driving still scares the crap out of me. Pull over at the next Rest Area and let me drive for a while. It's time I wore the pants in this family!"

Maggie threw her head back and laughed. "Well at least you're not a liar. Daddy said last night I needed to be more careful and not run you off before we even get there."

Kurtis nodded but didn't say that her daddy had read his mind.

~~~~~~~

Lydia and Jesse rode silently just enjoying the music and the scenery for most of the morning. At some point Jesse asked her what she was thinking about the new living arrangements. Remembering her struggle with honesty she made a special effort to speak the truth.

"I'm sorry to tell you this but I'm kind of worried about it. I like living with my boys and this will be my last chance to do that."

He was surprised. "I thought you were happy to be done with all their messes. You said…"

She interrupted. "I know what I said. I was trying to be supportive of Shawn helping Tessa. But honestly, I wish the boys were staying at my house til you and I get married. Don't get me wrong. I sure don't want them around after! We're going to need our privacy." She felt her face flush and wondered if she'd ever grow up.

Jesse noticed and laughed. "I agree. And I'm glad you feel that way. Especially once you start wearing your Victoria Secret wardrobe all the time."

Her mouth dropped open and she smacked his arm. "Anyway…" Lydia laughed and tried to remember what she was saying. "I'm gonna miss my boys. I can't believe how much I've missed Shawn. And I know things are changing between him and Tessa. But honestly I worry about having her in my house. I may end up having a 'Come to Jesus' meeting with her and it could cost me a son."

She was trying to decide whether to say anything about her fears regarding Maggie when Jesse spoke up. "I have similar fears about Maggie moving in with you as well."

Lydia looked at him surprised. "Really? Oh thank you Jesse! I love your sister but I don't know if I can take all the… helpfulness."

Jesse laughed. "Or the yammering."

Lydia laughed heartily at his word. It was spot on but not a word she would expect him to use regarding his beloved little sister.

"So what can we do about this? Speak to me ol' wise one." Suddenly she heard her words and put her hand over her mouth. "I'm so sorry Jesse. I never think of you as old. And I know that's a sore spot with you. That's just a phrase I use."

He laughed. "I'm over it. In fact, I think it was one of those tools Satan used to try to keep me from proposing. But you don't sit around feeling old because you hurt. So why should I?"

She nodded and reached for his hand. "That's right. 'Hold my hand, grow old with me. The best is yet to be.'"

He smiled. "I love that. Where'd you hear it?"

She shook her head. "I have no idea. But the thought of it makes me so happy." She picked up his hand and kissed it then asked again.

"So what can we do about the kids my beloved?"

Jesse thought for a moment. "I know Maggie was hoping to set up her furniture in my basement. There's a bathroom down there so really she could have her own apartment away from Kurtis and Shawn if they're upstairs."

Lydia shook her head. "Let's figure out how to keep the boys with me. Is there a way to have Tessa at your house?" She felt guilty for suggesting it. "I'm sorry Jesse. She's not your responsibility."

"Actually since my room is on the main level, she could take one of the bedrooms upstairs and have her own bathroom. I just didn't want her staying at the house with only me there. But since Maggie's coming," He thought for a bit more. "That will work. I can even set up one of the empty bedrooms as a den for her. We'll steal the boys' purple sofa from your house and find you another one."

He was still thinking when Lydia held up a hand to high five him. "Thank you so much sweet Jesse-man!" She smiled happily and thought,

Thank You Lord for helping me to be honest. This is a great reward!

Chapter 54

Shawn took a minute during lunch to call Tessa. "Hey Little Bird. How're you feeling?"

She actually answered with a civil tone. "I'm not as weak now, but I still can't keep anything on my stomach. Is that offer for a milkshake still good?"

Shawn was happy for the request. "For the duration! I'll bring you one everyday til Baby Bird comes."

She laughed but hushed him. "Can anybody hear you? No telling who all you've told already! You'd think you're the daddy!"

He was quiet then added tenderly. "Only if you want me. I'll never force you into anything. But I have to tell you, the thought of it makes me really happy."

She waited and wondered what to say as she tried not to tear up. "We'll talk tonight. You still up for chicken pie?"

Shawn noticed that she didn't shoot him down when he suggested again his role in raising the baby. "Yes ma'am. That sounds really good. It's cold out here in the garage. Thanks for sending the dumplins with me for lunch. Now that's real comfort food!"

Tessa smiled. "Don't you mean soul food? Get used to it baby. It's all I know how to do."

Shawn's heart nearly burst with happiness. She'd called him baby and even hinted that they'd be together in the future.

His voice broke as he ended their call. "Gotta go Little Bird. See you soon."

"Don't forget my milkshake White Boy. But make it vanilla. I'm kinda partial to white."

Shawn could barely utter a response. "Good to know Baby."

Chapter 55

By lunchtime nerves were once again testy in the second vehicle. As they pulled into the Rest Area Kurtis stepped from the driver's side of the Frontier and stretched while Maggie hurried to the bathroom without waiting on him to walk her up.

She thought to herself that the boy was likely the slowest person God had ever put on earth, except for Jesse. Though Kurtis kept up with Jesse, his relaxed driving style nearly infuriated Maggie as he nonchalantly allowed motorists to pass them. If he would ride closer to Jesse's Tundra Jesse would eventually get the message and move on down the highway. Instead Kurtis tended to lag back a few car lengths as if they had nowhere to be. And she had to pee!

As she walked quickly toward the restrooms she decided to tell Jesse that they needed to switch passengers. She'd rather have Lydia to talk to than Kurtis. He'd just have to be happy riding with Jesse for a change. She began to wonder what she'd ever seen in the boy.

Glancing back she noticed Jesse and Kurtis on either side of Lydia helping her walk up the slight incline. The stiff breeze caught Kurtis' Atlanta Braves ball cap and jerked it off. He caught it in midair and smiled that smile she found so handsome. His wavy blonde hair blew around his face and she watched as he smoothed it back and put his cap on. A couple college girls walked past Maggie from the drink machines and commented as they passed Kurtis.

"Go Braves!"

He smiled back at them then noticed Maggie watching from the entrance. She turned on her heel and went inside. Jesse laughed and Kurtis sighed.

"Jesse, I think we may need to switch how we're riding. Your sister is pretty ticked off at me. I don't think I can drive to suit her."

Jesse replied firmly. "Sorry son. Lydia's with me. You made your bed now lie in it. Figuratively speaking of course. By the way, NOBODY drives to suit Maggie."

Kurtis sighed. When they reached the restrooms he went inside and Lydia held onto Jesse for a moment. "Thanks Jesse. But if it will help I could ride with Kurtis to give his ears a break. That is if Maggie will ride with you."

Jesse laughed at her comment. "It's up to you Darlin'. You'll have her all night so I can take a turn now and you and Kurtis can catch up. I'll see what I can do to get her to ride with me."

"Thanks honey." Lydia hobbled inside praying that she didn't somehow end up riding with Maggie. At least it no longer looked like the girl would be moving in with her.

~~~~~~~

Maggie waited for Jesse in the lobby and nearly tackled him hoping to get a word before Kurtis came out.

"Jesse puh-leeeeseee help me! I'm losing my mind with Kurtis! It's bad enough I'm moving a million miles from home. But now I don't even LIKE the guy. Can I please have Lydia? Make up something so she'll ride with me! Please!"

Jesse tried not to laugh. "I think you need to ride with me a while. That way you can catch a nap. I know you trust my driving and it will give you a chance to relax. And if you can't go to sleep at least we can talk about your new living arrangements. I was thinking about letting you move into my basement."

She squealed with delight then caught herself. The women that made Kurtis smile so big were slightly older than her but definitely more sophisticated. Surely she could start acting more like a grown up.

She looked up as Kurtis helped Lydia toward them. He held her arm like a gentleman and laughed at something she said. Maggie had not heard him laugh in hours. Apparently everyone was more interesting and fun than she was.

When they were within earshot she announced, "I'm riding with Jesse for the next leg of the journey. Kurtis you drive my truck and try to keep up. I won't be there to help you navigate. Lydia, I'll get your pillows. Will you be alright in the smaller vehicle?" She was concerned that her plan may come unraveled with the question and hoped Lydia would be a sport.

"Yep. Good plan. I was getting sick of Jesse anyway. He's such a bear." She winked at him and Kurtis mouthed the words 'THANK YOU!' to Jesse as he headed to the vending machines.

Jesse was really having a difficult time keeping his laughter to himself.

~~~~~~~

When finally the road warriors had traveled a solid eleven hours they reached Mobile, Alabama. Jesse stopped at the same hotel he and Lydia had used going down and secured two adjoining rooms. Maggie woke from her nice long nap and stretched as Kurtis and Lydia watched from the other vehicle. They looked at each other and laughed.

"She'll be rested and ready to sit up late and talk with her roommate tonight." Kurtis teased Lydia. She shot back, "I think her boyfriend should take her to dinner and try to make up with her."

Kurt shook his head. "I don't think I'm qualified for the boyfriend role. I'm not sure what I do to tick women off but somehow I manage."

Lydia laughed. "Bless your heart."

He looked at her. "It's your stinkin' fault. I compare everybody to you and then I end up disappointed."

She was shocked. "Kurtis! What a sweet thing to say. I'm just glad you and Shawn can stay at my house a little longer. I'm gonna miss you guys."

Kurtis nodded. "Yeah me too. But don't worry. We'll be over every night after the wedding to check on you and Jesse." He smiled his mischievous smile as Maggie walked up to the truck. He opened the door and gave her an impromptu hug.

"Feeling better?" he asked.

She stiffened and gave him a look.

He took a step back. "I'll take that as a no." He laughed. "Can I treat you to a pizza tonight? We'll see if we can find something local."

She brightened a tiny bit. "I guess so. It's kind of early."

Kurtis looked at her sideways. "That's why I said 'tonight.' I thought we could go on a real date, like without family members." He pointed at Lydia and made a face. Maggie laughed and said, "Sure. Sounds like fun."

Jesse returned with the room keys. As Kurtis and Lydia moved their vehicle near the room she spoke to Kurtis.

"Blue and I used to fight like y'all sometimes. We actually broke up for a while in high school. Don't write her off just yet. Everybody needs room to grow. Blue was older than me too and put up with all kinds of crap. I still can't believe we got married when I was eighteen. It's a wonder he didn't kill me in my sleep."

Kurtis laughed. "Maybe that's why Jesse's making me and Maggie sleep in different rooms."

Chapter 56

Tessa's chicken pie was very different from the one Lydia had learned to make. Shawn loved it. But more than that, he loved how she waited til he took her hand and asked the blessing before she dipped it onto their plates. He peeked while he was praying to see if she had her eyes closed. She did.

Lord... it's been a good day. I got to keep my job. Tessa made a good supper and she's not hurling yet.

He heard her laugh and it gave him courage.

She's got her eyes closed like a good girl and she's lettin' me hold her hand. And Lord... there's a new little bird on the way. And she likes vanilla milkshakes. Help Little Bird and Baby Bird rest well tonight. Thank You so much. In the Name of Jesus we come, Amen.

Tessa had tears but she wouldn't look at him. However she held his hand longer than the prayer. Shawn slid his chair over close and put his arm around her but said nothing. Her head was still down and she swallowed hard. Eventually she said quietly, "Go ahead and eat while it's hot. I think I'll just sip on this shake for now."

Shawn gave her shoulders a soft hug then scooted his chair back to his place. "Mmm... this is really good. I like it better than the kind with peas and carrots."

She watched him eat and smiled happily. "I like cookin' for you. You always appreciate everything so much."

He took a deep breath and nodded. "Yep. Goin' hungry is something you don't forget too quick."

She looked at him wondering so he added. "I never knew my mom and my dad stays on the road for weeks at a time. So growing up I just went to a different friend's house every day after school and hoped to get fed. The weekends were tough though. I was one of those kids at school that got a backpack full of food on Fridays from the church. If I never see another Ramen Noodle I'll be fine. But I sure learned to appreciate a good peanut butter jelly sandwich."

He noticed her hair. "You look really pretty. It must be that baby glow they talk about."

She laughed. "I think that's sweat. I can't figure out if I'm hot or cold." She removed his jacket and placed it on the back of her chair. It was the first time he'd seen her in a strappy undershirt. Obviously she was not wearing a bra.

She noticed him looking but he quickly apologized. "Sorry." He tried to concentrate on his supper but it was hard. "I'm pretty sure you're cold." He laughed then looked up at her and apologized again. "Sorry."

She smiled. "What does it matter Shawn. I'm pregnant so obviously I'm one of those trashy girls who don't care. So why don't you go ahead and take me to bed? It's not like I haven't done it already."

Shawn put his fork down and sat quietly. He drank his tea and looked toward the window wondering what to say. Finally he rose and took his heavy work jacket from the coat hook and left.

The wind was cold. He pulled a hat from his pocket and started his truck. Toward the barn he drove, past the pond and up the hill. The sunset was beautiful so he slowed to a stop and just sat there with the heater blowing full blast.

God help! Why do I love her? Why Lord? What am I supposed to do? Everybody's gonna think the baby's mine anyway. But she's so broken and I don't want to make it worse. Help her love me. Can that please be Your will?

The trees made long shadows across his truck and the darkness began to settle in. He turned his truck around and slowed by the Claudia Garden. He left the gravel road and drove through the meadow grass. Pulling up near Lydia's prayer garden he parked and got out. Long gray stems of dead wild flowers fell across the ground. Brown coneflower seed pods leaned over waiting for tomorrow's hungry birds. Often Shawn had seen Lydia kneel there gaining strength just to put one foot in front of the other.

The soft damp earth was cold beneath his knees and quickly soaked through his work pants. It had been a long time since he'd cried. Kneeling there he made up for lost time as he poured out his soul to the Lord. No words would come so he just waited. Finally he returned to his truck and headed back to the house.

One more day.

Lydia would be home and she'd know what to do. She could also keep a secret. But something inside Shawn wondered if he might lose Tessa forever if he told anyone.

Lord… take away my love for her if You want to. Just show me what to do, especially tonight.

Chapter 57

Lydia thought about calling Shawn as she checked the weather on Jesse's phone. "The sun is setting at home."

She smiled at Maggie when she asked about her outfit and gave her a thumbs-up.

"I like it!" she whispered as she waited for Shawn to answer.

Shawn was just returning to his truck. "Hey Jesse. I was wishing I could talk to you."

Lydia waved good bye to Maggie and Kurtis as they left for their date. "I'm sorry Shawn. It's me still using Jesse's phone. Want me to have him call you?"

At the sound of Lydia's voice Shawn choked up. "No Liddy. I need to talk to you. Are you ever gonna get another phone?" His tone was odd and he seemed out of sorts with her. She could tell something was wrong so she waited a moment before answering.

"Honey, talk to me. What's going on?"

Shawn had a hard time speaking and it took a bit til he could reply. "I'm in a hard place Liddy. Please pray for me."

She waited and felt her own tears rising. "I will honey. Where are you right now?"

A shiver went through his body so he started his truck and turned on the heater. "I'm up at your prayer garden but I'm sittin' in my truck. It's turned cold all of a sudden."

She tried to brighten his mood. "Did you get to see the sunset?"

He relaxed a little remembering all the times they'd watched it together. "Yep. It was GLORIOUS!" He used her word with a flourish and she laughed.

"Glorious huh? That sounds about right. So I reckon God's still splashing His love all over the North Carolina sky. I don't think He much cares for Alabama. He makes them wait an hour on their sunset."

Shawn was quiet and knew she was trying to cheer him up. He breathed another prayer about how much to tell her. Somehow it didn't seem right to break the confidence he and Tessa shared.

Lydia asked quietly, "What's got you worried Shawn? This is not like you at all. Is Tessa okay?"

He sighed and thought about the question. "She needs a lot of prayer. I've been talking to her about the Lord but she hasn't listened yet. Pray for both of us Liddy."

"I will honey. Can I tell Jesse too? He's a really good pray-er."

Shawn laughed. "Yep he is. I'd appreciate it." He hoped it wouldn't come up about him staying at the house with Tessa so he tried to wrap up the call. "Hey Liddy?"

She waited on her man-child. "Yes?"

"I really miss you."

"I really miss you too Shawn… and I love you too. See you soon."

He hung up and wondered why he had such a hard time saying how much he loved her. Even as much as he wanted to tell Tessa, the closest he'd come was when he said 'What if I love you.' He wondered to himself what kind of lame statement that was.

Maybe that's what she needed; to hear that he loved her.

But in his heart of hearts he knew better. What she needed was not so much to hear it, but to see it.

Lord, help me show her how much You love her. God I need strength.

He put his truck in gear and slowly made his way home. He wondered what he'd find. Would she be mad that he'd rejected her? Would she try again like it was nothing? He hung his jacket and crammed his toboggan into the pocket. The table was cleared and the chicken pie was on top of the stove. He touched the side of the pan and found it had cooled. The house was cold too. He dipped some of the pie and put it in the microwave.

In the den he found her on the sofa wrapped in a blanket. He stacked wood into the fireplace with a few strips of kindling. It lit easily and began to warm the room.

She watched as he worked. His black hair had grown out some for winter and curled around the bottom because of wearing a hat. His beard was dark and scruffy from missing his usual shave two mornings in a row. He looked very rugged in his navy blue work uniform and she thought about how muscular he looked when she saw him without a shirt.

He poked at the wood with a cast iron tool that Blue had forged when he was about his age. "Sorry I let the fire go out. It'll be warm again in a minute."

She sat looking at him with those soft green eyes that melted his soul. "Be careful not to get it too hot in here. I'm liable to strip down to nothin' and then what would you do?"

He sat on the recliner and looked at her wondering if she had anything on under the blanket. Her feet stuck out the bottom and he noticed that at least she wore socks. For a brief moment he thought about dousing the fire just to teach her a lesson. Instead he stared at her with a look that made her wonder. He didn't seem angry and he sure wasn't coming over to take her up on her previous offer. It made her mad.

"Shawn! What is wrong with you? I'm a big girl! I've been sleeping around since I was seventeen and no man has ever turned me down. What is your problem?" She tested him.

He shook his head at her words. "Stop it Tessa. You're worth more than that to me." He rose and went to the kitchen retrieving his supper from the microwave. He sat at the table and ate in silence. Eventually she followed him there and made him another glass of tea. She heated water then sat beside him at the table and sipped something from a cup.

Thankfully she'd put his jacket back on. Shawn asked as he peered into her mug. "What IS that? It smells like... Thanksgiving."

She laughed. "It's ginger tea. It's to help with morning sickness. You're supposed to use real ginger root but I found some powdered in her spice rack." She held it up for him to sniff. He took a whiff and remembered the cookies Lydia sent home with him thinking they were his when in fact they'd been evidence that the stalker was in her house. He shivered.

Tessa looked at him. "You cold? Cause I can give you your jacket back if you want." She teased.

Shawn recognized it as her way of trying to make up so he tried to laugh at himself too. "Nooo... keep your shirt on Little Bird. I don't want to get all lusty again."

She laughed nicely at that. "Well at least you're not rejectin' me because you think I'm butt ugly."

He shook his head and spoke tenderly. "No girl. In fact, I think you're the prettiest woman I've ever met."

He turned his attention to his supper. "AND you know how to cook! This is so good." He tried not to look at her. Slowly she moved behind his chair and put her arms around his shoulders. She kissed his neck then moved to his lap.

"I need you Shawn. Please come." She kissed him and he gently returned the favor. He unzipped the jacket so she shed it and took his hand. Leading him to the bedroom she kissed him passionately and pulled him toward the bed.

Shawn looked at Lydia's bed and stopped. Through the kitchen to the back door he went again grabbing his coat on the fly. With keys in hand he headed to the truck then left. His heart pounded at the thought of her and yet he drove away. He couldn't decide whether to be angry or feel sorry for her. For a woman who seemed to feel so worthless, she certainly was secure in one area of her life.

He thought as he drove. Maybe that was it. Maybe that was the only time she felt like she was worth something. If only she could see herself like he saw her.

He realized too how close he'd come to giving in to his own desires. If she'd led him anywhere but that bedroom, he'd still be in her arms. His phone buzzed and startled him from his thoughts. Jesse's face popped up and he sighed.

"Hey Liddy." He shook his head again at the timing.

Jesse's deep voice laughed across the miles. "We've got to get that girl a phone. She's steelin' all my thunder."

Shawn sighed deeply. "Thanks for calling. Man I'll be glad when y'all get home."

Jesse could hear the stress in Shawn's voice. "I had a feeling you needed to talk. What's going on son?"

Shawn sighed again but considered his words carefully. "I'm headed to your house for the night. I hate leaving her alone but I need to. Pray that she'll be alright."

Jesse asked, "What makes you worried about her Shawn?"

Shawn thought for a minute. "I don't know why. It's just a gut feeling I guess. I don't know Jesse but I'm really worried."

"Are you sure you need to leave for the night? Don't go just because I put pressure on you. You're strong enough to do what's right. If you think she might harm herself then go back."

Shawn shook his head at the words. "No I'm not all that strong. Just pray Jesse. I can't stay there." He felt he'd said too much already so he hurried to hang up.

"Gotta go. See y'all tomorrow. Thanks Jesse."

~~~~~~~

He unlocked the door at Jesse's house and turned off the alarm. The big room was cold and dark except for the one lamp that had been purposely left on. The refrigerator was empty and Shawn thought of the chicken pie he'd tried twice to enjoy but had not. Remembering Tessa's tender kisses and warm embrace he longed for her.

He checked the thermostat and realized Jesse had turned the heat off before he left. Recalling the forecast for below freezing temperatures overnight he was glad he'd come. Water pipes could have burst causing tons of damage. He adjusted the settings. The gas furnace popped on and began warming the house.

He thought of his girl again. Was she really his girl? She'd just admitted to sleeping with numerous men and he wondered. Was he just one of many who would be loved and left? His heart hurt and he thought on Jesse's words. He'd never heard her speak of wanting to end her life. But her future looked very bleak. At least she had a safe place to live. Maybe Liddy would have a way of getting her to trust the Lord.

The fear of Tessa doing harm to herself was suddenly real. He thought of the guns in the house. But she wouldn't know where they were. Mentally Shawn took inventory. The antique rifle over the mantle would fire if she could find the bullets and figure out how to load it. That one was so difficult that he hardly worried about it. There was one in his truck but of course it was with him. Lydia kept Blue's in a safe in her closet. Then he remembered.

She also kept one hidden near her bed. But surely Tessa had not been in Lydia's room snooping around enough to find it. His heart did something odd at the thought. Shawn had only been in there a couple times, but Tessa seemed very familiar with the room only a few minutes earlier. He tried calling her having no idea what he'd say. But for the moment he just needed to hear her voice.

She didn't answer.

He sent her a text but received no reply.

Quickly he locked up and left for home. He tore through the back door and into Lydia's room where Tessa sat on the bed with a loaded pistol. Slowly he stepped toward her then stopped as she raised the gun.

She stared up at him with empty eyes and pulled the hammer back.

"Little Bird… please don't." Shawn spoke softly and took another step closer.

She placed the barrel of the gun under her chin. "I just wanted to say good bye in style Shawn. You're the only man I've ever known who's tried to love me. I'm sorry."

Shawn yelled, "NOOO!!!!" He dove for her just as she pulled the trigger. He landed on top of her and knocked the gun from her hand. It slid across the bed, hit the floor and discharged with a loud bang.

The two of them jumped with the noise then Shawn pulled her into his arms. "Oh dear God… Tessa! Why? Why can't you just let me love you through this?"

Silently he thanked God that the gun had misfired.

She let the tears flow finally and sobbed into his chest. He held her there as she cried and his own tears came again.

Eventually he whispered. "Little Bird… I don't TRY to love you… I can't help but love you."

She cried even harder at that. "Why Shawn? After all I've done…"

"I don't care! Please be my girl. That's all I want in this whole world. I'll quit school if I need to. I'll get us a place and take care of you. Just give me the word."

She relaxed against him and the tears stopped. He kissed her forehead and she asked, "Could you just hold me for a while? I promise to be a good girl."

He pulled her closer and flipped the side of the bedspread over her. She turned over and pushed her back into his chest. His arm draped over her waist and his hand landed on her tiny belly. With a deep sigh she seemed to melt into his strong embrace.

He wondered how long it would be before they could feel the baby kick. She jerked suddenly as if falling as she drifted to sleep. Drawing her closer he whispered, "I've got you. Rest well Lil' Bird."

Chapter 58

Jesse and Lydia found a mom and pop restaurant where they could enjoy a quiet supper together. Jesse realized how difficult it was to inquire about ingredients without ticking off the cook. Eventually Lydia figured out the safest thing to order and found the pot roast to be delicious. Jesse was very pleased with a giant homemade hamburger and fries. They each ordered a slice of pie to go, apple for Jesse and chocolate for Lydia.

As Jesse unlocked the hotel door for her, a couple walked down the hall so she motioned him into the room. He closed the door behind him and pulled her near. Looking down into her sweet face he spoke softly. "We're on the home stretch Darlin'." He kissed her gently.

She looked into his sparkling eyes knowing he referred to their wedding day. "Yep. Only seven weeks."

He pushed her hair back and corrected. "Six weeks and five days. I need to make you one of those paper chains so you don't miss it."

She laughed softly. "Yep. Probably wouldn't hurt. I'll be baking cookies as fast as I can and think... hmmm... seems like I was supposed to do something today."

He kissed her neck and whispered. "Maybe I can help you remember."

Her heart pounded and she mentally calculated how long it would be til the kids got back. She shook the notion from her head and he laughed. "Am I making you shiver?"

She smiled up at him and nodded slowly. "Oh yeah." She kissed him tenderly then added, "I was going to ask if you wanted to watch television with me but I think we'd better set a good example for our children. Good night Cowboy."

He sighed, "You make it awfully hard to leave girl." He turned to go then came back through the door. "Let me check your room first."

He looked in the bathroom behind the shower curtain and then under the beds. "All clear. Sleep well Darlin'."

He winced as he came up off his knee. She asked, "How long does it take to recover from the surgery?"

He sighed. "Only a couple days if everything goes well. I'll check on it next week. It would be nice to feel good for the honeymoon."

She smiled but said nothing. He saw her look and smiled as well. "I think you are looking forward to being Mrs. Jesse Mills."

She nodded as he left. "Yep."

~~~~~~~

Kurtis was happy that the local pizza place had a nice ambience. The small room was dark except for the candles burning on each table and the light from the stone fireplace. Candle wax dribbled down the sides of empty wine bottles and plaster walls added a nice touch. He was also glad they were able to agree on how to order their pizza. To him it was the beginning of what he hoped to be a miraculous recovery of their friendship.

"You look very pretty tonight." Kurtis looked at her and smiled.

She gazed back at him and decided he wasn't so bad after all. "Thank you." She actually reached across the table and took his hand. "I like your wavy hair especially without the ball cap."

He squeezed her hand and smiled. "Thanks. I'm letting it grow out but I don't really want to put it into a 'man bun.' So I usually just wear my Braves cap."

She laughed. "Man bun. You're so funny."

He nodded, "Yep kinda like 'does that milk smell funny?'" He was glad when she laughed again.

Her phone lit up her purse so she let go of his hand and answered. She spoke softly for a moment then rose to walk outside. It began to take a bit so when their pizza came and she wasn't back Kurtis walked out to check on her. He found her sitting at an outdoor table laughing with someone on the phone. She didn't notice him so he returned to their table and wondered whether to start without her.

Eventually he got tired of waiting and began eating. A few slices later he asked for a box and the check. He met her outside and stood waiting with box in hand. She looked up surprised and spoke softly as if not wanting to be overheard. Kurtis turned and made his way to her truck. The gentleman inside of him did his best to squelch the anger.

Still she talked as she walked slowly to the truck. Kurtis thought to himself that if the doors had not been locked he would've hotwired the truck and left her standing there. Finally she came and unlocked the driver's side door, got inside and hit the unlock button for him. As he climbed in she asked with eyes flashing, "So you just ate without me? That was rude!"

Kurtis nodded. "Yep. I thought so too."

She drove saner than usual and Kurtis wondered where she was going. Finally she stopped at a corner and demanded, "Well don't just sit there! Help me figure out how to get back to the hotel!"

He opened his door, came around to the driver's side and motioned for her to get out. She put the window down. "No! Get back in or I'll leave you."

Kurtis could feel the anger rising so he walked away.

At first she sat there looking at him then she began to follow. She put the passenger window down and drove beside him. "Kurtis just get in the truck and tell me how to get back."

He pointed. "Three blocks straight. Take a left. You'll see it on your left eventually. Lock your doors. Be careful in the parking lot. If you get lost you can always use your phone."

Suddenly she felt ashamed of herself. "I'm sorry. Come on Kurtis. Get back in the truck."

He motioned for her to go without him and realized he was probably madder than he'd ever been in his life... except for the time he and Shawn had fought at Liddy's house. He walked with a slow stride and refused to look at her though she drove next to him for about half a block. He was glad when she sped away. Ironically his phone buzzed in his pocket and Mykaela's cute face popped up.

He laughed as he answered it. "Hey girl! What's up with you?"

She laughed as well. "You sound chipper! Did you have a good Christmas?"

He thought for a minute before he replied. "It's been a learning experience. How about you?"

For some reason his answer made her laugh more than usual. When she answered he wondered what she'd been through. "ME TOO! I have to say I've missed you. Want to get a pizza?"

He smiled. "Just had one. But let's get together this week. I'll give you a call."

"Sounds good. Catch ya later." With that she was gone. Their short visit reminded him of one of the things he liked about her. She was definitely not into drama. He also realized that he missed her too.

~~~~~~~

As Kurtis walked he thought of how much he missed Shawn as well. A few blocks after he spoke to Mykaela he gave his buddy a call. It was obvious he woke him.

"Sorry man. Were you asleep?"

Shawn mumbled, "Hang on." He moved from his place beside Tessa. She cried out in her sleep and he quietly calmed her as he covered the phone.

"Okay go ahead." Shawn moved to the den and threw wood on the fire.

Kurtis could've sworn he heard Shawn talking to Tessa. He checked the time. "What're you doin' in bed so early? It's only like eight thirty there."

Shawn hesitated and Kurtis had a sick feeling.

"Shawn please tell me you were not in bed with her."

Shawn was silent as he continued to build the fire.

Kurtis kept walking as he waited for Shawn to answer. "What's going on man? Have you gone stupid or something? You hardly know the girl!"

Kurtis heard himself and realized how quickly he'd fallen for Maggie. Shawn reminded him of it when he finally spoke.

"Thank you for that keen observation Mr. HOP-ON-A-JET-TO-MEET-HER! Did you call for something specific or just to point out the obvious?"

Kurtis was quiet and wondered what to say. A big dog came out of nowhere and scared the life out of him. It barked viciously and was right on his heels. Kurtis froze then slowly turned trying to keep an eye on the dog. Backwards he walked and the dog retreated to his own space.

Shawn asked, "What's goin' on Squirt?! Where are you?!" He was genuinely concerned.

Kurtis moved quickly down the road then laughed with relief. "You haven't called me Squirt since about the eighth grade!" He broke into a trot. "I got mad at Maggie and decided to walk home. That dog came from behind a gas station and was right on me."

Shawn wondered if he heard right. "You're WALKING home? WHERE ARE YOU?"

Kurtis laughed again then sighed. "I'm in Mobile Alabama walking back to the hotel. If Maggie wasn't Jesse's sister I would have... I don't know. I wish I was in my Jeep. I would turn it around and take her back to Texas. She's driving me crazy... like literally. She drives like a psychopath, worse than Liddy ever did. And she talks about nothing until I want to pull my ears off and cram them down her throat. I have no idea how I'm gonna spend another whole day riding with her. If Liddy hadn't switched places and rode with me the last four hours of the trip I think I might've killed Maggie."

Shawn laughed hard at his friend. "I don't think I've ever heard you this worked up about anything." He continued laughing and it felt good.

Kurtis laughed too. "Okay. Give it to me straight. What's going on? I know Liddy and Jesse both told me to be praying for you. Please tell me you were not in bed with Tessa."

Shawn sighed. "It's a long hard sad story. I'll tell you what I can when you get back. Just keep praying Squirt!" He tried to lighten the mood before they hung up. "Now hurry back to the hotel and change your underwear. That dog scared the crap out of me and I'm not even there!"

Kurtis laughed but realized Shawn did not deny the charges. But he had asked for prayer so maybe he'd kept the pact they'd made with Blue when they were thirteen as 'Ironmen.'

"I'll keep praying for you. And if you call me Squirt again I can always go back to calling you Scrawny Shawn."

They laughed together but both knew something was wrong. Kurtis prayed when he ended the call. Seven more blocks on the dark unfamiliar street gave him plenty of time to invoke the Almighty.

Chapter 59

Lydia was propped on her bed watching HGTV. The pillow under her knees relieved some of the lower back pain but her head and neck were killing her. Maggie burst through the door and tossed the pizza box on the bed. She paced as she related to Lydia how insensitive Kurtis had been. Eventually she flopped on the bed and opened the box. She took a bite and tossed the piece back inside.

"That's awful!" She sighed heavily.

Lydia offered, "There's a microwave in the breakfast area right next to the lobby." She was glad when Maggie took the box and left.

Lydia walked gingerly to the door between the rooms and knocked. Jesse opened and noticed she held to the door.

"Is Kurtis in there?" She peeked inside their room.

"No, he's walking somewhere between here and *'Another Love Crashed and Burned.'* He called a while ago."

Lydia sighed and turned to go. Jesse stepped in and helped her to the bed. "When did you start hurting?"

"Right after you left. I knew I should've had you stay." She winked at him.

Jesse could tell she was upset and had heard part of Maggie's rant through the door. "Let's do our best to stay out of it okay?"

She nodded. "Honey I know this will sound awful, but I cannot ride with Maggie tomorrow. Will you take care of that for me?"

He gently stroked her back. "I sure will. That could save her from a butt whoopin' if I know my fiancée like I think I do."

Lydia thought,

Only if I don't kill her in her sleep first.

Jesse added. "Remember, do your best to stay out of it. I'll take care of the traveling arrangements. But for tonight, just settle into bed and pretend to be dead."

He leaned down and kissed her again then left.

~~~~~~~

Kurtis came through the hotel lobby feeling better. He'd talked with Jesse, and Mykaela, and Shawn but best of all he'd caught up with the Lord. Even as worried as he was about Shawn he had peace of mind knowing his friend's character. They'd been buddies too long to get into another fight. He'd find out what was going on when he got home.

It didn't even make him mad when he saw Maggie in the breakfast room eating pizza and chatting happily on the phone. He tossed up a hand her way and continued toward his room. He was surprised when she hurried to catch up with him.

She took his arm and pulled him to a stop. "Come finish this pizza with me. I don't like eating alone." She smiled at him hopefully.

He looked at her sideways. "Me neither." He didn't move.

She sighed. "I'm sorry Kurtis. Come sit with me and let's talk about it. I need to tell you something."

He obliged and noticed that she still held his arm as they walked. She was even quiet for a bit when they sat down. Apparently she was working up a true apology.

She rose to get him a drink from the hospitality bar. "Water or a soft drink?"

"Water's fine. Thanks." He watched as she brought it to him with a smile. She sat at the little table beside him and opened the box. "It may need to be nuked again. See what you think and I'll heat it up if you'd like."

He wondered what had come over her. "It's fine. So what's on your mind?" He pulled a slice out and began eating. He didn't look at her.

She took a deep breath. "I should have been more considerate at the pizza place." She sighed. "But that was Terrance on the phone; you know, my old boyfriend."

Kurtis nodded. "Yep. The one who dumped you right before Christmas." He wasn't ready to let her off the hook just yet.

She nodded. "He was going through a hard time with some things I didn't know about. I should've cut him some slack."

Kurtis nodded. "I understand that feeling." He continued eating and realized she was quiet. Finally he looked at her and she had tears.

"I'm sorry Kurtis. I know you and I aren't officially a couple, but I have to tell you that I might get back together with Terrance."

Kurtis looked away and pretended to be hurt. Inwardly he was jumping for joy. "So is this the part where you say, 'But we can still be friends'?"

She looked at her hands and sighed again. "I'm so sorry. You're such a nice guy. Please don't hate me."

Kurtis felt a little sorry for her so he put down his pizza, wiped his hands and patted her shoulder. "You're a good person Maggie. I think we'll make great friends." He smiled at her.

She stood and reached for him so he rose and hugged her. "Thank you Kurtis. Do you think you could drive more tomorrow? I'm so tired tonight I don't think I'll be as alert as I should be."

He returned her smile. "I'll be happy to. Maybe you can catch a nap and get rested up before we set up your new apartment."

She smiled happily. "I can't wait!"

Chapter 60

Shawn used the flashlight on his phone and headed back to Lydia's room. It dawned on him that he'd left Tessa there with the loaded gun still on the floor. Though he hoped and prayed she wouldn't try anything like that again, he was still very shaken.

She stirred as he came through the door. "What time is it?"

He sat on the bed beside her. "It's only about nine. We were sleeping so good. But I didn't think to turn my phone off. I'm sorry."

She sat up and stretched. "To tell you the truth, I'm just happy to be wakin' up at all." She reached for him and he held her close. He had no idea what to say. At least she seemed glad to be alive.

She turned on the lamp and sat looking at him. "What can I do Shawn? You keep talking like there's some magical way out of this. Lydia will be back tomorrow. Then what?"

Shawn was thankful she finally seemed open to his help. "Lydia will let you stay here and me and Kurtis will move in with Jesse. Or I'll figure out something for the two of us. It's up to you."

He suddenly recalled his conversation with Kurtis about Maggie. Tessa would not do well with her as a roommate. But before he had time to worry about it, Tessa spoke with determination.

"I can't live here with Lydia. She mothers me half to death. She probably thinks I'm pure as the driven snow. When she finds out about the baby she'll kick me to the curb."

Though Shawn knew Lydia would never do that, he had to agree that Tessa staying there was probably not a wise option; especially when he thought of Kurt's description of Maggie.

He took Tessa's hand and kissed it. "I need to ask you something." He paused and wondered how to phrase his question. "Do you believe in God at all?"

She laughed that hollow laugh that hurt his soul. "I feel sure He's up there somewhere and I wasn't too excited when I thought about meetin' Him today. But He don't like me and I don't blame Him. I think you're probably the only one on earth who's that foolish."

She was surprised that he pulled her close and held her in his arms. "Tessa, God ain't waitin' on you to clean your life up so He can love you. He already does. Just like me. I love you Little Bird. Do you think you could love me, or am I too butt ugly?"

She pulled away and looked up at him smiling. "Why do think I'm all over you? White Boy you are a good lookin' man!" She reached up and smoothed his hair. "I love those new curls around your neck and that beard you're growin'." She stroked his face gently and peered into his eyes. "You'd make an awfully pretty baby daddy."

Shawn's heart beat fast at her touch. He leaned down to kiss her and she teared up. Their embrace quickly turned passionate until Shawn whispered. "I need to tell you something." He took a deep breath, sat up and wondered if he could say it.

"The reason I keep pulling back from you is that I promised the man who used to sleep in this very bed that I would only make love to the woman I married. He died right after I made that promise. So don't take it wrong that I won't finish what we started tonight."

She shook her head. "You are the strangest man I have ever met. So you're telling me you're a virgin?"

For some reason her question embarrassed him so he just slowly nodded. Finally he said, "But I love you."

She still wasn't sure what to make of his words so she sighed heavily. Her phone lit up on the nightstand and Shawn noticed the screen said 'Father' but there was no picture.

She grabbed it quickly and jumped from the bed. As she moved toward the kitchen and into the sunroom he could hear her talking to someone. He rose and retrieved the gun from the floor near the closet and unloaded it. Down on his knees he looked for the bullet hole. Just below the curtain to the right of the window he found it. He stood to check and was thankful that it didn't show unless one knew where to look. He checked the gun again to make sure it was unloaded. Pulling the trigger a few times to see if it jammed, he silently thanked God that it had a few hours earlier.

If not... he shuddered to think of it.

Turning toward the bed he noticed a dirt stain where his muddy knee had landed. He tried wiping it clean with a wet rag but it was bad. He sighed and thought of Lydia and her crazy love for white. This would surely come back to bite him in the butt. He pulled the cover from the bed and hauled it to the wash. He squirted Dawn on the stain and rubbed it til it soaped up. The muffled words of Tessa's conversation drifted his way and he caught a few words.

She didn't have any contact with her real dad, so he wondered who 'Father' was. Maybe it WAS her real dad. That would explain not having a picture. He started the water for the washer and wondered whether to use cold, warm or hot.

Lord... I know this is crazy, but if I mess up Liddy's bedspread she will know I've washed it. And then she'll have to know why. Please help. How did I get into such a mess?

He switched the temperature to hot and sighed as he stuffed the heavy covers into the washing machine with her ever present plunger stick. He poured in more liquid detergent, closed the lid and walked back to the bedroom. He wondered where Tessa had found the gun.

Her voice startled him as he looked in the nightstand to see if perhaps it would fit in there.

"It goes between the mattress and box spring." Tessa spoke as she walked toward him. She lay back on the bed and reached down. "Right here. And point the handle out so if she checks it will be just like she left it."

Shawn realized that Tessa had a side to her that he'd not seen before. As if reading his mind she pulled a ten dollar bill from her shorts pocket. "And this is yours. I took it from your wallet while you were in the shower."

He tipped his head at her and wondered as she added, "You didn't even miss it did you? See, if I had taken it all you'da known somebody had stolen from you. But since I only took the ten you just wondered if you counted wrong or spent it somewhere else."

Shawn sat on the bed beside her and she sat up as well. "Like the first day I was here and there were two hundred dollar bills in the drawer. That's too easy to miss. But if it had been in twenties I could've took one and nobody would suspect."

He wondered why she was revealing her dishonesty. She answered his sad look. "See Shawn. You just THINK you love me, but you don't know me. The only reason you met me in the first place over at Jesse's was because me and my sister were there to see what we could pilfer without gettin' caught. But you wouldn't leave me alone long enough for me to go through his stuff. I'm tellin' you, you don't want me in your life and besides now you don't have to."

He looked at her still wondering and tried to keep his eyes where they belonged. At least she wasn't cold.

"What do you mean 'I don't have to'?" he asked softly.

"That call I just got. It was the real father of this baby. He's setting up an account to pay all the doctor bills. I put the squeeze on him for living expenses too. He seemed pretty worried I'd expose him. I don't mind keepin' quiet. He's probably got a girlfriend or a wife cause he don't want nothin' to do with the baby. So see? You don't have to move in with me or marry me or whatever else makes it right for us to have sex. I'm fine without you Shawn."

His heart hurt so bad that he had to walk away. The washer bumped loudly so he opened it and pulled the heavy bedspread from the side where it had shifted. Water soaked his clothes as he tried to distribute the weight inside the washer. He closed the lid and started it back up. Leaning on the washer he sighed deeply and tried not to tear up. The woman already questioned his manhood.

Again he took his coat from the hook and slowly headed out the door. At least this time he wasn't worried about her safety. Apparently she had it all figured out. The baby daddy had become the sugar daddy so Shawn was no longer needed.

She said so.

He swiped at a tear and wondered why it hurt so much. Down the road toward town he went not really thinking of where he'd land. If he was a drinking man he'd find a bar like his dad. But he was NOT like his dad. Lydia had spent years telling him so. For some reason he ended up at the grocery store. As he walked inside it occurred to him again that his pants were wet in front. He sighed and thought about how it must look. He grabbed a shopping cart and headed down the produce aisle for no apparent reason.

Gingerroot… so that's what it looks like.

He tossed a big chunk into his buggy. Around the bend he noticed fresh cut flowers in a large bucket. Colorful tulips nodded up at him as he passed. A large bouquet of dark purple ones seemed to call out. Gently he placed them in the kid seat of his cart.

Up and down the aisles he strolled *'as if he had good sense.'* He smiled at the phrase Liddy always said. A bottle of Ginger Ale was added plus a box of gingersnaps and a carton of vanilla ice cream. He headed to the checkout and hoped the ten was all she'd taken since he'd not thought to look.

Inside his wallet was a note. He stuck it in his shirt pocket to read later.

By the dome light in his truck he read her words to him.

I'm sorry Shawn. But don't grieve that I'm gone. Just be glad you didn't get stuck with me. Because I love you- Tessa

For a moment it gave his heart a jolt as her words to him were so final. Then it occurred to him that she'd left the note in his wallet before he'd knocked the gun from her hand. Still he hurried home and prayed as he drove. She'd admitted it. She loved him.

He had such peace that it seemed the Lord confirmed his plan.

Chapter 61

Through the back door he came with treasures in hand. He stopped at the laundry closet and pulled a basket from a top shelf. On top of the washer he arranged the gifts except for the flowers. Those he pulled from the wrap so they'd make a nicer bouquet. As he worked he thought,

No wonder she questions my manhood. Here I stand with wet pants, arranging a gift basket and flowers.

He smiled as he gathered everything and went to find her.

From the sunroom she watched as he carefully placed the items in the basket. She teared up when she saw the flowers and how gently he cut the cellophane away and snipped the bands to loosen them. In the cool dark room she waited as he walked the house looking for her. Swiping at a tear she turned on a lamp when he came back into the kitchen. He spotted her and smiled a handsome smile.

"I brought you a care package." He handed her the basket but held the flowers behind his back.

She couldn't speak. The tears kept slipping down her face and finally she looked up at him. "Shawn I'm so sorry. I don't know why I get so hateful."

She put the basket on the table beside her and stood, wrapping her arms about his neck. He hugged her with one arm then brought the flowers around to show her. "This will have to do for now."

He got down on one knee still holding the bouquet up to her. "You might not need me Little Bird, but I sure need you. Will you please marry me?"

She felt light headed so she sat down in complete surprise. She'd done everything she could to make the man hate her but he wouldn't. Apparently he really did love her.

She took the flowers from his hand and went to her knees in front of him. "Yes White Boy. I'll marry you. But you can't quit school okay?"

He kissed her tenderly and felt the tears coming again. "Girl you have no idea how happy I am!"

She smiled the prettiest smile he'd ever seen. "Nobody has ever brought me flowers. Never. How did you know that purple is my favorite color? And not that sorry-ass lavender neither. This dark purple right here is my all-time favorite." She hugged him again and he helped her up. Together they sat on the love seat and he asked, "Dark like the couch? That's called Blackberry. We'll take that to our new place. I don't think Liddy will mind."

For some reason it made her laugh. The man loved her! She'd never ever been loved like that before.

~~~~~~~

Tessa placed the flowers in a vase Shawn found over the laundry. She happily arranged them near the kitchen sink while Shawn checked the bedspread. He pulled it from the washer and tried to find the stain. When he couldn't he crammed the covers into the dryer. Tessa came behind him and patted him on the rear. "I like a man who knows how to do laundry."

She tossed a couple dryer sheets in before he closed the door. "Go change clothes White Boy then sit with me on the Blackberry. We've got some planning to do." She reached up and kissed him before heading to the den.

"I'm gonna grab a quick shower." Shawn called behind her. He thought to himself as he watched her walk away that he should probably make it a cold one.

Lord, You are gonna have to step up Your game if I'm gonna keep my promise to Blue tonight.

He smiled happily as he fetched clean jeans and a t-shirt and headed to the bathroom. The hot water felt so good but he could hardly wait to get back to her. At least he was clean even if he didn't take time to shave. And he wouldn't have to fret in the morning if she needed to be in the bathroom.

Dried and dressed he sat with her on the sofa as she checked her phone for places to live. "There's an apartment near the new playground. But the neighborhood is rough a couple blocks behind it."

She scrolled down the list in the classifieds. He could hardly take his eyes off her. "This is pretty and it's near the school. I could walk over and meet you for lunch in the cafeteria, or you could run home for lunch. But it's kinda high and it's not furnished."

Shawn finally spoke. "Don't worry about furniture. We'll find stuff. I wish Liddy hadn't donated all her baby stuff or we'd have enough for the whole nursery."

Tessa asked absent-mindedly, "Why'd she do that? Don't she want kids?"

Shawn suddenly thought about how this was going to feel for his adopted mother. "Yep. She's always wanted children. She lost her baby when Blue died. The doctor told her she's not likely to get pregnant again. But it took Jack leaving til she could finally let go of her baby stuff. You never know though. God might bless her and Jesse with a baby. I hope so."

Tessa looked up at Shawn and smiled. "You really want to be this baby's daddy don't you?"

Shawn teared up again and hated how much he'd shown his emotions in the last two days. "I really do. I won't tell a soul if you don't."

She leaned over and kissed him. "Congratulations White Boy. You're gonna be a daddy!" She laughed happily. He kissed her so tenderly that she teared up too.

He hugged her and whispered, "Thank you. I promise to be good to you both."

She looked at the handsome man before her. "I know you will. Probably TOO good." Almost as an afterthought she added, "And don't worry. This baby's gonna be three-quarters white, so you'll pass with flying colors."

Shawn asked, "Can I kiss her?"

Tessa looked at him and laughed again. "Honey you can kiss anything you wanta kiss. You're my fiancé!"

She leaned back and pulled her shirt up to expose her tiny tummy. He leaned down and gave a quick kiss to her belly and sat up embarrassed. Tessa laughed at his shyness. "You gonna have to do better than that if she's gonna know you're her daddy."

Shawn laughed nervously. "We'll get to know each other better later." He kissed his bride-to-be then leaned back and asked, "So how you wanta do the wedding? As soon as possible or in a couple months or what?"

She'd already been thinking about it. "I don't care what people think about me but for the baby's sake, the sooner the better. And Lydia and Jesse have theirs planned for Valentine's Day. So if we get ours out of the way it won't take anything away from their day."

Shawn was proud of her. "That's a good idea. Plus then we can move in together sooner."

She looked at him surprised. "So you're not moving in til the wedding?"

He laughed. "Nope. In fact I need you to help me keep my promise to Blue. So…"

She interrupted him. "So no sex tonight even though we got engaged and we're having a baby together?" She teased. "Dang! Most people just add the word fiancé and sex is a given. Alright White Boy. Whatever you say."

She pulled up a calendar on her phone. "Your family will be home tomorrow night. How about the next day which is Thursday, New Year's Eve? You have Friday off so we could have a long weekend for our honeymoon even if we don't go anywhere."

He couldn't believe she'd be willing to do that. "I like it! We'll start the new year right!" He thought for a second. "Want me to ask Jesse if he'll marry us?"

She nodded. "I like Jesse. That'd be good. And we can get married at his house if he don't mind." She thought for a moment. "You know they're all gonna think I'm pregnant if we do this. And they're all gonna assume you're the father."

He nodded. "They'll be right. You're bound to start showing eventually. Why not tell it like it's good news? Because to me it's great! You're gonna be my wife! And we're having a baby!"

She shook her head at him and smiled. "You have got to be the kindest man the good Lord ever made." He smiled happily, but mostly because she spoke of the Lord in a decent way.

"Okay woman, I've got to grab a couple hours sleep. I'm gonna go in to work early in the morning to get on the good side of my boss. He gets there around 5:30 so I will too. If we're getting married Thursday after I get off work, I need to make sure I've got all the repairs done so he don't ask me to stay late." He kissed her good night and stood to leave. "Don't get up to make breakfast. Just be still and take your time in the morning. Maybe you won't get so sick."

She stood too and pulled him into her arms. "Shawn I don't know why you love me… but I'm glad."

He held her close and rubbed her back as he whispered. "I told you. I can't help but love you." His kiss was tender and she knew the love he spoke of was true.

Chapter 62

Kurtis was surprised when Maggie handed him the keys to her truck first thing early Wednesday morning as they started the last day of their trip. Apparently she was very tired for she settled in and went right to sleep. The truck was quiet except for the radio which played very low. Kurtis silently thanked God for answering his cry for help. Maybe since SHE broke off their 'relationship' her brothers would not be lined up to kill him.

He and Jesse moved the trucks together like synchronized swimmers up Interstate 65 to Montgomery where they picked up I-85. Just seeing the signs for the highway he was used to driving at home gave him hope that eventually the journey would end.

Maggie never stirred. He glanced at her all cuddled down in a pillow leaning on the passenger door. He pulled the blanket up from the floorboard to cover more than just her arms. Dark brown curls fell into her face and she smiled in her sleep. He realized again how pretty she was and smiled as well. He really did like curvy girls. If only she wouldn't talk so much. The thought of her chatter made him laugh, but only to himself. The possibility of waking her kept him very quiet. Even as pretty as she was, she was best enjoyed in small doses.

Jesse and Lydia relished their time together. Though she too was settled into a blanket and pillows she didn't close her eyes. Being close to Jesse was something she didn't want to miss. She was already sad that they'd be back in their separate homes in only a few hours. Every chance she got she tried to draw him out so she could hear what he was thinking. Plus the business with Shawn had her wondering. If anyone would have insight as to what was going on with Shawn, it would be Jesse.

So she asked, "What do you think our boy Shawn is going through?"

Jesse kept his eyes on the road and wondered if he should tell her what he had put together so far. Eventually he shared hoping to prepare Lydia for the inevitable.

"I think Tessa has had to fight just to survive for so long that she doesn't know any other way. I think she's used to using people and her beauty has given her an advantage. So she's never felt loved for who she is as a person. But I also know Shawn and that's not how he views her. The boy is in love for the first time in his life with a young woman who's never really had anyone to care for her."

He sighed as he added, "It wouldn't surprise me at all to find them engaged when we get home."

Lydia looked at him shocked. "But they just met at your house on Thanksgiving. Surely not."

Jesse waited and thought before he added. "But what if the girl needs him to rescue her? Shawn pulled her from her uncle's house and she must not have anywhere else to go or she wouldn't have been there."

Lydia looked at Jesse surprised. "But we were going to let her stay at either your house or mine."

Jesse nodded. "But what if she didn't want that? She's not used to trusting anybody, and she probably hates the idea of being a charity case. I have a feeling she and Shawn have figured out a way to start keeping house together."

Lydia shook her head. "I don't think Shawn would do that to me. He and Kurtis had a pact with Blue to be honorable men. Blue called it their Ironman agreement." She smiled. "I've heard them tease each other about it especially while they've been in college. Kurtis even called Shawn to pick him up at a girl's house last summer when something happened. They still laugh about it."

She considered the possibility for a moment then added. "Shawn is a senior. He's only got one semester left. Surely he'd be wiser than to quit school after he's worked so hard."

She looked at Jesse and a few things started to add up from piecing together phone conversations she'd had with Shawn. Her face flushed and she spoke with resolve.

"I may have to kill her."

Gazing out the window she sighed heavily. "That girl, if she has messed up my boy's life…"

Jesse knew better than to laugh so he added softly. "Spoken like a true mother." He looked at her praying God would prepare her heart.

"Honey, Shawn is not a boy anymore. Think about his character. Be careful not to assume she's taking him somewhere he's not supposed to go. What if the Lord brought them together for a purpose?"

Lydia nearly interrupted him. She didn't want to hear it. "Tessa doesn't even know the Lord! Shawn deserves better!"

Jesse waited for a bit hoping Lydia could hear what he needed to say.

"Honey, none of us 'deserves' anything good. Every good thing comes from God but not because we deserve it. Maybe God put Shawn into Tessa's life so she could learn how to trust HIM."

They rode in silence for a while letting the words hang in the air. Finally Lydia replied with resolve. "I don't like it. What if she breaks his heart?"

Jesse sighed. "It's a good possibility. But God is not in the business of showing others His will for Shawn and Tessa. That's between Him and them. It's our job to love, no matter what."

She looked out the window watching the countryside fly by. Something inside told her Jesse was right. She remembered loving Jack when he messed up, even after he broke her heart. Shawn had loved her unconditionally, but Kurtis had stayed mad at her until it really hurt. As the memory of his anger came, Jesse spoke one more word of advice.

"Do your best not to respond with guns blazing. Shawn loves you so much and your support will mean everything. If I'm right, he's already made his decision. You won't change his mind at this point. But you could push him away. You've invested too much into the young man to lose him now."

Lydia couldn't stand the thought of it all. Her heart was sad and she just wanted to hurry home and find that none of it was true. But she had a feeling Jesse was right.

She took a couple deep breaths and silently prayed for strength. Jesse reached over and held her hand. "I'll help you through it no matter what girl. The number one goal is to love."

She nodded in agreement but couldn't speak. Her gut told her that Tessa would eventually break her son's heart.

She was sure of it.

Epilogue

About five hours into the journey they stopped for lunch just before Atlanta. Maggie stretched as she exited the truck. She staggered and Kurtis caught her arm.

"Whoa girl. Get your sea legs working!"

She looked at him and laughed. "I was sleeping so hard! I bet I look a mess."

Kurtis smiled and continued to hold her arm as they walked. "Actually I was thinking how pretty you are."

She squeezed his arm and returned his smile.

Lydia looked at Jesse and rolled her eyes. He couldn't help but laugh. He took her hand, leaned over and whispered,

"Hold my hand, grow old with me. The best is yet to be."

Lydia finally smiled. Things were definitely changing. She'd always known the day would come when her boys would meet women and move on without her. At least now she had Jesse.

With him she could definitely find hope for a happy future on Blue Meadow Farm.

~~~ * ~~~

Made in the USA
Columbia, SC
16 July 2020